D1008758

# United

# United

MELISSA LANDERS

everafterROMANCE

First edition August 2016.
ISBN: 9780997086805

First edition, August 2016

Cover designed by Gene Mollica

Library of Congress Cataloging-in-Publication Data
Landers, Melissa.
United: an Alienated novel/Melissa Landers. – First edition.
Summary: Star-crossed teenagers Aelyx and Cara must unite
their people against a common enemy or face extinction.
ISBN 978-0-9970-8680-5 (hardback) –ISBN 0-9970-8680-7
[1. Extraterrestrial beings—Fiction. 2. Student exchange programs—Fiction.
3. Love—Fiction. 4. Science fiction.]

This novel is dedicated to *you*, reader.
Thank you for loving my characters as much as I do.

# Chapter One

**United**

MAY THE SOURCE BE WITH YOU

SATURDAY, MAY 20
L'eihr: The Final Frontier

Greetings, earthlings!

No, your eyes aren't playing tricks on you—that's a new blog header up there. Welcome to UNITED, your exclusive source for sneak peeks into the first integrated L'eihr-Human colony. I hope you brought your sunscreen, because we're headed to the beach, baby! You heard me. The colony is set on a lush, tropical island located on the opposite side of the planet from the main continent.

Jealous?

It's not too late to apply for passage. . . .

We're looking for a few good humans to round out our first group of settlers, especially those with a background in agriculture or mechanical engineering. Your skills could help build a whole new society, and if that doesn't get your motor running, I don't know what will.

Remember, among the requirements for settlers are a full-scale IQ of at least 130, general wellness, and a healthy reproductive system. (Sorry. I don't make the rules.) You can download an application online and visit your local Earth Council office for a physical examination and mental screening.

I hope to see you around.

I'll be the one sporting a goofy smile and a perpetual sunburn.

*Posted by Cara Sweeney*

Cara closed her laptop, taking care to muffle the *click* so she didn't wake Aelyx, who was snoring lightly from the bunk they shared in her ship's quarters. He slept with one muscled arm curled beneath his head, his loose honey-brown locks hiding his eyes. As if sensing her absence, he grumbled and hugged her pillow to his chest, then gave a contented sigh and murmured something in his native language before drifting off again.

It made her smile.

In the weeks since they'd left Earth, she'd grown accustomed to sleeping in his arms, too. No matter how quietly either of them padded about the room in the morning, the other would inevitably wake within minutes. They'd become synchronized in their movements, much like the trio of moons that orbited the planet five hundred miles below their feet.

On silent tiptoes, Cara made her way to the porthole and gazed past the darkness of space to her new home. L'eihr was barely visible as a ring of light as it eclipsed the distant sun, but she could still picture it from her last visit—an orb of muted indigo dotted with thousands of tiny islands and two continents, one of which housed the entire population of their race.

Of course, that was about to change.

Once the medics were done quarantining them for Earth cooties, Cara and Aelyx would shuttle down to the colony and begin their new life together. The prospect made her heart flutter. They'd have the whole community to themselves for the first couple of weeks while she finished negotiating the colony charter. It would almost be like a vacation. And they were long overdue for some fun in the sun.

Thwarting coups and saving alliances was hard work.

"It's too early to get up." Aelyx's voice was rough with sleep in a way that never failed to make her tummy do backflips. When he stretched both arms above his head, it drew her gaze to the contours of his tawny chest and his flat slab of a belly, even more scrumptious without a "button." He yawned and murmured, "Come back to bed."

He didn't need to ask her twice.

Cara climbed beneath the covers and rested her cheek on the perfectly hollowed spot where his shoulder met his chest. His skin was warm, carrying with it the unique, spicy-sweet scent she'd grown to crave more than *h'ali,* the L'eihr equivalent of coffee. While he wrapped both arms around her and drew her close, she placed a palm over his heart to gauge the strength and rhythm of its beats.

"How's the ticker?" she asked, peeking at him through her lashes.

"Strong." He covered her hand with his and pressed down so she could feel a steady thump. "Healthy." A wicked grin curved his mouth, and with mischief in his voice, he nuzzled her ear and added, "Ready for anything."

3

Cara let her eyelids drift shut when he gently took her earlobe between his teeth. She didn't know if she had the strength to turn him down this time. Two weeks ago, a L'eihr weapon had stopped Aelyx's heart. It was a miracle she'd been able to get it beating again, and since then, she'd insisted on giving him a chance to recover before they played their respective v-cards.

Keeping those cards in their pockets hadn't been easy—for either of them.

But with his lips brushing a wayward trail down the side of her neck, Cara was feeling awfully ready, too. Chills broke out across her skin in delicious contrast to the heated blood rushing through her veins. Then he bit that magical place at the top of her shoulder, and her resolve folded faster than a stadium seat.

"Are you sure?" she whispered. "I don't want to send you back to the great beyond."

Aelyx paused long enough to lock their gazes, sharing a brief snippet of his emotions through Silent Speech. A rush of desire flooded over her, and after that, there was no more chitchat. . . .

Until a few moments later, when their com-spheres buzzed an alert.

"*Fasha,*" Aelyx swore, raking a hand through his hair. He rolled onto his back and groaned loud enough to vibrate the pillow. "How do they always know?" He jabbed an index finger toward the unused top bunk. "I wouldn't be surprised if there's a camera up there."

Cara took a second to steady her breathing before answering the summons. Its signature frequency told her the call came from The Way—L'eihr's governing body, which now included her as the Chief Human Consultant. Her colleagues weren't spying. She and Aelyx simply had rotten luck.

"One of these days, we'll catch a break." She handed over his sphere, and together they spoke their passkeys while tugging the blanket high enough to conceal any exposed skin.

An image of the head Elder flickered to life, stooped in her miniature form atop the mattress. If Alona was surprised to see them together under the covers, she didn't let it show. Her faded chrome eyes betrayed no emotion as she lifted two fingers in the usual L'eihr greeting and droned, "I have wonderful news."

You'd never know it from her tone, but that was normal for the Elders. They'd practically bred the life out of themselves several generations ago. That was why they needed humans to diversify the gene pool. Cara returned the greeting and waited for her leader to continue.

"Your quarantine is complete," Alona said. "I've sent a craft to shuttle you to the colony, where the head of the development panel will greet you." She raised a brow at Cara. "I assume you remember Devinder from your former involvement on the panel?"

Cara suppressed an eye roll. She remembered him, all right. The old guy was so uptight he practically squeaked when he walked. "Yes, ma'am."

"He is now our tenth member of The Way," Alona said. "As the two of you are equals, I expect a greater level of collaboration between you."

Translation: no more bickering. "Understood," Cara told her.

"Excellent." Alona's lips quirked in what might have been a smile. Or indigestion. It was hard to tell with the Elders.

"What about Jaxen and Aisly?" Cara asked. The genetically altered clones had attempted to overthrow The Way, taking several lives and nearly destroying the Earth–L'eihr alliance in the process. Afterward, they'd vanished without a trace, which led Cara to believe they had more support than she'd originally thought. Maybe enough support to take them off of Earth and back to L'eihr. "Any news?"

"A few possible sightings, but nothing concrete enough to share." Then Alona dismissed her by asking, "Do you require further assistance?"

"No, ma'am."

"Then you may depart at your leisure." With a brief two-finger salute, Alona's image vanished in a wisp of gray.

Cara heaved a sigh and sat up, then glanced over her shoulder at Aelyx. "We'd better hurry." One thing she'd learned during her portion of the student exchange was *at your leisure* really meant *immediately*. Even though her position in The Way gave her more power than most citizens, she couldn't disobey a direct order from Alona. Not without consequences.

Aelyx pinched the bridge of his nose and squeezed his eyes shut. By now, Cara knew what he was doing—reciting Earth's periodic table of elements, probably forward and backward, judging by the pained look on his face.

As soon as he reopened his eyes, Cara latched her gaze onto his silvery irises and used Silent Speech to repeat what he'd told her weeks ago when she had needed reassurance. *Soon we'll be in our new home—no roommates, no bunk beds, no classes. Just you and me and miles and miles of beach.*

6

He flashed a weary smile. *At this point, I'll believe it when I see it.*

"Come on," she said aloud, tugging on his wrist. "I'll race you to the washroom." She winked and added, "Winner gets anything they want."

With that, Aelyx maneuvered around her and bolted for the door, then smacked the keypad and ran into the hallway. Never mind that he was clad in nothing but his boxers. For all their stoicism, L'eihrs had no modesty. Cara laughed and pulled on a clean uniform, pleased with herself for putting a spring in Aelyx's step.

Two cups of *h'ali* later, they stood in the docking station with their duffel bags planted at their feet. The shuttle was late, so they linked arms and let the hiss of recycled air through the vents fill the silence. Soon the sound of boots against metal turned their attention to the doorway, where Aelyx's best friend, Syrine, strode into view, dragging her own duffel behind her.

Syrine offered a smile, but it didn't touch her eyes, which were bloodshot and puffy from weeks of crying. A sympathy pain needled at Cara's sternum. Syrine had lost her *l'ihan,* a young soldier named David, who'd served as her bodyguard and died protecting Aelyx during the attempted coup. They'd brought David's body with them to bury on the colony. L'eihrs typically cremated their dead, but Cara had intervened for an exception in this case.

It was the least she could do.

"Shuttling to the continent?" Cara asked, because she didn't know what else to say. She already knew the answer. Syrine was an emotional healer and more fragile than the other clones. She needed the kind of help they couldn't provide on the colony.

The girl gave a slight nod and tugged on her ponytail in a nervous habit she'd recently picked up. "I won't be gone long. Will you wait until I'm back before burying David? I want to be at his memor—" Her words cut off with a hitched breath.

Aelyx jogged to meet Syrine and took her pretty, heart-shaped face between his hands. There was a time when something like that would've made Cara jealous, but not anymore. Syrine needed a friend, and no one knew her better than Aelyx. The two exchanged a few quiet murmurs before Cara turned away to give them some privacy.

She chewed her bottom lip and stared at the cargo hold, where a cryogenic box held David's remains. His was another senseless murder, just like Syrine's first love, a young L'eihr exchange student who'd died in China.

So many losses. It wasn't fair.

But despite that, Cara had hope—both for herself and Syrine—that they could put the past behind them and move forward together, stronger than before. Joining the colony was the first step to a brighter future.

And the future began today.

# Chapter Two

Sometimes after waking from a nightmare, a cloud of fear and sorrow followed Aelyx into the realm of consciousness, and he'd have to keep reminding himself that the negative emotions weren't real. They were nothing more than a mental mirage—a trick of his psyche.

He felt that way now.

Today was the first time Syrine had spoken openly to him about David's death, and even though they'd parted an hour ago, her grief had bled into Aelyx's heart and lingered there like a shadow. No matter how tightly he held to Cara's hand, he couldn't shake the feeling that she might vanish if he took his gaze away from her. The experience had left him more than a little shaken.

It had also put his problems into perspective.

Had he really wasted one moment of his time with Cara brooding because of sex? What right did he have to complain about waiting a little longer when Cara was living and breathing, strapped into the seat beside him as they sped to their new home?

To hell with the ache in his gut. He was the luckiest L'eihr alive.

"Look at me," he said to Cara while lifting their linked hands to his lips. When she turned her gaze away from the window, he told her, "I love you."

Her face broke into a smile, enlivening her electric blue eyes and dimpling one freckled cheek. Her look of pure happiness intensified the pain in his belly. At times like these, she was too beautiful to bear.

"Love you more." She nodded at the window and gave a little bounce of excitement, causing her safety restraints to squeak. "We're almost there. Can you believe it *now*?"

Her enthusiasm prompted him to peer past her through the glass, though there wasn't much to see. The morning sun hadn't yet burned away the thick layer of fog clinging to L'eihr's ocean waters, so the view resembled roiling tendrils of smoke trapped beneath glass. Still, a thrill tickled his chest when the shuttle descended into the mist. Regardless of whether he could see the colony, it was down there, and he would stand on its sandy shores within minutes.

"Funny how this is my home planet," he said, "but you're the one who's been to the colony." Aside from his visits to Earth, he'd never travelled beyond the continent's third precinct. "Seems backward."

Cara sniffed a humorless laugh and slanted him a glance. "Since when has anything between Earth and L'eihr been normal?"

"Point taken."

"But don't worry," she said. "I think you'll like the setup.

The panel tried to blend both cultures so it won't feel too foreign to anyone. There's even a—" She stopped with a gasp and pressed her forehead to the window. "What's that?"

Aelyx leaned in, following the direction of her gaze. The mist had cleared enough to reveal a shadow gliding beneath the surface of the water. As it was twice the size of their shuttle, Aelyx understood why the creature had drawn Cara's attention. He recognized the rounded form at once, even though he'd never before seen one in the flesh.

"It's a *priva*. They feed on microorganisms through slits in their skin. They're very gentle, like a cross between a manta ray and a humpback whale."

Cara breathed out in awe, and then the animal was gone as the shuttle sped onward.

Before long, something even more thrilling than an oceanic mammoth came into view: a cluster of beige islands, the largest of which showed signs of civilization in the form of tall multistory structures constructed from the same gray stone used at the capital. Aelyx pressed nearer to the glass, squashing Cara in the process.

She groaned, but there was laughter in her voice. "Guess I should've given you the window seat."

"Is that it?"

"Yep." She sat straighter, beaming with pride. And for good reason. The community was charming, at least from a hundred meters above the ground.

Dozens of paved paths wound around the buildings in a linked trail. Upon closer inspection, he realized the paths were roads with a few compact vehicles parked along the shoulder. He identified the main dormitory by its position at the center of the community, bordering an expansive park and what appeared to be a swimming pool. But that couldn't be the case. Recreation wasn't a priority for L'eihrs, only duty.

"Is that what I think it is?" he asked.

"If you think it's a solar-heated pool, then yes." She delivered a light elbow nudge. "I negotiated one full day a week for leisure time."

"Impressive."

Cara pointed at the barracks. "That's called the living center. Our unit will have a bedroom and a small lounge, but no bathroom or kitchen." She heaved a sigh. "I fought for more privacy, but the panel insisted on having communal washrooms and a dining hall because it'll force everyone to interact."

That made sense to Aelyx. His upbringing in the Aegis had offered him very little privacy, but resulted in close relationships between the students. "Sounds like a good compromise."

"I'll remind you of that at two in the morning, when you have to trek down the hallway to pee."

Laughing, he scanned the tiny settlement and continued north to a flat expanse of unoccupied land that stretched across half the island. The soil had been disturbed in tidy rows, which indicated vegetation had recently been planted.

"Crops?" he asked.

"Mmm-hmm. The goal is to be self-sufficient."

As the shuttle prepared to touch down on the beach, Aelyx spotted a family of *mahlay* guarding their collective nest of eggs buried in the sand. The small creatures darted nervous glances at the craft, then used their talon-spiked flippers to drag themselves into the safety of the nearby underbrush. It made him think of Vero, his house pet at the Aegis, particularly all the places the animal had buried scraps of food. Vero had once hidden a full serving of *l'ina* beneath Aelyx's mattress. The stench had lingered for days, driving his roommates to sleep in the lobby. A pang of wistfulness tugged at Aelyx's stomach. He wished he could bring Vero to the colony, but the animal belonged to all the students.

When the shuttle landed, Aelyx unfastened his harness in record time and rushed to the door. He jumped to the ground, grinning as the sand shifted beneath his boots, and then he immediately lifted his face to the sun. The gentle caress of warmth made him groan. He'd missed this. Manhattan in winter had been his own personal hell.

Right away, he noticed the air was different here than on L'eihr's first precinct—humid and thick with the slightly bitter scents of salt and sea. The island trees bore a light curve, and their oversize beige leaves fanned out directly from each trunk to absorb nutrients from the air. The effect made them resemble tall shrubs instead of trees, but he supposed they were attractive in their own way. In his absence during the exchange, he'd nearly forgotten that the colors of Cara's world didn't exist on his home planet. It had taken him a year to grow accustomed to the vibrant greens of Earth's trees, and now he almost missed them.

But not enough to go back.

He turned to find Cara standing behind him, watching him with a cautious expression. Clearly his opinion mattered a great deal to her.

*Does it feel like home?* she asked him privately.

Truthfully, no, it didn't. But after being away from L'eihr for so long, it felt good to stand beneath a familiar sky. That was enough. And since he couldn't lie through Silent Speech, he told her *I'm sure it will.*

The shuttle pilot startled them by abruptly lifting off, and in the blink of an eye, the craft was gone. That's when it occurred to Aelyx they were alone on a balmy island.

A tempting idea came to mind.

"Come on," he said while kicking off his boots. "I'll bet the water's as warm as it looks." He toed off both socks and tugged his tunic over his head, but Cara just stood there biting her lip. She was probably afraid to remove her clothes. Humans had such prudish views regarding the naked form. "It's nothing I haven't seen before," he assured her. "Besides, we're alone."

"Actually . . ." She gulped when he dropped his pants. "We're not."

Aelyx glanced past the shoreline to the settlement in the distance. He didn't see any signs of life, not that it mattered. "The clones have showered together since childhood. Your nudity won't shock anyone." And to prove it, he shed his undergarments.

Cara's eyes went round while her face flushed. After blinking a few times, she dropped her gaze to the sand. "I . . . uh . . . have to find Devinder so we can go over some colony business, remember?"

"Oh." Aelyx had forgotten. It kept slipping his mind that Cara was part of The Way. Her appointment to the government had been so abrupt, and, quite frankly, bizarre. It also meant he had to obey her every command, but he refused to dwell on that small detail. "Go ahead, then." He thumbed at the gently crashing waves. "I can find ways to occupy myself."

"I'll make it up to you," she said as she backed away. "Promise."

Aelyx waded into the water, discovering it *was* as warm as it looked. "Don't worry," he told her. "We have all the time in the world."

## Chapter Three

Resisting the urge to jut out her bottom lip, Cara watched Aelyx's glistening body slice through the waves with the same lithe movements as a dolphin in pursuit of mackerel. He made it past the breakers within seconds and set off down the shoreline to explore the northern tip of the island, where silky sand gave way to uneven slabs of stone. Clearly the Aegis had taught him to swim—quite well—but he looked more like an Olympic athlete than a vacationer frolicking in the water.

Cara wished she could join him and show him how to have fun . . . and maybe have some fun of her own. She couldn't remember the last time she'd felt the pull of an ocean tide, and she'd never been skinny-dipping, not even in the murky lake back home.

Aelyx, the workaholic, had beaten her to it. How ironic was that?

When she finally turned away and crossed the dunes,

she caught a glimpse of the ancient ruins crumbling at the southern end of the beach, and her footsteps came to a gradual halt. The piles of sand-colored blocks held her gaze, mocking her with reminders of Jaxen and Aisly, who were cloned in a L'eihr laboratory with exhumed remains from the old tomb.

*Not just cloned*, she reminded herself. *Supercharged.*

Jaxen and Aisly had been enhanced with DNA from an advanced, secretive race of aliens called the Aribol, which gave them mind control, and the hybrids weren't Cara's only concern. The Aribol had been showering L'eihr with mechanical probes for months. Nobody knew what the aliens wanted, but one thing was clear: Even with a strong alliance, humans and L'eihrs were outmatched.

She mused that back in Midtown, her friends were getting ready for prom—browsing magazines for trendy updos and the perfect strappy pumps. She was launching a colony and worrying about an alien invasion.

Never a dull moment.

Determined to stay positive, she made her way past the dunes to the paved sidewalk and set off to find Devinder. She strode into the fringes of their vacant community and scanned the storefront signs, which were engraved with symbols for those who didn't speak L'eihr. One shop displayed a stick figure with a needle in its arm—the medic—that was obvious enough. But the adjacent building wasn't as simple to identify. Its sign revealed a tablet with a few lines of nondescript writing on the screen. She hadn't seen anything like it during her time at the Aegis, so she made a mental note to request a guided tour before the first colonists arrived. Humans would look to her for guidance, and she needed to know how to direct them.

A few minutes later, she found Devinder seated on a park bench outside the living center, one arm resting on the seatback as he gazed out at the ocean. He spotted her and stood, then strode to meet her in the sluggish, labored steps unique to his generation. His gray-streaked hair was gathered at the nape of his neck in a low ponytail, and his chrome irises had lost some of their gleam, but Cara knew better than to underestimate him. He was like the Jell-O fruit salad her mom used to make—soft on the outside with a surprisingly tart interior.

Devinder pressed two fingers to the left side of her throat, and she reciprocated, careful not to hold the contact for too long and accidentally make a romantic advance toward him. She'd made that mistake before.

*Welcome back*, he told her. *I've heard your visit to Earth was eventful.*

*That's putting it mildly*, she said. *But before we go on, do you mind if we speak aloud? I'm not very good at Silent Speech.* It wasn't a lie—not really. She was still learning the nuances of mental communication, but that wasn't the real reason for her request.

Devinder reflected for a moment, then scrunched his forehead. "You believe I'm so tight that I squeak when I walk? I don't understand. What does it mean?"

*That* was the reason. She couldn't control all of her thoughts, and embarrassing snippets tended to leak out at the worst moments. Cara's cheeks went up in flames while she searched for a response.

"And the shop you passed," Devinder added, pointing in

the direction she'd come, "is the cultural archive. Comparable to your library system."

"That makes sense." She grabbed the opportunity with both hands and shamelessly changed the subject. "I hope you'll take me on a tour before the colonists arrive."

"It would be my pleasure." He gestured at the nearest bench. "We have much to discuss before then."

"Can we begin with island defense?" she asked, reflexively glancing toward the ruins at the south end of the beach. "What kind of protection will we have against an invasion?"

She half expected Devinder to dismiss her as a worry-prone human, but he didn't. Strangely, that made her feel worse. "The colony will be allotted one capital guard squadron."

Cara felt her eyebrows rise. "That's it? What can a dozen guards possibly do?"

"Their presence here is not intended to protect the colonists from an outside force, but to maintain order and administer Reckonings."

"*Reckonings?*" All thoughts of alien attacks vanished when Cara realized The Way intended to implement their method of justice on the colony. She'd fought vehemently against Reckonings—corporal punishment in the form of an electric lash. "I thought we agreed the *iphet* has no place here."

"No. We agreed to suspend the death penalty."

"But most governments on Earth don't lash their citizens. Settlers won't stand for it."

Devinder splayed both hands while shaking his head. "Miss Sweeney, we've invited humans here to integrate with the clones, to reproduce with them. If a human colonist commits an infraction, do you believe the guilty party would

19

prefer deportation—leaving behind their offspring—to a few moments of physical discomfort?"

"But why does it have to be one or the other? Why can't we consider alternative disciplinary options, like work penalties?"

"Do you mean assigning harsh labor as a means of punishment?"

Cara nodded.

"But the result of that penalty is also physical discomfort," he pointed out. "Much like the *iphet*. I fail to see the distinction."

She opened her mouth to argue, but he'd stumped her by making a halfway decent point. After a few moments, she told him, "But the settlers from Earth will respond better to labor than a lash. Can't we at least try it?"

He pursed his lips and watched her. "All right. I suppose there's no harm in trying your method. We can always revert to the *iphet* if necessary."

"Thank you. I appreciate your being flexible."

A half smile lifted the corners of his mouth. "I am not incapable of compromise. You yielded on the matter of assigned occupations, so I'm happy to return the favor."

Cara bit her tongue. She hadn't *yielded* at all—she'd been outvoted. Now she had the delightful task of informing the colonists that they had no say in choosing their own jobs. "Has the panel discussed who'll oversee daily life here?"

"Yes," he said. "Alona has suggested you take a leader-ship role."

"Me?" Cara's hand flew to her chest. "What kind of role?"

"As a liaison for the human colonists."

"Like a go-between?"

20

"Essentially, yes," he told her. "Humans will come to you with their concerns, and you will present them when The Way convenes."

"What about the clones? Who'll represent them?"

"We propose that your *l'ihan* fill that role."

Cara perked up. That was a great idea—the perfect way to make Aelyx feel involved in his new home. "I'll talk to him about it. Do we know how many clones have signed up to join the community?" Most L'eihrs of Aelyx's generation would rather drag ass over a field of rusty nails than pair off with a human.

"Not enough to form a match with each immigrant, but I'm certain that will change with time."

"Oh, speaking of time," Cara said. "I'd like to take a few days off, if you don't mind."

Devinder lowered a brow in confusion.

"For leisure," she clarified. In the last year, she and Aelyx had survived riotous mobs, alien hybrids, and worst of all, high school on two planets. "I need a break—just a short one."

"Of course. I often forget how much The Way has asked of you."

With that settled, they discussed issues ranging from inoculation procedures to interspecies matchmaking strategies. By the time the conversation was over, the sun had begun to sink over the horizon. She walked Devinder to his shuttle, and after a two-fingered goodbye, used her com-sphere to contact Aelyx.

"I'm done with my meeting," she told his miniature hologram, which appeared to be indoors. "Where are you?"

"In the living center." He cradled a bowl between his

21

hands and spoke with one cheek full. "I didn't know which room was ours, so I palmed each keypad until a door opened. By the way, it's number sixteen. Come on. I made dinner."

Cara winced. It was no secret that she hated L'eihr food. "What's on the menu?"

Tilting his bowl toward the sphere, he revealed a heap of buttery penne noodles that made her mouth water. "Look what I found in the dining hall pantry."

"Imports!"

"And lucky for you, pasta is one of two meals I can cook."

She smiled, recalling that the other was toast. "I'm on my way."


Twenty minutes later, she groaned with satisfaction and rested a hand on her belly, which was full of starchy goodness. Not wanting to leave the comfort of the cushioned futon, she looked around for a place to rest her bowl, but came up empty.

The apartment wasn't designed for eating. It consisted of two small rooms: a living area furnished with a futon and a data table, and their bedroom, which contained a storage bureau and two interlocking cots that made a double-size bed. The cots were designed to keep couples in close proximity while giving L'eihrs the option of sleeping apart, as they were accustomed to doing in the Aegis dorms.

And much like the Aegis, the walls were painted light gray with minimal clutter. A year ago, Cara would have found the décor barren and cold. Now the tidiness felt comforting.

"Here," Aelyx said, reaching for the bowl. "I'll take it."

"No, you made dinner." Cara retrieved his dish from the

floor. "You shouldn't have to clean up, too." She stood and strode toward the kitchen sink before remembering there wasn't one. Then she made a move for the bathroom that didn't exist.

This was going to get old fast.

Aelyx grinned. "Change your mind?"

"Psh," she scoffed. "I'm not too lazy to hoof it to the kitchen."

In socked feet, she padded down the long hallway leading to the dining hall, grateful that at least their apartment was on the first level. Movement sensors illuminated a set of dim running lights installed along the floor. The bulbs incorrectly predicted her destination and lit a path to the nearest washroom, then recalculated when she continued straight.

It didn't take long to reach the dining hall, its rows of parallel metallic tables and benches also modeled after the Aegis. She continued to the industrial kitchen and squinted in the darkness for the sonic purifier chute. Countless hours of sanitation detail had taught her exactly what to do. Once she found the chute, she chucked the dishes inside and returned to room sixteen.

Aelyx had moved to the floor, where he lounged in front of the data table and swiped at its glossy screen. In response, it displayed an overhead view of the island. He enlarged the image and focused on the northern tip, then spun it around so a flawless stretch of beach came into view. It was a recording from his com-sphere, so vivid that Cara could make out the shadows of a few *mahlay* dragging across the sand.

Aelyx patted the spot beside him on the floor. "I want to show you something." When she joined him, she rested her head on his shoulder and watched the screen. "I went exploring today and found a spot you can't reach from the trails." He pointed past the dunes, where the landscape disappeared into darkness. "You can't see it, but there's a cave back there with a small freshwater pool. It's warm and quiet. The perfect place to escape if we want to be alone."

"We're already alone. But you can take me there tomorrow if you want. I'm officially on vacation for the next few days."

"Really?" Aelyx rotated to peer down at her. "We've got the whole island to ourselves?"

She tucked a wayward lock of hair behind his ear and inhaled the scent of sea salt emanating from his skin. She could breathe him in for hours and never tire of it. "Every last inch."

He pulled his com-sphere from his pocket, then motioned for hers. Once he had them both, he rested them on the data table. "So we're finally off duty."

"What are we going to do with ourselves?"

A spark flickered behind his eyes, and he flashed a grin that set her own lips curving in response. Then his gaze dipped to her mouth and held there.

Just like that, the mood shifted.

Each of their breaths seemed amplified in the new silence, the air around them charged with anticipation. A gradual warmth unfurled inside her belly, and when Aelyx licked his lips as if tasting her there, she knew the conversation was over.

He didn't lean down to kiss her. Instead, he tipped her chin with an index finger, slowly lifting her face toward his while burning her up with those molten silver eyes. When their lips finally met, it was a whisper of contact—just a teasing sweep that left her wanting more. Aelyx licked her upper lip, then inched back, forcing her to chase his tongue until she straddled his lap and took what she wanted.

He tasted of salted butter and pent-up need, an enticing blend that sent her pulse into overdrive. Cara couldn't get enough of him. It was as if a void had opened up inside her, and nothing but his touch would fill the blackness. She deepened the kiss, wrapping herself around him until she couldn't tell where she ended and he began. The distant crash of ocean waves faded, and she went deaf to everything but the rush of blood in her ears. Aelyx filled her senses, claiming her mouth while his hands grasped the back of her tunic. Soon those hands released the fabric and slipped beneath, skimming the bare flesh along her spine.

Cara broke from the kiss long enough to pull off her tunic, then helped Aelyx do the same. Skin-to-skin, he settled two fingers at the base of her throat to count the frenzied beats of her heart.

"One-twenty," he whispered against her mouth. "I think we can do better."

He opened his mind to her for a moment, just long enough for Cara to feel an ache of desire low in his core. She knew what he wanted—and what she wanted, too.

She rested a palm over his heart, wondering if it was fully healed from the accident. "Are you sure you're ready for this?"

He swallowed hard and studied her from beneath heavy lids, his chrome eyes darkening while his mouth curved in a grin. "You're not planning to jump on my chest, are you?"

Cara matched his smile. "I've never done this before, but I'm pretty sure that's not how it works."

"Then I'm ready." He asked her silently, *Are you? If not, we can stop.*

By way of answer, she stood up and led him into the bedroom.

They peeled off the rest of their clothes and settled on the linked cots. This wasn't like their reunion on Earth, when they tore at each other in a rush of desperation. Now their entire future stretched out before them. They slowed things down and shared lingering kisses as if they had a lifetime to get this right.

Because they did.

Despite their inexperience, it didn't take long for them to figure out what they were doing. He moved inside her slowly at first. There was some pain, but it was duller than Cara had expected, and mingled with an urgent sort of pleasure that drove her hips into a steady rhythm that matched the pace of her breathing.

He held her gaze the whole time, whispering *I love you* in broken L'eihr. She didn't need the words because with each lapse of control, his sensations slipped out through Silent Speech, and in those moments, they were one person, thinking and feeling and moving in flawless synchrony. There was no distinction between his touch and hers, between his body and hers, only unified bliss. It was unlike anything she'd ever experienced—unearthly and spectacular, just like Aelyx.

After, they lay together, limbs tangled, for a while, the only sound an erratic pull of breath into their lungs. She rested a hand on his chest and timed his heartbeats, which seemed strong and steady. She smiled to herself. They'd actually done it. Now that the rush was receding, she tried to pinpoint whether she felt any differently. At once she decided *yes.* There was something new at the base of her heart, as if an extra chamber had grown there, one that filled her veins with emotion instead of blood. It was hard to describe and slightly scary, because now she had more to lose than ever.

She wondered what Aelyx was thinking, and if he felt differently, too.


Aelyx had won at life.

If an *iphal* should take him again, he'd be ready, because nothing could surpass what he'd done with Cara. It had been worth every second of the wait. He only hoped she couldn't see him grinning like a madman at the ceiling.

"Hey," she whispered, tickling his skin with the light sweep of her fingernails. "You okay? A credit for your thoughts."

Aelyx tightened his arms around her and buried his face in her hair. "A million credits couldn't buy anything as amazing as that."

She shrank into his shoulder as if embarrassed. "Not too bad for our first time, huh?"

"Well, remember our first kiss? I told you we were gifted."

Cara's body shook with quiet laughter. "That's right. And I said the world wasn't ready for our talent."

"Which explains why we had to relocate across multiple galaxies."

Her fingertips halted their lazy skate across his chest, her mood seeming to shift.

When she didn't respond, he asked, "A credit for yours?"

"I'm just worried. About a lot of things, like your heart." She paused to place a kiss on his chest. "It would break me to lose you again. And then there are the colonists. I don't know what—"

"Hey, we're off duty, remember?" He smoothed the hair back from her face and used a thumb to caress her cheek. He wished he had Syrine's gift. If he did, he would absorb Cara's anxiety and bear it himself. "I need you to do something for me."

"Anything," she said without hesitation.

"Three days." He paused to deliver a pointed look. "That's all the time we have before our lives are consumed again. That time belongs to us, and we deserve every moment of it. Can you give me three days with no worries?"

Her blue gaze turned soft, almost apologetic, and she slid a bare leg over his hip. "Live in the moment," she mused. "I can do that."

"Promise?"

"I don't just promise." She extended her little finger. "I pinky-swear."

He grinned at her offering, then hooked a finger around hers. "Now I know you're serious."

They fell asleep to the lullaby of ocean waves, and in the days that followed, awoke to sunlight streaming through the open window. Each morning they ate their breakfast on the beach, and Aelyx reserved some spare crumbs to trap a *peca*. With the amphibian in hand, he showed Cara how to lure fish by holding it beneath the water and tickling its belly. In response, the *peca* emitted a series of ultrasonic chirps that drew a few specimens within reach. Aelyx eventually caught a fish, but released it, as he wasn't in the mood to clean and cook it.

He showed Cara the cave he'd discovered, and by the

28

second afternoon, she grew brave enough to shed her uniform and skinny-dip in the freshwater pool. Then they lay on the warm stone slabs and let the sun dry their skin before devouring the picnic lunch they'd assembled from the kitchen imports. When the sun hung low in the sky, they linked hands and strode back to their apartment, where they spent the evening playing chess and sharing stories of their time apart.

Because Cara was still tender from their first night together, the only thing they did in bed was sleep. But Aelyx didn't mind. He simply loved having her near—and all to himself. He could honestly say that those three days were the best of his life.

But as leisure time had a tendency to do, it passed too quickly.

On the fourth morning, they awoke to the noise of shuttles alighting on the beach and supplies being hauled into the living center. Then Cara received a transmission on her com-sphere. It was Devinder, informing her that the first group of human colonists had arrived on the transport and begun quarantine procedures.

After disconnecting, Cara bit her lip and set down her sphere. With a sigh, she rested her chin on Aelyx's chest. "Time to get up. Devinder wants to meet us in town to go over some new policies."

Aelyx suppressed a groan. "A far cry from skinny-dipping at the cave."

"No joke." A pair of lines creased her ivory brow. "But if the colonists are already in quarantine, that means they'll be here next week." That pair of lines turned into a trio, and her breathing accelerated. "There's so much to do before then, I get dizzy just thinking about it."

Aelyx pulled her close, nuzzling the spot on her shoulder that always gave her chills. But her muscles were too tense for the contact to produce the desired effect. He wished she weren't so anxious. After all, he was here to share the responsibility as the L'eihr representative. "No worries, remember?"

She shook her head. "That was a limited-time offer."

"It was fun while it lasted."

"Come on." She threw aside the sheet and sat up, then tugged at his elbow until he did the same. "Duty calls."

She didn't even offer to race him to the washroom.

The vacation was officially over.

# Chapter Four

**United**

MAY THE SOURCE BE WITH YOU

TUESDAY, JULY 25
Growing Pains

There's an old saying that you can't make an omelet without breaking a few eggs. Or as my dad likes to put it, "If you don't screw up at least once a day, you're not trying hard enough." Either way, the point is basically the same: you can't have success without failure.

By that logic, this colony will be a masterpiece.

It's been a couple of months since the first immigrants arrived, and I won't lie—we've had some pretty spectacular fails. Like the time we discovered half the human colonists are allergic to L'eihr seafood. (Who knew faces could swell so big?) Or when a dead bird got stuck in the drinking filtration system and gave us all salmonella poisoning. It probably goes without saying that projectile vomiting isn't very romantic, so matchmaking efforts between humans and L'eihrs have been a bit hampered by recent events. But we've had some wins in that department. The software created for us by the experts at e-Compatibility has already resulted in a few love matches, and I'm confident that many more will follow.

We'll get the hang of this whole "alien integration" thing. Because we don't make stupid mistakes on our colony. We make spectacular ones!

*Posted by Cara Sweeney*

Cara logged off and stuffed another bite of *l'ina* sandwich into her mouth, littering the laptop keyboard with crumbs. She tried to blow them away, but her mouth was too full, so she made a mental note to deal with it later. Right now she had to get back to the administrative building before the colonists assembled in the lobby noticed she was gone and came looking for her.

Because they would.

A few minutes ago she'd snuck into her apartment for a quick working lunch, typing with one hand while feeding herself with the other, but experience had taught her there was no place to hide from her people. Not even the shower stalls were safe. It was somewhat disturbing how accustomed she'd become to taking complaints while shaving her armpits.

She grabbed her sandwich and made for the door, but stopped short when she discovered a petite brunette waiting on the other side. Cara recognized the woman, having seen her once or twice in passing. She was young for a colonist, about twenty-three, with an angled bob hugging her jawline and a pair of misty, red-rimmed eyes that formed an instant link to Cara's heartstrings. Maybe she was homesick. It was a bigger problem than anyone wanted to admit.

"I saw you come in through the window," the woman

said, fidgeting with her hands. "So I know you want to be alone, but . . ." Her gaze faltered. "I really need to talk. I'm Mary, by the way."

Cara made a concerted effort not to glance at the clock or think about her appointments. Helping people like Mary was part of her role as human representative. "No problem." She gestured for Mary to come inside. "Are you missing your family? Because I can give you extra time in the conference pods. As much as you need."

"No," Mary said as the door closed behind her. "I mean, yes, but that's not the problem."

"What's bothering you?"

Mary smoothed her tunic, watching the floor while she spoke. "It's my job."

Cara mentally groaned. Of course it was.

"I knew we wouldn't get to pick for ourselves," Mary went on. "I read your blog before I applied. But you kind of made it sound like the intake test would match us to our perfect careers, and—"

"And that's not the case?"

"Not even close. They put me in sanitation."

"Cleaning isn't glamorous, but every job is important here."

Mary quickly clarified, "Oh, it's not that the work's beneath me. I'm not too good to clean. It's the isolation. I'm on a crew with one other person, a L'eihr guy, and most days we go a whole shift without saying ten words to each other." She tucked a lock of hair behind one ear and lifted a shoulder. "I thought coming here would be some great adventure, but more than anything I feel lonely. I'm not asking for special treatment, and I'm not afraid of hard work. I just want to be around other people." She peered up with wide eyes. "Isn't there anything you can do?"

As much as Cara wanted to say no, there actually *was* something she could do, and everyone knew it. As a member of The Way, her decision was law. No L'eihrs would question her if she reassigned Mary's occupation. Humans, on the other hand, would go berserk. If word spread that she was willing to change people's jobs, it would open the floodgates for a hundred more requests. She'd told the truth when she'd said every role was important. The reality of it was there were some jobs nobody wanted to do . . . like cleaning.

"Please?" Mary pressed. "I really want to stay, but this isn't what I signed up for. Give me something else. *Anything* else. I promise I won't complain."

The longer Cara looked into those sad brown eyes, the more her willpower crumbled. "Well, I guess the agriculture department can always use another—" Before she could finish her sentence, Mary threw both arms around her. "Let's keep this quiet," Cara mumbled around a mouthful of hair. "If anyone asks, we'll say there was a mistake with your test results."

After a multitude of thanks, Mary practically skipped out the door to tell her supervisor the news. Cara started to follow, then changed her mind and decided to leave the same way she'd arrived—through the window.

As she strode along the outskirts of the front lawn, she pictured Mary's smile and found herself beaming. It felt good to make a difference, to boost someone's quality of life with one simple act. Maybe it was a small victory, but she'd needed the win, so she reveled in it while munching on her sandwich.

While walking, she watched the activity taking place on the park field as colonists used their lunch break to fulfill the daily exercise quota. One group of humans had formed a scrimmage game, flag football from the look of it, while another group jogged laps around the field perimeter. It seemed all of the L'eihrs were either engaged in games of sticks on the opposite end of the park or swimming in the nearby saltwater pool.

Cara's prideful grin fell. Aside from one interspecies couple sitting on a bench overlooking the ocean, she couldn't see any humans and L'eihrs interacting. There were no fights, but it was clear that cliques had formed. She wished she knew what to do about it. This was the sort of problem that couldn't be fixed by shuffling job assignments.

Her day took a turn for the worse when she snuck back into her office and found a pair of pristine boots propped up on her data table, belonging to a young blond man who was currently perusing her data tablet. He glanced up at her with narrowed eyes, as if she'd been caught trespassing instead of the other way around.

Cara's jaw clenched. *Jake Winters.*

He was her least favorite human being on the planet—a twenty-something Los Angeles big shot who'd made millions from an Internet startup company, and then gotten bored, sold it, and applied to join the colony. Cara didn't know why he'd come here. He didn't seem to like her very much, and the feeling was mutual.

"Make yourself at home," she said sarcastically while snatching her tablet from him. At least he had the decency to remove his boots from her table, though he didn't surrender her chair. "We need to have a serious talk about boundaries, Jake."

"What we need to talk about," he countered, "is why you're playing favorites."

"I already told you Aelyx doesn't get special treatment."

"Who said anything about your boyfriend?" Jake stood up extra tall in a clear attempt to use his three-inch height advantage against her. Not that it worked. She glared right back at him. "I want to know why Mary Shapiro can change jobs, but the rest of us have to suck it up and play the hand we're dealt."

Cara's mouth dropped open. How could he have possibly heard so quickly? She'd barely left the living center five minutes ago.

Jake's answering smirk said he enjoyed catching her off guard. "I was with the agriculture supervisor when the call came in. I heard everything, so don't bother denying it."

Cara released a thousand mental swears while a riot broke out in her stomach. Of all the people to overhear that call, it had to be an instigator like Jake. "There was a problem with Mary's—"

"Test results," he finished flatly. "Yeah, I know. Well, guess what. There's a problem with mine, too."

Behind her, the door hissed open and Aelyx stepped inside, pausing to survey the tension with a sweeping gaze. Cara felt a brief moment of relief at seeing him until she noticed the parallel lines between his eyes and realized he hadn't come here bearing good news.

"What's wrong?" she asked.

After another sideways glance at Jake, he moved closer to

her and used Silent Speech instead of speaking aloud. *Why did you transfer the human female away from the sanitation department?*

Right away Cara sensed his urgency, which surprised her. He was upset about her decision, and so were several other L'eihrs. *You heard about that, too?*

*Just now, yes. Her supervisor contacted me with a complaint.* He then shared a brief stream of consciousness that explained everything. Mary's former crew partner—the L'eihr who'd barely spoken to her—harbored a secret crush, but he wasn't sure how to proceed. He'd hoped to use their shifts together to understand more about her. In reassigning Mary, not only had Cara hindered a potential match; she'd also made the L'eihrs in the sanitation department worry she'd shown favoritism toward a human. They were growing resentful of the number of L'eihrs holding service-related positions within the colony.

Cara's eyes began to water. She couldn't win.

Aelyx cupped her chin in a comforting gesture, but she felt his frustration. He wished she had talked to him first instead of making a snap decision. *I'll find a way to smooth it over. Your intentions were pure. Maybe if you transfer the L'eihr male to the same department, he'll withdraw his complaint.*

But then she would have to replace two slots in sanitation instead of one. *No, I'll put Mary back in her old job.* She wasn't looking forward to that conversation. Mary would be crushed. Besides, reversing the decision so quickly would make Cara look every bit as incompetent as Jake already thought she was.

"Don't tell anyone what you overheard," she said to Jake. "There's been a change of plan. Mary's going back to sanitation."

*"What?"* he cried. Despite his former objection, clearly he'd hoped to use Mary's transfer as a springboard for his own.

"This should make you happy," Cara told him. "Now you know I'm not playing favorites." While he sputtered in shock, she swept a hand toward the door. "Next time you want to talk to me, make an appointment like everyone else."

Jake stormed out in a rage. Aelyx dropped a supportive kiss on her head and followed, leaving her alone to clean up the mess she'd made.

Eight hours and several awkward conversations later, Cara sank onto her futon in hopes of decompressing from the stressful day. But her backside had barely met the seat cushion when a series of rapid-fire knocks clattered on her apartment door, hard enough to rattle the keypad. There was a special kind of anger behind those knuckles that told her exactly whose hand they were attached to. When she answered the door, she saw that she was right.

"Jake," she forced through her teeth while smiling tightly. She took notice of the half dozen others lingering behind him in the hall, immigrants from Earth whose names she hadn't learned yet. "And friends. What's the emergency?"

"We're tired of—"

"This *is* an emergency, right?" Cara interrupted. "Because we talked about setting boundaries. Evenings are for family and—"

"Oh, please." He slipped around her into the apartment. "Your boyfriend's not even here. I saw him in the lounge with a bunch of other L'eihrs."

As the group followed him inside, Cara counted backward from ten to one, determined not to pop off and say something she would regret later. She'd already exceeded her daily allotment of unprofessionalism, and the last thing she wanted to do was give Jake more ammunition to use against her.

"Don't just stand there," he said to the others. "Speak up."

There was a beat of hesitation, followed by shuffling feet. Then six pairs of eyes turned to the floor and the complaints began flying.

"I hate my job."

"There's nothing to do here."

"I want an apartment on the first floor."

"The food's disgusting."

"There's no privacy in the bathroom."

"These uniforms are tacky. Why can't we wear jeans?"

Despite her best efforts, Cara couldn't stop her upper lip from hitching. If whiners grew on trees, this place would be an orchard.

"Back home," Jake said, puffing his chest, "I was the leader of a multimillion dollar corporation. So explain to me why I'm stuck on the maintenance crew while you call all the shots." He glared at her and added, "What're you, like, twelve?"

There was a collective intake of breath, and the room went uncomfortably silent. Everyone seemed to know Jake had crossed a line . . . with the exception of Jake himself, whose chin lifted another inch. All eyes shifted to Cara as if waiting to see what she'd do next.

Her face heated, mostly with fury, but with hurt, too. These people had no idea how hard she'd fought for the freedoms they took for granted, or how much she'd sacrificed for this colony. As the group continued watching her, she knew her next move was pivotal. If she let Jake talk down to her, it would undermine her power. She had to make an example out of him.

"Starting tomorrow," she said, "you will report to the guard station at the end of your regular shift. I'm assigning you a week of nighttime work detail." She took a step toward him, raising her face to his. "If you have a problem with that, you can choose a Reckoning instead. But I'll warn you: That lash stings like a bitch."

She made a show of glancing around at the others. "Anyone else want to disrespect me or challenge my authority tonight?"

None of them argued or spoke up for Jake, who stood there frozen and white-faced. But as his friends ducked their heads and strode into the hallway, Cara noticed more fear in their eyes than respect. She felt a pinch in her stomach. This wasn't how she wanted to lead.

Once they left, she spoke to Jake in a calmer voice. "The L'eihrs made me one of their leaders because of my actions, not my age. You don't have to like it, but if you want to live here, you have to accept it."

"What if I don't want to live here?"

They stared each other down for a few moments. She was about to offer him a ticket to the next Earthbound transport when the door slid into the wall with a *hiss*, and someone new walked inside, a L'eihr girl with a beautiful heart-shaped face.

Cara did a double take. It was Syrine. "You're back!" she called with a smile. She hadn't spoken to Syrine since their last day on the transport. The therapy seemed to have worked. Syrine looked more peaceful—still softened by grief but not ruled by it.

Syrine glanced back and forth between Cara and Jake. "And just in time, I see."

Cara huffed a dry laugh. No matter how powerful Syrine's gift, her skills were no match for Jake's assholery.

"Are you a guard?" he asked. "Because I didn't break any rules."

Syrine shook her head and approached him. "I'm a special kind of healer. I can remove negative emotions and clear your mind to help you see the root of a problem."

"Like mind control?"

"Not at all. I provide clarity and comfort. The rest is up to you."

Jake didn't seem convinced, but he allowed Syrine into his personal space and held her gaze as she peered up at him with wide, silvery eyes.

"Now relax," she said, and in response, his shoulders eased down.

A minute later she broke contact, and Cara noticed the slight shift in her mannerisms that said she'd absorbed Jake's anger and was working to process it out of her system. Once the tension had left her jaw, she faced Jake with her usual calm.

"You're frustrated because you want to make a difference here, and you fear you're not needed. But you're wrong. You have an agile mind, good for problem solving. That's why you tested into the maintenance department." Syrine paused, wrinkling her forehead. "And there's a L'eihr girl you like, but she won't talk to you, no matter how hard you try to impress her. You think L'eihrs are cold, and you're wrong about that, too."

His cheeks turned pink.

"Human mating rituals won't work on her," Syrine said. "They didn't work on me, either. My *l'ihan* was human. His pursuits annoyed me at first, until he risked his life to save me. That was the first time I saw him for who he was—selfless and brave. He died before I had a chance to say that I loved him, but I did. Even in death, he has my heart." She touched Jake's arm, a rare move, as L'eihrs weren't accustomed to casual contact. "My people aren't cold. Show this girl who you are, and she'll respond."

Jake's face flushed crimson. Instead of thanking Syrine, he shook off her hand and backed toward door. "Stay out of my head," he muttered, and then charged out of the room without a backward glance.

Cara made a noise of disgust. "What a jerk."

"Not really," Syrine said. "You judge him too harshly." She fingered the pendant at her neck, a pear seed floating inside a tiny glass sphere. Cara didn't know the specifics, but the seed was a treasured reminder of David.

Sympathy plucked at Cara's heart. "I did what you asked and waited to plan David's memorial. Now that you're here, maybe we can—"

"No!" Syrine snapped. Her eyes went round and wild in a way that prompted Cara to take a step back. "I'm sorry. I didn't mean to yell at you. I just don't want to talk about that right now."

"It's okay," Cara said. "Whenever you're ready."

She didn't stand in the way as Syrine mumbled apologies and made excuses to leave. Cara tried convincing herself the outburst was related to Jake's anger, but she couldn't help wondering if Syrine had left the continent too soon.

When Aelyx came home, he looked almost as rough as she felt.

Cara tapped a finger against her cheek in mock reflection. "*Be a representative for your people*, they said. *It'll be fun*, they said."

His expression melted into a warm smile, and she knew what he was thinking because she felt the same way. No matter what they had to put up with during the day, the nights together were worth it. "Representatives?" he asked, making a show of looking around. "I don't see any of those in here."

It was a hint to leave her work outside, one she willingly took. She rose to join him at the doorway, where he gathered her in an embrace that dissolved all her worries faster than sugar melting on the tip of her tongue. She squeezed him while emotion rose up inside her. Every time she thought she couldn't love him any more intensely, her heart grew and demanded to be filled. It was the very best kind of hunger, which resulted in neither of them getting much sleep. But that was all right. She could sleep when she was dead.

An hour later, they were tangled up on the futon, too exhausted to move.

Or so she thought.

Aelyx tightened his arms around her and nuzzled the side of her neck in a hint that he'd found an extra pocket of energy and wasn't ready for the night to end.

"Again?" she whispered. "Don't you ever get tired?"

"Not of you."

"It's unnatural. No one has that much stamina."

He flashed a wicked grin, and all of a sudden she wasn't so tired anymore. "Is that a challenge?"

Just as she hooked a leg around his hip, her com-sphere buzzed an alert. Its frequency told her The Way was calling, which struck her as odd, because they'd never summoned her this late before. As Aelyx retreated to the bedroom, she pulled on her pants and tunic, then spoke her passkey while finger-combing her hair. She hoped the lighting in the room was dim enough that the Elders wouldn't know what she'd been up to.

But one look at their waxen faces, and she knew they wouldn't care.

Something was wrong.

"We need to convene at once," Alona said. "There's no time to send a shuttle, so you and Devinder will participate from your quarters." Her gaze shifted to the stretch of futon on either side of Cara. "Are you alone?"

Cara nodded. Aelyx was close enough to overhear from the other room, but she would tell him everything anyway.

Devinder's hologram appeared, and Alona repeated to him what she'd told Cara. Then she called the meeting to order by abruptly dropping a bomb on them. "The Aribol have made contact. They requested a remote meeting that will begin momentarily."

"We're having a conference call with the Aribol?" Cara blurted.

"Essentially, yes."

"But how? The probes they launched didn't speak any of our languages."

"It seems the probes were intended to collect our speech

patterns, among other data, for this very purpose," Alona said. "The fact that the request was recorded in a variety of human languages indicates probes were sent to Earth as well as L'eihr."

That was news to Cara. She hadn't heard of any probes landing on her home world. The governments of Earth must've covered it up. They were good at that.

"Do we know what they want?" asked Devinder.

"No," Alona told him. "But their request was more of a demand."

Cara had a bad feeling about this. If the Aribol wanted to make contact, why hadn't they sent a representative to visit Earth and L'eihr? That would've been the friendlier thing to do.

Maybe they weren't friendly.

A high-pitched whine rang out in the background, and all eight Elders stiffened visibly in their seats. "The transmission is about to begin," Alona said. "Remember: We fed false information regarding our weaponry systems and our population size to their mechanical probes, so choose your words carefully."

She spoke her passkey, and the image of a man's head and shoulders flickered to life, floating like a specter in front of the Elders.

Cara leaned closer to the hologram, drinking in every detail. Until now, no one had known what the Aribol looked like. There was even some argument as to whether they existed. This creature was undeniably real, but Cara doubted she was seeing his true form. His face resembled a ceramic mask, oval and unnaturally smooth, and his shoulders lacked the contours of muscle or bone.

"Greetings, children," he said without moving his lips. His voice sounded computerized, as if filtered through translation software. Maybe the Aribol didn't communicate with words. That would make sense, considering their rumored psychic abilities.

"I am the head Elder," Alona said. "Those of us gathered here compose The Way, our governing body. With whom are we speaking?"

"My name and face are beyond the comprehension of your Noven brains. For the sake of simplicity, you may call me Zane."

"Noven?" asked Alona.

"The collective name we give the children we've seeded throughout the universe. All of you are descended from a single race."

Cara's brows jumped at the revelation. She'd suspected this, but had never had any proof. She wanted so badly to ask where the Noven race originated. Her bet was on Earth, where the remains of ancient primates indicated mankind had evolved slowly over time. Unless the ancient primates themselves had been seeded on Earth . . .

"So the legends are true," Alona mused. "Humans and L'eihrs share a common ancestor."

"Yes. Your kind is a quaint species."

"*My* kind?" Alona said. "Is that to say you and I are unrelated?"

"Correct."

"Why refer to us as your children, then?"

"Ah." His voice raised a pitch as if in amusement. "An understandably confusing term, meant in a figurative way. My people have grown fond of your race; we've come to view you as progeny. But we are a singular species. We share no lineage with any of the beings we've discovered." As Zane spoke, he turned to take in all ten members of The Way. When his shadowy eyes passed over Cara, they caught and held for a moment before moving on, almost as though he recognized her. Maybe she'd imagined it. "We rarely intervene in our children's lives, but for the protection of all, we must make an exception in this case."

"How so?"

"We cannot allow an alliance to exist between Earth and L'eihr."

Cara's stomach dipped.

"Over the millennia," Zane continued, "your civilizations have developed more aggressive tendencies than other Noven. The merging of your planets poses a threat to delicate races we've seeded in nearby galaxies. Through exploration, you may discover these races and decide to overtake them."

Alona said what Cara was thinking. "We are a threat to no one."

"That is not for you to decide."

"But we haven't done anything wrong," Cara told him, unable to stay quiet any longer. "There's no evidence to back up what you're saying."

"This is a proactive measure to maintain peace," Zane said. "We will allow humans and L'eihrs one month to return to your respective planets and then surrender all interstellar travel technology. If you refuse to comply, both civilizations will have to be neutralized."

Cara sputtered, too stunned to speak. The Aribol weren't simply demanding the end of the alliance—they wanted a permanent separation of humans and L'eihrs. Not only would she lose her home and never see Aelyx again, but both societies would suffer. L'eihrs needed humans to breathe new life into their gene pool, and L'eihr technology had saved Earth on more than one occasion. Agreeing to Zane's terms might save them in the short term, but it could also lead to their extinction.

"Please reconsider," she begged. "At least make an exception for humans on the colony who want to stay. Some of us have found *l'ihans*—life partners. None of us are violent. You don't know what you're asking."

Zane stared blankly at her for a moment. "I am sorry, young human, but there can be no exception. It is better to leave your mate than to bring about the destruction of your kind. We don't enjoy punishing our children, but we do, when necessary."

"How do we know you have the means to destroy us?" Alona asked.

His façade swiveled toward her. "Here is a demonstration to eliminate any doubt."

There was a beat of silence, followed by a clamorous roar from the sky. Cara rushed to the window and peered up. She didn't see anything at first, but then debris began to enter the atmosphere in great balls of fire that streaked through the darkness and landed in distant ocean waters.

"That was your spaceport and your Voyager fleet," Zane told them casually, as if discussing what he should order for dinner. "One transport craft remains intact for use in complying with our demands. I urge you to obey. We've neutralized entire worlds for less than this."

And with that, his image vanished.

Cara couldn't blink, and her lungs seemed to have

stopped working. Her mind kept jumping the tracks from one train of thought to another: *Was anyone on board those ships when they exploded? Was the spaceport empty? Why didn't the Aribol just kill us all and be done with it? What are Aelyx and I going to do? Maybe we can live in hiding. But wait. We're famous on Earth. If we both disappear, people will know we ran away together. What if someone tells? What if the Aribol make an example out of us, like I did to Jake?*

"Miss Sweeney."

At the sound of her name, Cara jerked to attention. "Sorry," she told Alona. "I'm still in shock."

"I'd like to hear your initial thoughts. Your instincts have proven useful to me in the past."

Cara blew out a long breath and tried to calm down. As she processed the news, her first reaction was that something didn't add up. There was no reason to believe humans and L'eihrs would attack other worlds. And Zane had said the Aribol didn't like to interfere. So why would they sit back for thousands of years of war and genocide on Earth and then step in now? There had to be a different reason, an ulterior motive for banning the alliance. "Maybe they're the ones planning a takeover. Maybe they're trying to weaken us for an invasion."

Alona remained silent for a while, both hands folded on her lap. "An interesting theory, though they didn't ask for the surrender of our weaponry systems."

Devinder pointed out, "And we exaggerated our defenses to the mechanical probes by showing them multiple images of *iphal* cannons. The Aribol believe we're heavily armed."

"My gut's telling me something's not right," Cara insisted.

"What do we know about the Aribol? Can we track Zane's transmission to see where it came from?"

"I already did." Alona brought up a digital screen and swiped at the data with an index finger. "His signal originated from a galaxy our Voyagers discovered last year. We've yet to explore it."

*Last year?* Cara frowned. Wasn't that when the probes had begun falling?

"As for what we know," interjected a male Elder seated to Alona's right, "the Aribol are a mystery. One of our scholars, Larish, compiled ages of research and rumor to form his own theories about their kind, but they're just that—theories."

Cara knew Larish. He was a middle-aged academic who specialized in humanities. She'd visited him months ago, when she'd first suspected that Jaxen and Aisly were part Aribol. According to Larish, the race predated every known life form in the universe, they possessed extreme psychic abilities, and they wielded technology advanced enough to blow her "Noven" mind. She'd always assumed the Aribol were a bunch of bored ancients who amused themselves by playing god.

Looked like she was right.

"We need more information," she said.

"Agreed." Alona peered at her fellow Elders. "In addition to the transport, we have one Voyager ship the Aribol missed. It's away on a mission. I'll call it home and send it to investigate Zane's location. To be safe, all humans will return to Earth at once."

Panic squeezed Cara's windpipe. "All humans? Can't some of us stay behind to help the Voyager crew?"

Alona frowned. "Perhaps, but you won't be among them.

50

I need you on Earth to act on behalf of The Way." As if reading Cara's thoughts, she added, "You may bring Aelyx with you. If we're forced to meet the Aribols' demands, he can return to L'eihr before the deadline."

"Do you mind if I assemble a team to come with me?" Cara asked. "Including Larish? He can inspect the probes that were sent to Earth."

"You may," Alona agreed. "If I require his input, I'll confer with him remotely."

The meeting adjourned, and as soon as Cara's com-sphere shut down, Aelyx rushed in from the bedroom and swept her into a hug that lifted her toes off the floor.

"I won't leave you," he murmured in her ear. "No matter what happens."

She hugged him close and nodded into his shoulder, but deep down, she knew neither of them would risk the lives of billions in order to stay together.

She didn't want to think about that right now.

"Let's call an emergency meeting in the dining hall," she said. One month was barely enough time for a L'eihr transport to make it to Earth and back. Every minute counted. "We need to be out of here before dawn."


Devinder relayed the news in his native language to the colonists, and those who didn't speak L'eihr used translator earpieces to listen. When he was done, Cara stood up and added a few words of her own.

"I know life here has been an adjustment, and we don't always see eye-to-eye. But no matter how you feel about the colony, ending the alliance is bad for all of us. If you agree, I hope you'll volunteer to join the Voyager ship when it returns. They need all the help they can get; they lost a lot of explorers today." She glanced around the room. "Are any humans willing to stay behind?"

To her immense surprise, Jake Winters was the first to raise his hand. "I will."

His response inspired a few of his friends, who lifted their arms and echoed his words. Their willingness prompted even more to do the same, and before long, half the human colonists had volunteered for duty.

"Thank you," Cara told them. "Everyone else, you have five minutes to pack a bag, then report to shuttle number three. Our transport is fueled and waiting."

The room cleared, and Aelyx jogged in from the lobby to meet her. "I just spoke to Elle on the continent. She's going to join Larish and meet us on the ship."

"Good." Cara was grateful to have Aelyx's sister on the team. Elle worked mostly as a medic, but she had other skills, too. She was the one who'd taught Cara how to block her thoughts, which had saved her from Jaxen's multiple attempts at brainwashing. There was only one problem. "Did you tell Syrine?"

Aelyx cringed. Elle and Syrine were former best friends who'd turned into enemies years ago, when they'd allowed a boy to come between them. "I was going to let her find out for herself."

Cara shook her head at him. Leave it to a guy to underestimate frenemies.

The sound of footsteps drew her attention to a young L'eihr girl, who was hurrying toward them with worry etched on her face. As soon as the girl reached Cara, she skidded to a halt and locked their gazes to use Silent Speech.

*There's a problem,* she said in a rush. *I was going to tell you in the morning, but now there's no time.*

*What's wrong?* Cara asked.

*I work in the medical center. After supper, I received an alert that the cryogenic chamber had been opened. When I went to the lab to see what was wrong, I discovered the human body had been moved to the crematorium.*

It took a second for Cara to figure out who the girl was talking about. *David's body? The soldier we brought here from Earth?*

The girl nodded. *I contacted the crematorium, but it was too late. The remains have been incinerated.*

Cara massaged her forehead. This was why she'd wanted to bury David sooner rather than later. Burial was a foreign concept to the L'eihrs. An error like this was bound to happen.

At that precise moment, Syrine appeared by Cara's side with a duffel bag slung over one shoulder. "I'm ready." She glanced around at the group. "Is something wrong?"

"No," Cara lied, because now wasn't the time to explain something so delicate. She would tell Syrine on the transport, when they were alone. She locked eyes with the medic and pushed a hurried thought into her mind. *Keep this quiet until we leave.* Then she took Aelyx's hand and led him toward the lobby. "We have to pack. Meet you at the shuttle."

Inside her apartment, Cara stuffed a week's worth of uniforms into her bag while doing her best not to look around—at the joined cots where she and Aelyx had slept in each other's arms; at the futon where she'd rested her head on his lap and read *Jane Eyre* to him; at the data table where they'd played virtual chess; at the collection of seashells sitting in a bucket by the door.

At the home they'd made together.

"Ready?" Aelyx asked, his own duffel bag in hand.

Cara nodded, because her throat was too thick to let words pass. She resisted the urge to grab a handful of shells as a memento, telling herself this wasn't really goodbye. The colony was her home, and one day soon she would return to it.

When she strode out the door, she didn't look back.

## Chapter Five

By the time they reached Earth's atmosphere, their one month deadline had shrunk to a mere sixteen days. Aelyx had never felt more helpless in his life. He couldn't wait to disembark for the shuttle to Manhattan so he could actually *do* something for a change.

"Perhaps they don't possess physical bodies . . ."

Something besides theorizing with Larish.

"Of course they do," Aelyx replied. He had nothing against the scholar, but ideas would only take them so far. They needed facts about the Aribol, and as of yet, the Voyagers hadn't uncovered any. "How else would they build the technology to destroy our spaceport?"

"Their minds are powerful. Maybe they enslaved another race to do it."

Aelyx pinched the bridge of his nose. He couldn't take any more. He left Larish and crossed to the other side of the transmissions room, where Cara was engaged in a terse conversation with Jake Winters's hologram.

"The L'eihrs won't listen to me," Jake hissed, his blond brows forming slashes over narrowed eyes. It was almost magical how his bitterness transcended the distance of multiple galaxies. "I have an idea for probes that would measure brainwave activity instead of energy output, but my software codes aren't compatible with their system. I need a L'eihr to work with me."

Syrine strode to Aelyx's side with labored steps that told him she hadn't recovered from the news of David's cremation. He couldn't blame her. In a way, it was as if she'd lost him a second time. And because Aelyx knew her so well, he also knew she didn't want to talk about it. So he wrapped an arm around her shoulders, and they resumed listening to the conversation. Their images must not have appeared within Jake's line of vision, because he didn't seem to notice them.

"Did you ask *nicely*?" Cara said.

"Yes!" Jake flung a hand in the air. "They ignored all my..." He trailed off and feigned a casual smile at the exact moment a young L'eihr female walked behind him. The flash in his eyes made it clear he liked the girl. As soon as she passed out of view, Jake's lips curved downward again. "They think humans are idiots. I can tell."

*Well . . .* Aelyx thought, tipping his head, *a few of them are.*

Syrine crouched by Cara's side and entered the conversation. "Stop that girl," she said, pointing. "The one who just passed you. Her name is Ayah."

Jake hesitated, then turned and called out to the girl. He waved her over, and soon her hologram appeared alongside

56

his, though at a distance that indicated how uncomfortable she was in his presence. She glanced at Cara and Syrine.

"Yes?" she asked in L'eihr.

Syrine spoke in their native language. "This human wants to make a prototype that could find the Aribols' home planet. He needs help understanding our systems. Will you work with him?"

Ayah winced. "I don't like him. He's loud, and he stands too close when he talks."

"I'll tell him to give you space," Syrine said. When that didn't yield results, she added, "I would consider this a favor. Remember when I helped *you* during your breakup with—"

"I remember," Ayah blurted, her cheeks darkening. "I'll do it."

Syrine grinned and addressed Jake in English. "Ayah is happy to assist you with the project." She held up an index finger. "But remember, our ears are more sensitive than yours. Use a soft voice when you speak to her, and keep an arm's length of distance between you."

Jake's skin turned the shade of ripe berries, but he thanked Syrine and delivered a wobbly smile. When the transmission ended, Aelyx tried to catch Syrine's eye so he could ask why she'd gone out of her way to help Jake with the target of his affections, but she wouldn't hold his gaze long enough for Silent Speech. He couldn't blame her for that either. If their situations were reversed, he would want to keep his grief private, too.

Cara pocketed her com-sphere and looped an arm through his. "Hey, I forgot. Did you get through to the ambassador?"

Aelyx nodded. "He's expecting us, but I'm not sure about the sleeping arrangements." There were three guest bedrooms in the Manhattan penthouse, and eight bodies in need of beds: Aelyx, Cara, Elle, Syrine, Larish, and Cara's family, who'd flown in to meet her.

"It's no biggie. Most of us have been roommates at some point." Cara gestured at Elle, who had just entered from the hallway. "She bunked with me and my brother in the Aegis."

Elle turned her eyes toward them, and her gaze brightened. Her abnormally long eyelashes gave her a deceptively meek appearance as she smiled at them, but upon noticing Syrine, she scowled and returned to the corridor.

Syrine sniffed dryly. "Tell Elyx'a"—Elle's given name—"that she and I won't be sharing quarters."

"Tell her yourself," Aelyx said. "I'm tired of being your go-between."

Syrine spun around, flicking him in the face with her ponytail before charging away.

"Must be tough," Cara observed while resting her head on his shoulder. "Caught in the middle of all that drama between your best friend and your sister."

"Not really. You keep forgetting—"

"That Elle is more like a friend than a sister, and nuclear families don't exist at the Aegis," Cara finished. "Blah, blah, blah. Just admit it's annoying."

"It is," he conceded. "We should lock them in a room until they forgive each other."

"Oh, sweetie," Cara said, patting his arm. "You don't know much about girls, do you?"

Aelyx smiled as an echo of grief tugged at his stomach. "That's what David used to say." He missed his friend. David had made mistakes, but only because he was under duress. In the end, he'd done the right thing, and that was all that mattered. "If I can forgive David for trying to kill me, why can't Syrine and Elle move past a love triangle?"

"It's basic Girl Code. If you and your bestie share a crush, neither of you can have him. Exes are off-limits, too, though my former BFF didn't get the memo on that."

A simultaneous chime sounded from their com-spheres, informing them that the shuttle was ready for boarding. Aelyx had requested a specific craft, one he could pilot himself. It was a small ten-seater, equipped with cloaking technology that would allow him to hide it in plain sight. That way they'd have access to rapid transportation if they needed to fly across the globe to meet with world leaders.

Everyone returned to their respective rooms to pack their duffels, and then the team met in the hangar. Aelyx made Syrine and Elle wait until last to board, so they'd have no choice but to share a seat. They turned their glares on him instead of each other, which he supposed was progress. He offered the copilot's seat to Cara and took his place behind the wheel, and then they were off, speeding away from the transport into the clouds.

He used his com-sphere to inform the head of his security detail, Colonel Rutter, that he was en route, and once the colonel cleared Aelyx to enter military airspace, he began his descent and landed the shuttle on one of the base's vacant helipads.

Cara's parents were already visible though the front shield, both of them bouncing and waving from the mouth of an adjacent hangar, where they stood with a dozen or so uniformed soldiers. No sooner had Aelyx cut the engine than Cara threw open the passenger door and bounded across the tarmac toward her family, her scarlet braid trailing in the breeze. Bill Sweeney caught his daughter in his bearlike arms and twirled her in a dozen circles before he set her down and she stumbled dizzily to embrace Eileen.

Aelyx stepped outside and cringed at the change in temperature since his last visit. New York in spring had been tolerable, but now the air was stifling hot and so humid he could almost drown from breathing it. By the time he caught up with Cara, the front of his tunic was damp with sweat.

Eileen didn't seem to mind. She launched herself at him in a crushing hug and then planted sticky kisses on his cheeks. "We missed you so much," she said, pulling back to brush the lint off his tunic and smooth the strands of hair that had escaped his ponytail.

Aelyx let her fuss over him, glad for the attention. As a clone, this was the closest he would ever come to having a mother. "I missed you, too."

A soldier snuck up behind Cara and captured her in a headlock. Aelyx stiffened until he recognized the boy as Troy Sweeney, her older brother. Troy had the same electric blue eyes as Cara, but he'd inherited their mother's black hair instead of their father's red. He scrubbed his knuckles over Cara's scalp until she squealed and thrust an elbow in his belly. Then he ruffled her already mussed hair and called her dorkus.

Aelyx shared a glance with Elle and tried to imagine having that kind of sibling bond with her. Clearly she was thinking the same thing, because she told him privately, *If you ever do that to me, I'll smother you in your sleep.*

"Elle," Troy breathed, yanking off his camouflage hat and flinching to attention. His pupils widened and his teeth flashed in a lopsided smile. His reaction was nearly identical to that of Jake Winters, and Aelyx had to clamp his lips together to trap a laugh. He'd forgotten about Troy's unrequited crush on Elle.

Aelyx nudged Elle and asked, *Have you picked out names for your offspring yet?* She burned a glare into his head, and he responded by making kissing noises, which earned him a punch on the arm.

"Uh-huh," Cara muttered. "You're nothing like human siblings at all."

"I didn't know you were coming," Troy said to Elle while sliding an annoyed look at his sister. "Someone forgot to mention it."

Cara rolled her eyes. "Excuse me for being preoccupied with saving the world from alien domination."

"Speaking of which," interrupted Colonel Rutter, who'd been silently observing them from the fringes. "Not a word about these Ari-bol"—mispronouncing it Airy-Ball—"to anyone outside the group. HALO will lose their damn minds, start rioting in the streets again." Aelyx grimaced as he recalled last year's run-ins with the fanatical group Humans Against L'eihr Occupation. Colonel Rutter motioned toward three black SUVs parked nearby. "We should probably get a move on before rush hour hits; otherwise it'll be gridlock on the bridge."

"I'd like to fly the shuttle to the penthouse," Aelyx said. "Cloaked, of course, so I can keep it docked there."

"Me, too," Cara added.

"All right." Rutter jutted his chin at Troy. "Sergeant Sweeney, go with them."

"Yes, sir."

"As for the rest of you," Rutter continued, "no one

sets foot outside that penthouse without an armed shadow. Understood?" He glanced around the group until he found Syrine, and then his no-nonsense tone went softer than a butterfly's wing. "Why don't you ride with me, hon? I've got a box for you in my car."

Syrine darted a glance at Aelyx while she fidgeted with her pear-seed pendant. Colonel Rutter had been David's commander, the one who'd assigned him as their bodyguard last winter. David hadn't left any family behind, so the box probably contained his possessions.

Syrine managed a smile that didn't reach her eyes. "Thank you for thinking of me."

Aelyx slid an arm around her. "I hope his deck of trick cards is in there. It was his favorite thing in the world, aside from you."

"*Trick* deck?" she asked. "You mean . . ."

"Every time he guessed your card, he was cheating," Aelyx finished with a grin. "I can't believe you never noticed." He leaned down and whispered, "Are you going to be okay? If not, you can ride with me in the shuttle."

"I'm fine," she whispered back. "I want to see what's in the box."

Colonel Rutter clapped his palms together. "All right, folks. Let's roll." He gestured at the shuttle. "Or fly, as the case may be."


The shuttle arrived in Manhattan well ahead of the SUV caravan, and Aelyx began circling the penthouse building while searching the adjacent streets for the most secluded place to dock the craft. He eventually settled on an alleyway between two restaurants, then landed the shuttle in front of a Dumpster overflowing with black garbage bags.

As soon as Aelyx climbed out, the stench of rotting food assaulted his nostrils. Cara and Troy jogged away from the Dumpster while he stayed behind to finish the docking process. Holding his breath, he pushed a button on his key fob, and in response, the shuttle rose fifteen feet into the air and stopped, invisible and safely out of reach.

Two soldiers were already waiting at the sidewalk. They led the way to the penthouse building, and Aelyx took Cara's hand and followed with Troy bringing up the rear. Aelyx kept his head down and his eyes trained on the pavement. He could almost pass for a human with his light brown skin and hair, but his silver irises gave him away every time. He wished he'd worn sunglasses for concealment. His fans meant well, but they didn't always respect personal boundaries, and he was in no mood to dodge undergarments thrown at his face.

He'd nearly reached the building's entrance when Cara stopped suddenly and dragged him to a halt. He glanced behind and found her gazing at a stack of magazines on a nearby newsstand. Arranged in rows, each copy was an identical edition of *Squee Teen*, featuring both of their faces on the cover and promising readers a look "Inside the Star Couple's *Perfect Life* on the Colony!"

Cara let go of his hand and picked up a magazine. As she thumbed through the glossy pages, Aelyx recognized the pictures they'd posed for months ago, when she'd agreed to the exclusive interview to entice more immigrants to the colony. There was a wide-angle photo of their living room and another that showed them cuddled on the futon, gazing into each other's eyes from above their mugs of spiced *h'ali.* She'd refused to allow the shoot in their bedroom, but the magazine's centerfold oozed romance in a montage of couple shots—the two of them strolling hand-in-hand on the beach; wading in the ocean with their bodies silhouetted against the sunset; pausing beneath a canopy of trees to share a kiss in the rain.

Aelyx's heart turned heavy. It truly had been a perfect life.

He caught himself using past tense. *Is,* he corrected. *It is a perfect life.*

The newsstand owner, an ebony-skinned man with spectacles perched on the end of his nose, glanced up from his cell phone, and his eyebrows twitched. He looked from Cara to the magazine and back again, then nearly dropped his phone in his haste to stand up from his stool and fish a pen from his pocket.

"Will you sign it to my daughter?" he asked, waving a black marker back and forth between them. "Her name is Talya. She's your biggest fan. She's going to die when she finds out I met you!"

When Cara couldn't tear her gaze away from the magazine, Aelyx picked up another copy and took the man's pen. He scrawled: *For Talya. Much l'ove, Aelyx and Cara* and then handed it back as the man snapped a picture with his phone.

From behind, Troy muttered, "We can't stay here."

Aelyx noticed they'd drawn the attention of several passersby, and he cupped Cara's elbow to move her along. She patted herself down with one hand as if looking for money to buy the magazine. The man told her, "Take it—I insist."

She thanked him, and they made their way to the penthouse building. No one spoke during the elevator ride to the top floor, but Aelyx knew Cara well enough to understand what she was thinking. Of all the obstacles they'd overcome to be together—prejudice, distance, violence, hate—this hurdle seemed nearly too high to jump. It chilled him to the marrow to imagine losing her now.

He squeezed her hand, as much to ground himself as to comfort her. When she raised her freckled face to his, he swore, *I won't stop fighting for us. Not ever. That life is still ours.*

She tucked the rolled-up magazine beneath the elevator handrail. *You're right. I don't need this.*

Troy exited the elevator first and glanced up and down the hallway before waving the rest of them forward. He told his fellow soldiers to stand guard in the hall, and while the men saluted one another and exchanged words, Aelyx knocked on the door.

The ambassador answered, looking much the same as he had last winter—his withered form stooped but his eyes as sharp as ever. *Welcome back, Aelyx*, Stepha said. *It's good to see you again. I only wish it were under better circumstances.*

As Aelyx led Cara and Troy into the foyer, his senses prickled and his footsteps slowed. Something about the ambassador's greeting struck him as odd. Stepha had called him by his given name instead of using the L'eihr term for brother. But more than that, the ambassador's mind seemed different. Aelyx was still puzzling about it when he turned around and discovered Stepha with a com-sphere in one hand and an *iphal* in the other—the same weapon that'd stopped Aelyx's heart several months ago.

"They're both here," the ambassador said into his sphere, then tossed it to the carpet while aiming the weapon at Aelyx's chest.

Aelyx dove for the floor, yelling for Cara and Troy to

run. The *iphal* made no sound, but its energy pulse distorted the air above him like waves of heat rising from asphalt. He scrambled on all fours to take cover behind the sofa as the ambassador shuffled across the rug in pursuit. Aelyx's pulse throbbed in his ears. He darted a glance around the sofa but couldn't see Cara or Troy. In desperation, he peered behind him for a weapon he could use, but it was too late. Stepha had reached the front of the sofa, and he leaned over it to take aim.

Aelyx thought fast. Gripping the base of the sofa, he flipped it over, knocking the ambassador backward and skewing his shot. Stepha's frail body crashed to the floor, and Aelyx trapped him there beneath the upended piece of furniture. Troy quickly reappeared and began prying the *iphal* out of Stepha's hand. The ambassador struggled to free himself and regain his weapon, even as his breaths rattled within his chest. Then the door burst open, and two soldiers stormed inside with their pistols drawn.

"Don't shoot," Aelyx yelled. He noticed Cara peeking out from behind the kitchen wall and told her, "Call an ambulance. Something's wrong. I think he might've punctured a lung."

"A punctured lung?" Troy repeated. "*That's* what you think is wrong?"

Aelyx shook his head to clear it. His adrenaline was still surging, making his limbs tremble. "Stepha's not in his right mind. I sensed it when he answered the door. It's almost as if someone got inside his head and . . ." He trailed off with a gasp. "Jaxen."

"Don't forget his sister, Aisly," Troy added with a note of disgust.

"She's not really Jaxen's sister," Aelyx said.

"Doesn't matter. That bitch has skills."

"But Jaxen is the only one who wants me dead," Aelyx pointed out. He recalled the message Stepha had sent right before he'd fired the weapon. *They're both here.* "Either way, whoever did this is probably coming here now."

Troy radioed Colonel Rutter to tell him the area wasn't secure, and the colonel replied with instructions to meet him at a safe house. Troy pocketed the *iphal* he'd confiscated and ordered, "Let's go."

Aelyx lifted the sofa off the ambassador. "What about him?"

"The men will stay with him until the ambulance arrives."

Aelyx backed away from the scene, unable to take his eyes off of Stepha until Troy delivered a rough shove that sent him stumbling into the foyer. Cara grabbed his hand, and the three of them jogged back to the elevator.

During the ride down, Cara rubbed a hand over his chest. "I thought I was going to have to use a defibrillator on you again."

"It's a new record," Aelyx said. "Less than an hour on this planet, and already someone's trying to kill me."

When the elevator stopped on the ground floor, Troy stepped out to scan the lobby. Finding it clear, he ordered them to follow, and they darted out the building doors and into the light of day . . . where they immediately stopped short at the sight of a thousand fans clogging the street.

Word had spread about Aelyx's return.

The sidewalk was so thick with people that he couldn't see a path along it. L'annabes dressed in low ponytails and mock gray-tan uniforms bounced in place, waving magazines and signs that read TAKE ME TO YOUR LEADER! and PROBE ME,

AELYX! There were plenty of protesters, too. He'd long ago learned to recognize the vitriol in their shouts. Police worked to keep the crowd behind temporary metal barricades, but the masses surged forward, making the bolts creak. Then someone spotted Aelyx and cried his name, and all hell broke loose.

A chorus of screams filled the air while cameras flashed, forcing him to shield his eyes. In front of him, Troy spread both arms and took a step back, prompting him to do the same. He was about to take Cara's hand and retreat into the lobby when something happened that defied the laws of science.

Abruptly, hundreds of people at the front of the crowd went hurtling backward, as if an invisible broom had swept them into a dustpan. Their bodies collided with those behind them, setting off a domino effect that resulted in half the mob lying on the pavement.

Voices went silent, and Aelyx blinked in shock.

What had just happened?

The masses began untangling their limbs and standing up, trading empty glances with one another. Some of them looked to the police for guidance, but those men were busy hauling their own bodies off the ground. There was a general murmur of confusion, and then a whooshing noise sounded from above.

Aelyx turned his gaze skyward, and things began to make sense.

Jaxen glided toward them, his long ponytail rippling in the breeze as he stood atop a hovercraft that bore a slight resemblance to a human surfboard. Aelyx didn't recognize the technology as anything that existed on Earth or on

L'eihr, and he wondered where Jaxen had obtained it. The instant Jaxen met Aelyx's gaze, his face broke into a manic grin that made him appear deranged. There was something new in Jaxen's eyes, a recklessness that prompted Aelyx to tuck Cara farther behind him.

"You're alive," Jaxen bellowed, hovering nearly within reach. "Good. I'll do the honors myself. You tried to kill me once, and as humans say, one good turn deserves—"

Troy fired his pistol at Jaxen in three quick blasts.

Aelyx flinched. All around him, heads ducked and bystanders screamed. But when he opened his eyes, Jaxen was still standing above them, his grin impossibly wider than before. That's when Aelyx noticed the object in his hand, a staff supporting a softball-size orb that glowed milky white. The orb seemed to have absorbed the bullets, or at least shielded him from them. Aelyx had never seen anything like it. There was no chance Jaxen had built this weapon on his own. Either he'd stolen it, or someone had armed him.

"Handy device, don't you think?" Jaxen said. "It's a Nova Staff, given to me by our mutual friend, Zane." Aelyx barely had time to process this revelation when Jaxen spoke again. "It harnesses energy and stores it, so I can do this." Then he pointed the orb at Cara's brother, and Troy flew back several yards, where he collided with a cluster of police officers and flattened them like bowling pins.

Cara screamed and tried to run to him, but Aelyx held her still. The safest place for her was inside the penthouse building. If they could make it to the elevator, they could hide on any number of floors. He inched her toward the door, but Jaxen stopped them with another sweep of his staff. Aelyx felt a blow to the chest, and the next thing he knew, he slammed against the concrete.

He heard shouts from the crowd, fans crying his name. Someone yelled, "Oh, my god! That guy's trying to kill Aelyx!" and in the span of two heartbeats, the crowd broke through the barricades and attacked Jaxen. They leaped up and grabbed his hovercraft, tipping it to and fro. Jaxen tried to strike back, but each time he raised his staff, he was forced to flail his arms for balance.

Aelyx didn't waste another moment watching. He pushed up from the ground and grabbed Cara's hand. The two of them raced for Troy, and after helping him to his feet, they half limped, half ran around the corner and didn't stop until they reached the shuttle.

Once they were safely inside, floating high above the chaos and cloaked by an invisible shield, Aelyx sat back against the pilot's seat and tried to steady his shaking hands. The relief of cheating death twice in the span of ten minutes caused him to laugh—a bizarre response, as he found nothing humorous about the situation. Quite the contrary, it disturbed and confused him to learn Zane had armed Jaxen. How had such a partnership formed, especially considering Jaxen had once intended to use humans in a war against the Aribol?

Only one thing was certain. Aelyx would never again complain about unwanted attention from the L'annabes. They were his heroes.

# CHAPTER SIX

In the movies, government safe houses were depicted as grubby apartments with sagging furniture and bad lighting that made everyone look jaundiced. For some reason, the feds were always playing poker in these films, or maybe reading the newspaper, while mafia informants paced the floor, twitching at every sound. Cara knew she wouldn't find any of Colonel Rutter's men playing cards—not unless they craved a boot up the tailpipe—but she hadn't expected the safe house to seem so . . . homey.

Nestled on a heavily wooded lot outside the city, the two-story log cabin looked more like an off-season ski lodge than a government hidey-hole. The house was shaded by a canopy of tree branches, and even offered a wide wraparound porch, perfect for watching the sunset and sipping lemonade. Maybe the armored Humvee parked on the driveway didn't scream *nature*, but if Cara closed her eyes and ignored the chattering soldiers on patrol, she could hear cicadas and birdsongs high in the trees, and detect notes of pine on the breeze, mingled with hints of musk from the bay.

"This is better than summer camp," she told Aelyx as they crossed the front lawn. "I should let the military hide me more often."

He huffed a dry laugh and kicked aside a pinecone. "Be careful what you wish for. The last safe house was a motel room the size of a closet. Six people, one toilet, twelve hours of tedious small talk."

Maybe the movies were more accurate than she'd thought.

Inside the cabin, her parents and a few others were standing in the living room, huddled in front of a flat screen television mounted on the wall. The TV's sound was muted, but Cara recognized the newsreel at first glance. In slow motion, the footage showed Jaxen wobbling on his hovercraft until he finally stabilized well enough to knock the crowd back with his staff. The caption along the bottom of the screen read ROGUE ALIEN WREAKS HAVOC IN MANHATTAN!

Cara watched Jaxen zoom off into the distance. "I guess that answers my question. He got away."

Her dad glanced over his shoulder at her, then turned off the screen. He went quiet for a moment, a surefire sign he was upset. "It's playing everywhere."

Cara gave her parents an extra peppy grin so they wouldn't worry. "I'll bet. It's not every day an alien hybrid gets his ass handed to him by a mob of angry fangirls."

Her casual act didn't fool them. Mom latched onto Dad's side and pressed her cheek to his chest while he stroked her hair and rubbed her lower back to comfort her. Her parents tended to become . . . *physical* . . . during times of stress, and the way they clung to each other told Cara she'd better claim the bedroom farthest from theirs before it was too late.

Some noises couldn't be unheard.

"I'm more interested in the weapon he used," Larish said, wrist-deep in a bag of pork rinds. It was an odd contrast to see someone of his generation—stiff and unemotional, not a hair of his graying ponytail out of place—munching on fried pigskins. Cara wondered if he knew what he was eating. "I've never seen anything like it."

Aelyx rubbed the knot on the back of his head. "Wait until you hear who gave it to him—our 'mutual friend' Zane."

At that information, Larish posed a question Cara had already asked herself: Why had the Aribol sent Jaxen to do their dirty work? More than that, she thought Jaxen had seemed . . . *off*, for lack of a better word. A few months ago, he'd been so obsessed with her that he'd stolen her DNA and asked her to rule by his side. Today he'd barely looked at her. Not that she was complaining; it just didn't make sense.

Nothing about this did.

"I studied the probes that landed on Earth," Larish said. "They're identical to the others, so that's no help." He paused with a pork rind suspended an inch from his lips. "When was the last time Jaxen and Aisly were seen on Earth?"

"The day of the alliance signing," Cara told him. "Why?"

"I'm curious how the staff came into Jaxen's possession. Was it sent to him? Or did he travel to the Aribols' home planet? Because if the latter is the case, then—"

Aelyx gasped. "Then the planet's location would be stored inside his ship's navigational system. We could tell the Voyagers where to go."

"Down to the exact coordinates."

Cara had never considered that. It could also explain Jaxen's odd behavior. Maybe the Aribol had altered his mind. "Jaxen and Aisly went totally off the grid. They could've been with the Aribol the whole time."

Larish crunched away, deep in thought. "But how did they find the planet to begin with?"

"Too bad we didn't think to ask," muttered Troy, who was sporting a wicked goose egg of his own, not to mention a black eye and two scraped elbows. His injuries reminded Cara that they had an expert medic at their disposal, but when she glanced around the room, she realized Elle wasn't there, and neither was Syrine.

"Where's Elle?"

At the mention of her name, Troy perked up and sucked in his stomach.

Mom pointed at the ceiling. "Checking on her friend." She added with a sympathetic shake of her head, "Whatever was in that box really upset the girl."

Aelyx furrowed his brow and glanced at the stairs. Cara told him, "Go ahead and check on Syrine. I have to contact Alona anyway." Standing on tiptoe, she whispered, "And while you're up there, call dibs on a room for us—one far away from wherever my parents are sleeping."

Aelyx's cheeks colored, and he glanced at her dad. When he returned his gaze to hers, he shared a stream of consciousness that made her smile. Memories flitted through his mind of the day her father had caught them making out in her bedroom. The trauma had obviously left a mark, because Aelyx was terrified to touch her with Dad under the same roof.

*Not for that,* she told him. *If we want to be alone, we'll have to sneak into the woods like normal teenagers.*

And with that settled, they went their separate ways.

She slipped out the back door and found a quiet spot at the rear of the yard, where the grass thinned and gave way to fallen pine needles. The sun had nearly disappeared from the summer sky, bathing the landscape in its gentle glow. But the illumination was more than enough to reveal the strain in Alona's clasped hands when her hologram appeared.

"You have news," Alona said. It wasn't a question. "Disturbing news, according to the lines above your eyebrows."

Cara rubbed a finger over her forehead and described everything that had happened, down to the last detail. "I haven't seen Aisly, so I don't know if she's involved." Or if the Aribol had given her a weapon, too. She hoped not.

Alona considered in silence for a while. "Did Jaxen seem to have a larger goal when he confronted you? Aside from killing Aelyx?"

"Not that I could tell, but he must have a purpose here." The Aribol hadn't armed him so he could return to Earth to settle an old grudge. "The other ten hybrids," she asked, recalling that The Way had rounded them up, "are they alive?"

"Yes," Alona said. "We found no reason to believe they colluded with Jaxen, so we're allowing them to live in a controlled environment."

"Have they been acting weird lately?"

*"Weird?"* Alona repeated. The word sounded funny in her accent.

"Different than usual."

"I don't interact with them, but I'll make an inquiry." Alona unclasped her hands and used one to massage the other. It was a rare tell, a show of anxiety that knocked Cara's confidence down a notch. "On the topic of unusual behavior, the Earth Council has refused to accept my last three transmissions. I need you to find out what the problem is. We can't discuss strategy without communication, and our time is growing short."

"I'll go first thing tomorrow," Cara said. The Earth Council office was in Manhattan, a short flight away in the shuttle. "Any word from the Voyagers?"

"There's been no progress."

"Well, if Jaxen visited the Aribol and if we can find his ship, we might be able to access his flight log and—"

"Miss Sweeney," Alona interrupted. "I heard two *if*s and one *might* in that statement. I understand your concern, but please remember that finding the Aribol will only provide us with more information. In all likelihood, we'll never be able to defeat them. Now that Jaxen is involved, there's reason to believe the Aribol are gathering their own allies." The wrinkles around her mouth deepened. "The colony was my dream, long before you were born. Nothing would pain me more than to divide our people, but that's what I have to prepare for."

Cara shook her head. It was too soon to quit.

"Two days," Alona said. "That's all I can spare before I call my people home. Even that much is a risk, considering the length of the journey."

Their conversation ended, and the sun slipped over the horizon, leaving behind a purple bruise of twilight and the reminder of another day gone. Numbly, Cara shifted to her feet and stared into the wooded shadows.

Two days. Two sunsets.

What could she possibly hope to accomplish in that time?

She was so deep in thought she didn't hear the light crunch of boots until they were right behind her. But she knew who they belonged to. The cadence of those steps was more familiar to her than her own heartbeat. She whirled around and threw her arms around Aelyx's neck. She didn't have to tell him what she needed. He gathered her tightly in his arms, and the night seemed a little less dark.

"How did you know?" she whispered.

"Know what?"

"That I needed you."

"I didn't," he confessed. "I came out here because I needed *you*."

His words melted her heart, because they reaffirmed what she already believed: They belonged together. Their love was an actual force of nature, a spiritual gravity that bound them like planets in orbit.

God help anyone who tried to take him away from her.

Tomorrow she was going into the city, and she wouldn't leave until the Earth Council pulled their heads out of the sand. She dared Jaxen to try and stop her. Let him wield his staff. No weapon on earth was stronger than the will of a girl in love.

When dawn broke, Aelyx was dressed and ready. He tiptoed down the hall to wake the others while Cara finished grooming herself in the washroom. He didn't share her opinion that cloying hairspray and chalky cosmetics would increase the Council's respect for her, but she'd dismissed him, claiming he didn't understand how human minds worked.

That much was true.

He shook Troy's shoulder and then nudged Elle, who dozed in the adjacent bed. He knew the two of them had briefly shared a room in the Aegis many months ago, but he wondered if there was another reason his sister had agreed to sleep here. He made a mental note to tease her about it later. Unnerving her gave him an odd sort of satisfaction.

When he reached the door to Syrine's room, he paused, unsure of what condition he would find her in. Yesterday she'd opened more than just a box. In lifting that cardboard lid, she'd reopened a wound on her heart. Among an assortment of dog tags, photographs, and paper currency, she'd found David's trick cards with the queen of spades resting on top—the last card he'd ever pulled from the deck. Then she'd begun crying and hadn't stopped. Aelyx had done his best to comfort her. She'd let him hold her hand and coach her through *K'imsha*, an ancient meditative art, but she'd refused to share her thoughts with him.

He pushed open the door and found her lying in bed with both hands positioned on her stomach and her eyes closed in a meditative trance. She blinked as if sensing him and sat up with a peaceful grin.

"Feeling better?" he whispered so as not to wake Larish, who slept nearby on an inflatable mattress. He wasn't coming with them. "It looks like the *K'imsha* helped."

"It always does." She shifted her glance to the cardboard box on the floor. "But I think I'll leave the lid on that for a while."

"Probably a good idea." He offered his hand. "Help me with breakfast?"

Twelve eggs, ten slices of toast, and two pots of coffee later, they were on their way to the United Nations building in Manhattan, where the Earth Council was located in an office near the top floor.

The flight took only minutes. Aelyx spent more of his time hovering above the building while Colonel Rutter assembled a squadron of soldiers on the ground. From the shuttle's vantage point, it seemed there were more security personnel on the sidewalk than citizens. Clearly the government was taking no chances today.

*Good.*

After landing and cloaking the shuttle, they made their way inside the building through the security entrance. Syrine and Elle walked in front with Troy while Aelyx held back to keep pace with Cara, who was slowed down by her ridiculous shoes. Her heels echoed in a noisy *click-click-click* through the corridors, but strangest of all was the sight of her in a fitted black skirt and suit jacket—"professional" clothing retrieved for her last night. She'd even twisted her hair into a matronly bun at the base of her head. Every time she glanced at him, his fingers twitched to shake loose her curls.

Without incident, they rode the elevator to the Earth Council offices, but a pair of guards stopped them at the lobby doors. Unlike Troy, in his camouflage uniform, these men wore black suits and ties. They didn't seem to appreciate the company, sweeping the hallway with their gazes instead of making eye contact.

Cara made a guttural noise of frustration. "Secret Service."

It took Aelyx a moment, but he recalled from his attendance at the student exchange gala that Secret Service agents were assigned to protect the American president. Aelyx glanced through the glass lobby doors for the woman, a tall, middle-aged politician with a short cap of graying hair, but he didn't see anyone except the receptionist.

Troy showed his credentials to the men. "I'm here to escort Cara Sweeney and her team to the Council meeting."

One guard inspected Troy's identification while the other touched his earpiece and murmured to someone out of sight. A minute later, the second man tensed visibly and whispered to his partner while watching Cara. Then that same man pulled out a pair of restraints and told her, "Put your hands behind your back."

Cara retreated a pace. "No. I haven't done anything wrong. I'm the Chief Human Consultant, which makes me part of this Council, and I'm not going anywhere except to the conference room."

"We need backup," said the first man while the other advanced on Cara and snatched her wrist. He twisted it hard, causing her to cry out in pain.

Before Aelyx could advance a single step, Troy punched the offending agent in the throat. The man doubled over for breath, allowing Cara to squirm free. Aelyx knew the other guard would retaliate, so he knocked him against the doors and stole the firearm from his holster, then handed the weapon to Troy, who'd already drawn his own pistol.

"I probably shouldn't have done that," Troy said, a gun in each hand. "But since I already dug myself a hole, you might as well go inside. I'll hold them here."

As Cara hurried through the doors, Aelyx pointed at the elevator bank and told his sister, "Push the emergency button. It'll stop the motor for a few minutes." Then he glanced at Syrine. "See if you can find a way to jam the stairwell door. I'm going inside with Cara."

In the lobby, Cara was locked in a wrestling match with the receptionist, their high heels wobbling and slipping on the glossy floor. Then Cara kicked off her shoes and shoved the woman aside while Aelyx ran ahead of her and looked around for the conference room. With no signs to direct him, he began haphazardly throwing open office doors while the receptionist screeched for someone to call security.

When Cara caught up, her feet were bare and her once-tidy bun was in tatters. "So much for making a good impression," she said, and pointed to a mahogany door at the end of the hall. "That's the one. I signed the alliance pact in there."

They rushed into the meeting room, and he slammed the door behind them, instantly bracing against it so no one could follow them inside. Around the long conference table, heads swiveled toward the sound, their eyes vacant as if entranced. At the far end of the table sat the president, facing a young L'eihr girl, locked in what appeared to be Silent Speech. But then the girl broke contact and faced Aelyx with vivid blue eyes, and he recognized her at once.

*Aisly.*

Now he knew why the Council had cut off communication with L'eihr. Aisly had tampered with their minds. "Stop her," he told Cara as the door bucked from the outside.

Cara was already circling the room.

Aisly whipped her gaze back to the president. "Cara Sweeney is a threat to national security," she said in a rush.

"She and anyone who helps her should be killed on sight. She's right behind you. Defend yourself!"

Cara had almost reached Aisly when the president stood abruptly, tipping her chair into Cara's path. The woman launched herself at Cara and tackled her to the floor. Panicked, Aelyx ran to help. He grabbed the president and heaved her aside, but in doing so, he left the door unprotected.

He glanced up and Aisly was gone.

"Go!" Cara said, still lying on her back. "We have to make her undo—"

Aelyx didn't need to hear any more. He pulled Cara to her feet and then ran out the door in pursuit of Aisly. She was faster than he expected, already beyond the reception desk. Aelyx shouted for someone to stop her, but Troy was too busy handcuffing the Secret Service agents. By the time Aelyx reached the hall, she was tearing toward the stairwell.

"Syrine!" Aelyx yelled.

Syrine wedged an axe through the door handle, then snagged Aisly around the waist. Aisly swung an elbow, catching Syrine in the face. Once free, she dislodged the axe handle and opened the door. A shoving match ensued, and both girls disappeared into the stairwell.

When Aelyx reached the door, he threw it open and found Syrine on the ground, cradling her head. Aisly was nowhere to be seen, but an echo of stampeding boots told him the Secret Service's reinforcements had arrived. He dragged Syrine into the hallway and shut the door, then slid the axe handle back into place.

Cara and Elle jogged into view, while Troy finished shackling the guards. All of them exchanged empty glances that signaled they'd reached the same conclusion.

They were trapped.

Aelyx glanced at the only exit points—two floor-to-ceiling windows at each end of the hall, thirty stories above the ground. From beside him, bodies slammed against the stairwell door, and a faint hum from the elevator indicated it was now in motion.

"Any brilliant ideas?" Troy asked. "That don't involve me spending twenty years in Leavenworth?"

Aelyx remembered the key fob in his pocket. He ran to the nearest window and held the fob toward it, then pushed the shuttle's retrieval button. "Is that glass bulletproof?" he asked Troy while jogging backward.

Troy drew his pistol. "Let's find out."

He fired a series of blasts, sending shards of glass raining to the floor. Aelyx dragged a decorative plant from the corner and used its brass pot to knock aside the remaining glass. He heard the shuttle approaching and pressed a button to disable its cloaking device. The craft came into view by gradual degrees, first its nose, followed by its wings, bay, and tail. When he couldn't maneuver the port wing any closer, he used his fob to open the pilot's door.

Aelyx pointed at the wing. "We'll have to walk across it to get inside."

Troy's face paled a shade as he stared at the ground. "Will it hold us?"

"It's stabilized. Watch." Aelyx leaned through the window frame and planted both palms on the warm metal wing. He shoved down with all his weight, but the shuttle remained fixed in place. "Want me to go first?"

Troy nodded vigorously.

Heights had never bothered Aelyx, so he gauged the

wind speed and climbed onto the wing, keeping his knees bent when he stood. In a few short steps, he reached the pilot's seat and gripped the roof to maneuver himself inside. After loosely fastening his safety harness, he extended an arm to help Syrine, who'd already followed in his footsteps. He pulled her inside, and she climbed over his lap into the backseat. Cara went next, moving steadily on her hands and knees, and then Elle crossed the wing in two swift bounds. That left only Troy . . . who seemed to have stopped breathing.

Three hundred feet below, sirens wailed as police cruisers converged at the base of the building. From somewhere in the distance, Aelyx heard the choppy whir of helicopter blades.

"Hurry," he said, motioning to Troy with one hand.

Troy didn't move.

The stairwell door burst open, and a flurry of soldiers and gunmen swarmed into the hall behind Troy, shouting for him to drop his weapon and lie down on the floor. Troy froze. Moving only one arm, he extended a pistol and let it fall. Cara called to him from the backseat, but he didn't seem to hear her.

"Listen to me," Aelyx yelled. "Jump and grab on to the wing. I promise I won't let you fall."

Troy laced his fingers together at the back of his head.

"Jump!" Aelyx shouted over the chaos unfolding in the hallway. Someone fired a warning shot. That seemed to get Troy's attention. "Do it now!"

Troy's chest expanded as he drew a fortifying breath. His face crumpled in a grimace, and then he ran for the window and leaped onto the wing. Aelyx lifted the shuttle sharply, using the force of velocity to keep Troy in place. Gunfire popped from below. With bullets pinging off the hull, Aelyx soared until they cleared the roof, and then veered directly above it, out of the range of fire. He hovered there, a few inches from the rooftop, and reached out to shake Troy's arm.

"You can look down now."

Troy pried open one eye and then the other. He peered over the wing, and when he saw the roof's flat surface within reach, he dropped onto it and proceeded to lose his breakfast. The noise of helicopters grew nearer. Troy spat once more onto the roof and climbed inside the shuttle. Aelyx cloaked the craft, and for the second time in less than a day, they fled for their lives from the city.

## Chapter Seven

From her window in the backseat, Cara noticed Central Park approaching. She reached forward and grabbed Aelyx's arm. "Wait, stop the shuttle."

He slowed to a midair halt and turned to face her, his chrome eyes searching her as if checking for damage. "What's wrong?"

"Where're we going?"

"To the safe house."

"Why?"

"*Well,*" he said in the patronizing voice of a kindergarten teacher, "Aisly just signed your death warrant—"

Troy raised his hand. "And I might've committed treason."

"—so I'm taking us where we're least likely to be shot on sight."

"But we're invisible," Cara pointed out. "And the shuttle's

quieter than most taxis. As noisy as the city streets are, no one will hear us."

Elle caught on, sitting up straighter. "So why not go back and look for Aisly? If she took the stairs from the thirtieth floor, she couldn't have gone far."

"I remember what she's wearing," Cara said. "Gray shirt, black leggings. If we hurry, we can find her. She might lead us to Jaxen."

Syrine massaged her temples again. She'd been doing that ever since Aisly attacked her in the stairwell. "Forget her; she's gone. I think we should go to the safe house before your president announces what Aisly put in her head. The soldiers might not help us after that. Larish is still there, and all of our things."

"I'll call Colonel Rutter and explain what happened," Cara said. She leaned forward and squeezed Aelyx's arm. "We might never get this chance again."

He didn't reply, but instead gripped the wheel and made a hard left turn that tipped her sideways. The shuttle rocketed back to the United Nations building, and in seconds they were floating above a traffic jam of police cruisers, fire trucks, SWAT vans, and armored cars. High above them, helicopters swept the city skies, but Cara kept her gaze fixed on the sidewalks, searching for Aisly's petite frame and her long, brown ponytail.

Troy pressed his forehead to the front passenger window. "I don't see anything this way."

"Same here." Cara glanced through the windshield. "Make a left at this intersection, and we'll try the next block."

They didn't find Aisly there either. To give them a wider view of the surrounding streets, Aelyx lifted the shuttle, and

Cara squinted at the people below, scanning for anyone in gray. She was starting to worry Aisly had taken a cab when Troy tapped an index finger against his window and said, "I think I see her."

"Where?"

He pointed ahead. "There, past that bus stop, on the right-hand corner."

Aelyx brought the shuttle around, and Cara perched on the edge of her seat to peer out the windshield. She held her breath in anticipation while they soared closer. As soon as she spotted the profile of Aisly's small, upturned nose, she exhaled in relief.

*Gotcha.*

"Hold back a little," Cara said to Aelyx. "We don't want her to hear us."

They slowed to a virtual crawl and trailed Aisly as she strode down the sidewalk, her ponytail swinging to and fro. Like Jaxen, her behavior seemed a bit bolder than usual, but not as extreme. She passed a silver breakfast cart and stopped, doing a double take. She said something to the vendor and stood on tiptoe to trap his gaze, probably telling him to give her a free bagel. Cara was right. The man handed over a paper-wrapped pastry and a cup of coffee, and Aisly continued on her merry way.

While they crept behind her over the next block, Cara used her com-sphere to call Colonel Rutter. She didn't expect him to answer on the first buzz. She barely had time to set her sphere on the console when his miniature hologram appeared, demanding, "What did you do, Sweeney? Everything's FUBAR over here!"

"FUBAR?" Cara looked to her brother for a translation.

"F'ed up beyond all recognition," he supplied.

"Oh." She cringed. "I guess you heard."

"That you're public enemy number one?" Rutter hollered. "Damn right, I heard! By now, every corn-poking yokel in America has heard. The anti L'eihr folks are going nuts—this is exactly what they've been waiting for."

"It was Aisly," Cara said. "She got to the president and the Earth Council before we could stop her."

The colonel muttered a long string of curses that required no translation whatsoever. "That explains a lot." He rubbed his jaw a bit too hard, stretching his weather-beaten skin. "The president just held a press conference. She said the Earth Council revoked all L'eihr visas. It's an immediate expulsion for all nonhumans."

"But she's brainwashed."

"Doesn't matter. She's commander in chief. I can't disobey a direct order from her, and neither can any US soldier." The colonel's eyes shifted to Troy. "By the way, Sergeant Sweeney, I'm relieving you of your post, effective immediately. When the Marines court-martial you—and make no mistake, they will—at least it won't be for dereliction of duty."

Troy saluted the colonel. "Thank you, sir."

Rutter dipped his chin. "As for the rest of you, unless you can unscramble the president's eggs by tonight, I'm personally escorting Larish and the ambassador to the L'eihr transport tomorrow at zero six hundred hours." He glanced around the shuttle, nodding at Aelyx, Elle, and Syrine. "I suggest you meet me there. I can't protect you anymore, and I don't want you kids going home in body bags."

At those words, a beat of silence hung in the air. The colonel was right. There was no place remote enough to hide from the full force of the American military, at least not for very long. Their only hope was to convince Aisly to undo the damage she'd caused.

"I'll hold on to this," Rutter said, lifting his comsphere. "My commander might've ordered me to neutralize you, Sweeney, but she didn't say I couldn't talk to you in the meantime."

Cara understood the subtext. He would help her as much as he could. "Thank you. We'll be in touch."

The call ended, but it put a damper on the mood. Nobody spoke as they tracked Aisly across three more blocks. Then she crossed another street and stopped suddenly to dig inside her pocket.

"She's answering a call," Cara said.

Aisly's device was too small to see, but she was definitely talking to someone, most likely that *fasher* Jaxen. After tossing her coffee cup onto the sidewalk—never mind the recycling bin at her elbow—Aisly stepped off the curb and hailed a cab.

"This is about to get interesting," Troy murmured. "Everyone keep your eyes on that taxi."

They followed the car through a sea of identical yellow cabs until it reached the outskirts of the city and merged onto the expressway. There it was easy to track. Cara breathed more easily as they sped along the highway. It felt good to move faster, to do more with her rapidly diminishing time.

The trip lasted longer than she expected, taking them all the way upstate. Her stomach growled for lunch when the taxi finally pulled to a stop in front of an industrial complex that appeared to be some kind of factory—NITRATE SOLUTIONS, according to the sign. No cars stood in the parking lot, but

90

judging by the semis and trailers parked in the loading area behind the main building, the company was still in business.

"Are we lost?" Cara asked. Maybe the cab had stopped to radio for directions. But then Aisly stepped out of the car, and the taxi drove away. "Guess not."

Aelyx hovered outside the property line, just above the trees. "What's she doing here of all places?"

Cara poked her brother, the only one of them with a smartphone. "Look up Nitrate Solutions and see what they make."

Troy shook his head. "I shut down my phone so the government can't track the signal."

"I don't like this," Syrine said. "Let's go back to the safe house."

"She's going inside," Elle announced, pointing through the windshield.

Sure enough, Aisly had managed to unlock the front door. Either that or someone had let her in. Regardless, Cara hadn't followed all this way to turn back.

"Set us down," she told Aelyx. "Between the five of us, we can take her."

"Unless Jaxen's in there with his staff," Troy added.

"So we'll park somewhere close," Cara said. "Worst case scenario, we'll run back here and go invisible again."

Syrine kept muttering that she had a bad feeling about this. She started massaging her head with more pressure than before.

"Did you look Aisly in the eyes?" asked Cara.

"Of course not. I know better than that."

Cara chewed the inside of her cheek. Maybe Syrine should sit this one out. "You and Elle stay here and try to contact

Larish. See what he can find out about Nitrate Solutions. The rest of us will go inside."

With that decided, Cara stepped out of the shuttle, along with Aelyx and Troy. The asphalt scorched her bare feet, forcing her to hop on alternating tiptoes until Aelyx noticed her plight and swept her into his arms.

"Next stop, the shoe store," he said as he carried her across the parking lot. The moment didn't last long, but there in his embrace, Cara remembered what she was fighting for.

"I don't know," she teased, wiggling her bare toes. "I could get used to this."

Troy skewered them with a glare. "If you two are done making me want to vomit, maybe we can focus here?" He thumbed at the door. "Remember to keep your heads down. Our best weapon is the element of surprise."

They slipped inside, and Aelyx set her down on the cool lobby tile. From there, they proceeded through a pair of swinging doors that led to a short hallway and a thicker set of doors marked CAUTION: DOUBLE HEARING PROTECTION REQUIRED IN THIS AREA. There was no noise, but an unpleasant scent clung to the air, an odd mix of sewage and chemicals, similar to portable toilets at a fair. The narrow walls were covered in occupational safety procedures and government regulations. This was definitely a manufacturing plant, though Cara didn't see any clues to indicate what kind.

Troy pushed open the doors a crack and peeked through. "Looks empty," he whispered, and they continued inside to the main factory.

The concrete floor was gritty, dusted with sand or dirt. All around, enormous machines stood dormant, each unit connected by long stretches of motionless conveyer belts.

Cara glanced around for a label machine or finished products to tell her what was made here, but a faraway *clink* caught her attention, and she snapped her gaze toward the sound.

Aelyx and Troy heard it, too. All three of them stared at the far end of the room near the ceiling, where a set of metal stairs led to a catwalk that stretched into the next part of the factory. They'd just started for the stairs when the distant echo of voices sounded from the rear of the building, and Cara tugged both boys to a halt.

She pointed between herself and Aelyx, then toward the sound of the voices. She hated to split up, but it was the smart thing to do. Troy nodded. He gestured toward the stairs and touched the com-sphere in his pocket, a message that he'd check in when he found something.

As Cara crept across the factory floor, an eerie chill puckered her skin into goose bumps. She'd toured plenty of factories during field trips, but there was something unnatural about the silence of the machines and the angular shadows they cast on the floor. She reached for Aelyx's hand, but pulled back and wiped her sweaty palms on her skirt. When she stretched out her arm to him again, he wasn't there.

She spun around and found him facing the opposite direction, his muscles tense and his backbone locked.

"What is it?" she whispered.

"Your brother," he whispered back. "He buzzed me on my sphere, but not long enough to connect. I don't know what it means."

"Maybe he pocket-dialed you."

Aelyx hesitated. "I'm going to check on him." He pointed at a nearby stretch of conveyor belt. "Hide under there until I get back."

Cara wrinkled her nose. As dirty as the floor was, God only knew what kind of science experiments were growing underneath the equipment.

Aelyx sighed. "Just don't go anywhere, okay?"

"Okay."

After she watched him jog away, she turned an ear toward the nearby corridor. The voices were clearer now—one male, one female—and distinct enough that she could tell they were speaking L'eihr. She understood enough of the language to pick out a few words: *put them there . . . along the support walls . . . nothing left standing.* The female didn't sound like Aisly, and more than that, Cara wondered why two L'eihrs would talk to each other when they could use Silent Speech. She peeked over her shoulder, torn between waiting for Aelyx and moving closer to investigate.

In the end, temptation won the battle.

She inched silently down the corridor, keeping her back to the wall and her ears alert. The voices had fallen silent, but an occasional scrape of shoes told her at least one person was still near. The hallway led to a warehouse at the back of the property. At the far end of the room, two mammoth garage-style doors were open, revealing the tractor-trailers Cara had seen from the shuttle. Sunlight cut through the doorways and illuminated the loading bay, but the rest of the warehouse—a maze of wooden pallets and cardboard boxes wrapped in plastic—remained in shadows. It wasn't until she heard a rattle that she was able to spot someone.

About ten yards to the left, a redheaded girl stood facing a closed maintenance closet. The girl was dressed like Aisly in a gray tunic over black leggings, but she was much taller and definitely not a L'eihr, as evidenced by the long, scarlet braid hanging between her shoulders. Since the girl couldn't see her, Cara tiptoed from the mouth of the hallway to a forklift parked in the center of the room, then ducked behind it for a closer look.

The redhead seemed frustrated, tugging on a handle that wouldn't open. There was a sign affixed to the door. In bold lettering easily visible from Cara's position, it stated PUSH, DON'T PULL. As the girl stared at the words, she grabbed the handle and jerked it back with a grunt. When that didn't work, she growled and stomped a foot.

Whoever she was, she couldn't read English.

Cara was still puzzling over it when a voice from behind drawled, "Hello, *Cah*-ra." She slapped a hand over her heart and whirled around to find herself face-to-face with Jaxen, who stood there with both hands in his pockets, grinning at her as if they'd bumped into each other at a party and he wanted to ask her out.

"Jaxen," she breathed. She noticed he didn't have his staff. That was one point in her favor. "Always a pleasure."

"I see you've found my new friend." He lifted a hand to indicate the redhead. "How appropriate that you were drawn to her."

Cara didn't answer him. She was too busy taking note of the exits and calculating the quickest path back to the shuttle.

"I believe an introduction is in order." He motioned for the redhead to join them. "This is Rune. I named her myself. It's the L'eihr word for *improvement.*"

Cara was vaguely aware of the girl's presence, noticing in her periphery when she reached Jaxen's side. Then she looked at the girl in earnest and did a double take. Or maybe a triple-take. It was hard to tell because her brain couldn't reconcile what her eyes were trying to tell her.

It was as though she'd stepped in front of a mirror. Rune was identical to her, right down to the freckles on her nose and the slight cowlick at her left temple, the one no amount of hair gel could ever tame. Cara stared, unblinking, at the girl, who didn't seem at all shocked by their freakish physical resemblance. Rune simply looked her up and down, tipping her head at Cara's hips as if asking herself *Do my thighs really look that big?*

Then it clicked. This was Cara 2.0. A replicate. Since Jaxen couldn't have the real thing, he'd created an "improvement" to bend to his will.

But wait. That was impossible.

Even with her stolen DNA, it would take nine months to incubate a clone, and then an infant would emerge from the womb, not a fully-grown seventeen-year-old girl. No one could generate an instant carbon copy of a human being. Cloning didn't work that way.

"What did you do?" Cara mumbled, still transfixed by her own face, which was now glaring back at her in annoyance.

"Isn't it obvious?" Jaxen asked, and turned to admire the girl. "I cloned you. I admit; I had some help. The Aribol possess remarkable technology, among which is the ability to manipulate the aging process."

Cara remembered her conference call with Zane and how he'd seemed to recognize her before they'd met. Now it made sense. He'd helped create the clone, and in return, Jaxen had agreed to wreak havoc on Earth—something he probably would've done for free. What she didn't understand was why the Aribol thought they needed him.

"I'm pleased with the results," Jaxen said, even as he straightened the clone's braid and brushed the front of her tunic as if unsatisfied. "I was afraid she would be too different from you—that she wouldn't have your spark. But she does. Her passion is so fierce it rivals even your own. So I named her Rune."

*Improvement.*

Cara huffed a sarcastic laugh. "This is what you consider an upgrade? She can't even read." Her voice raised a pitch as hysteria set in. "And in no timeline of any alternate dimension should there exist a version of me who is illiterate!"

Jaxen shrugged. "She's young. Just a few months old." His hand wandered down her back and settled low—disturbingly low—at the base of her spine. "I've been using that time to teach her . . . other skills."

Cara gasped so hard she nearly collapsed her own lungs. "You sick, perverted pig!"

In true Jaxen form, he threw back his head and filled the warehouse with echoes of laughter. It went on and on, his ribs shaking until he cradled his stomach as if the hilarity had given him a cramp. "*Cah*-ra, *Cah*-ra, *Cah*-ra," he said, wagging an index finger at her. "Get your mind out of the gutter. I was referring to her motor skills, like walking and hand control. I can use my talents to transfer concepts to her mind, but still, these things take practice."

Suddenly, there was a blur of flesh, and a fist connected with Cara's eye. Her head snapped back, and she stumbled, only to take another punch to the mouth and fall to the concrete floor, where she landed hard on her ass.

"Oh, yes," Jaxen added. "I also taught her to fight. She's quite good at it."

Cara dabbed at her lip, tasting blood. She glared at her clone, and Rune glowered back while angling her body toward Jaxen, clearly irritated that another girl had amused him. Cara 2.0 was a cast-iron bitch. But instead of giving in to her temper, Cara forced herself to stay calm. She doubted she could reason with Jaxen, but she might be able to stall him long enough for Aelyx and Troy to find her.

"Whatever you taught her," she said from the floor, "she still isn't me."

"In time she'll be better than you," Jaxen murmured while preening the clone. "So much better."

"Keep telling yourself that." Cara pretended to rub her sore tailbone while pressing the com-sphere in her pocket, issuing a group summons. "Why are you doing this—helping the Aribol? I thought you wanted to fight them."

"Well, that was before The Way turned against me, wasn't it?"

"In all fairness, you turned against them first."

"Irrelevant." Jaxen flicked his wrist dismissively. "The point is Aisly and I had few options. We found an emissary probe, and our partial Aribol genetics allowed us to access its contact function. So we proposed an alliance of sorts. As you humans say, politics makes for strange bedfellows."

"So you're not brainwashed?"

He laughed. "My mind can't be compromised, *Cah*-ra. It's another benefit of my genetics."

"But you told me you loved Earth."

"I do. That's why I'm here: to make sure it's not destroyed."

"By terrorizing my people and brainwashing the president?"

"By keeping humans compliant," he specified, as if there were a difference. "You can't deny mankind has a turbulent history. Once you send Aelyx and the other L'eihrs back where they belong, the threat will be over."

Somehow Cara doubted that. She was willing to bet the hybrids' deal with the Aribol included a position of power on Earth. They wouldn't leave this planet so easily.

"Otherwise I'll kill every one of them that remains."

Now *that* she believed.

A beep sounded from a band around Rune's wrist. "It's time," she said in L'eihr.

Jaxen nodded and told her, "Meet Aisly at the ship. I'll be there soon."

The clone jogged across the room and jumped out the nearest loading bay, then vanished behind the trailers parked on the lot. After she'd gone, Jaxen crouched down until he was eye-level with Cara. He regarded her with a bittersweet regret that reminded her of a guy gazing at his ex after a few too many beers.

"*Cah*-ra," he said softly, reaching for her cheek before pulling back. "Despite the fact that I've replaced you, I still believe the universe is a better place with you in it. That's why I'm going to advise you to leave." He glanced at a digital clock on the wall. "Within the next sixty seconds, to be exact." He stood and backed toward the loading bay. "I'm sure our paths will cross again."

Then he disappeared out the bay door, and Cara thought back to the words she'd overheard earlier: *put them there . . . along the support walls . . . nothing left standing.*

She scrambled to her feet. It was a demolition.

Aelyx skidded to a halt at the mouth of the hallway with

Troy right behind him. "You were supposed to stay . . ." He trailed off, squinting into the distance. "Is that Jaxen?"

Cara ran past him and snagged his sleeve. "Back to the shuttle! The building's about to blow!"

She tore through the factory, her bare feet slapping on the floor. Boots clomped from behind and quickly overtook her. Soon Troy was leading the way while Aelyx kept pace with her. As soon as they reached the front parking lot, he threw her over one shoulder and bounded across the blazing asphalt.

Elle and Syrine must've received the summons, because the shuttle doors were already open. Aelyx tossed Cara into the backseat, then took his place in front along with Troy. In moments, the doors sealed shut and the craft lifted off the parking lot.

No sooner had they risen above the treetops than an explosion boomed from the factory and sent the shuttle careening in the other direction. Cara collided with knees and elbows as they rolled over and over. Once Aelyx righted the craft, they rose above the hail of flaming debris, and Cara glanced out the window at what little remained of Nitrate Solutions.

"Is everyone okay?" she asked. "That was worse than I thought."

Elle wriggled out from beneath her and rotated a stiff shoulder. "Larish said fertilizer was made here. It's highly explosive."

"Fertilizer?" Cara wrinkled her forehead. "Why would Jaxen care about that?"

"War strategy," Troy said. "First you divide your enemy from their allies. Then you remove the essentials—like food.

Without fertilizer, our crops won't be able to . . ." He paused when he caught a glimpse of Cara. "Whoa, Pepper, who did that to your face?"

Aelyx whipped around, his silver gaze wide.

Cara gently probed her swollen eye. "Would you believe me if I said . . . me?"

Troy lifted a shoulder. "Stranger things have happened. A couple hours ago, the president gave you a proper beatdown."

She told them about Jaxen and the clone he'd created with Aribol technology.

For a moment, Aelyx went quiet. *Angry* quiet. "The clone could have killed you. Why didn't you wait for me like you said you would?"

"It's a good thing I didn't," she argued. "Jaxen's the one who warned me about the explosion."

He released a breath through his flaring nostrils. "Well, regardless, now that we know he's been to the Aribols' home planet, all we have to do is find his flight log."

"And then what?" demanded Syrine. "Transmit the coordinates to the Voyagers so they can go there and provoke a war?"

Cara shook her head. "So they can go there and negotiate. Or find a weakness to exploit. Or do *something* besides sit back and let the hybrids take over. We just need more time to—"

"What we *need* is to admit we're outmatched," Syrine insisted. "You can stay here and chase Jaxen. I want to go home."

Cara looked to Aelyx for support and discovered one corner of his lips curved ever-so-slightly upward. She knew that scheming grin. He'd worn the same one last month when he'd tricked a group of human colonists, herself included, into believing a nutrient-rich dip called *n'ala* was exactly like hummus. He'd conveniently forgotten to mention the main ingredient was insect paste.

"Syrine is right," he said. "It's time to give the Aribol what they want. First thing tomorrow we're boarding the transport home."

## Chapter Eight

The moon had risen in a sliver of radiance over upstate New York, but the suburban streets were no less crowded as people left their homes to enjoy a respite from the scorching heat of day. For the last few minutes, Aelyx had been watching them. Perhaps it was paranoia, but he perceived a heightened sense of alertness in their strides, an urgency when they spoke to one another. He wondered how many of them believed the president, and how many had the mental tenacity to question their leader.

He supposed it didn't matter. Either way, he couldn't show his face.

He turned and walked back to the shuttle, which was docked behind a thrift store. Nearby, Cara rummaged in a clothing donation bin for shoes and a more comfortable outfit to wear. Only her skirt-clad backside was visible, wriggling back and forth with each of her movements. Aelyx grinned and leaned against the hull to enjoy the view. In times of hardship, one had to appreciate the basic pleasures in life, to *stop and smell the roses*, as humans said. So he admired Cara's roses until her brother approached, and then he cleared his throat and pretended to inspect the shuttle wing.

Troy lifted two paper bags, each smelling of fried potatoes. "Five heart attacks in the making. I'm not a hundred percent sure the cashier didn't recognize me, so we should probably go."

"I'm waiting for Elle to return from the grocery." Aelyx peered around the building and spotted her on the sidewalk, a plastic bag in hand. She'd concealed her face with a hat from the donation bin, but he recognized her brisk stride. "There she is."

As Troy always did when Elle was near, he stiffened and made an obvious effort not to check behind him. "Hey," he whispered, moving closer. "Can I ask you something about your sister?"

Aelyx nodded. Considering all the things he'd done with Troy's sister, he could hardly refuse.

"Has she . . . you know . . . moved on from losing Eron?" Troy asked. "Is she seeing anyone back home?"

Reflexively, Aelyx glanced at Syrine in the backseat. He advanced a few paces out of earshot and motioned for Troy to join him. Syrine had loved Eron too, and as fragile as she was, she didn't need the reminder of another loss. "I don't know," he said. Elle didn't share those details with him. "But the last time I engaged in Silent Speech with her, she seemed to have recovered from her grief, so she—"

Troy shushed him and waved at Elle as she reached the shuttle. She lowered a brow in confusion and waved back, then climbed into the backseat. "So," Troy whispered, "she might be ready to move on?"

Aelyx was growing annoyed with this topic. "Assuming the Aribol don't annihilate both our races, and assuming you join the colony *and* convince her to leave the capital, you might stand a remote chance with her."

Troy grinned and delivered a slap on the back. "Thanks, man. Good talk."

That might've been the nicest thing Troy had ever said to him.

Cara padded over, holding up a pair of simple black flats and a bundle of denim. "I won't think too hard about who wore these before me or how often they bathed." She sniffed the air a few times. "Do I smell curly fries?"

"And hamburgers." Aelyx opened the passenger door for her. "Dinner awaits, with a side of cardiovascular disease."

"Mmm. My favorite kind."

Aelyx flew them one state over, and they ate dinner floating in the airspace above a national forest. He'd never developed a taste for American food, finding it overseasoned, but tonight he'd reached the advanced stage of hunger that made anything a delicacy. He devoured his meal and sat back in the pilot's seat, resting a hand on his stomach.

After Cara finished eating, she changed into jeans and a T-shirt, then reached a hand toward her brother in the back. "Let me use your cell."

"They can track us if it's turned on."

"One minute," she said. "Then I'll shut it off and we'll go someplace else. The shuttle's crazy fast. We'll be in the next time zone before they notice our signal."

Troy passed her the smartphone, and moments later, she

cupped it between her palms, her face illuminated by the screen's pale glow. Aelyx noticed a smudge of dirt streaking the length of her nose, and he reached out a thumb to clean it. He changed his mind at the last second and left the smudge intact. It made her seem younger, more like a girl of seventeen and less like a Chief Human Consultant bearing the weight of two worlds on her shoulders.

"Wow," she breathed, gazing in wonder at the phone. "We're trending. We even have our own hashtag."

Having no idea what a hashtag was, Aelyx leaned over for a glimpse of the screen. She rotated the phone and showed him a picture of the two of them together, captioned by the words *Aelyx is bae! He and Cara are my IRL OTP! Don't let the government tear them apart! Let's do everything we can to #SaveCalyx*

He understood about half of that.

"It's everywhere." She powered off the phone, continuing to gaze at it. "The fandom's going nuts. This could really work in our favor."

"What's a Calyx?" he asked.

"Cara plus Aelyx. It's our ship name."

"Ship? Do you mean a sailing vessel or a method of mailing packages?"

She laughed and patted his knee. "I'll explain later. Right now you should probably show me how to fly this thing."

As his entire plan hinged on her ability to pilot the craft, he agreed. Fortunately the controls made flying effortless; all she had to do was learn them. So they switched seats, and he spent the next few hours teaching her how to steer and accelerate, and most important, the subtle nuance of approaching an object without striking it.

She absorbed the information quickly, which didn't

surprise him. Cara was one of a kind among humans . . . or perhaps two of a kind now that she'd been cloned. Aelyx tried to push away the thought. It made him uneasy to know another version of her existed, even more so to think that Jaxen had warped the very best part of the girl. Passion was of little worth without love to soften its edges.

Syrine drew him back to present company with a complaint. "I wish you hadn't told me what you're about to do. It's a crime against The Way. I'll be punished when I get home if I don't report you first."

He turned to face her while Cara continued practicing. The others might not understand Syrine's concern because they didn't know what had happened last winter. He'd disobeyed their leaders, and she'd made the mistake of trying to defend him. As punishment, she'd had to administer his Reckoning—twenty lashes with the *iphet*.

"No one will punish you," he told her. "Alona said we have two more days. Technically, we aren't disobeying her orders."

"The Way doesn't care about technicalities, and you know it." Syrine folded her arms and addressed Cara. "If you're so confident, then contact Alona and tell her everything."

Cara laughed without humor. "Sometimes it's better to beg forgiveness than ask permission."

"That proves my point."

"Give it a rest, okay?" Cara called over her shoulder. "Right now it feels like the whole world is against me— because it kind of is—and the last thing I need is my friends jumping on my case, too."

Aelyx found that a bit harsh. "She's not against you. She's only worried, and for good reason. You weren't raised on L'eihr. You don't understand what it's like to be taught obedience to The Way from birth."

"Please," Cara scoffed. "I was raised Catholic. I win."

Troy snickered and reached forward to bump fists with his sister.

"Maybe we should stop bickering and focus on the plan," Elle suggested. "There's very little margin for error, and if you don't mind, I'd prefer not to die in the cold void of space."

Syrine heaved a sigh and stayed quiet after that.

The rest of them went over the plan, and then over it a dozen more times. They covered every detail, leaving nothing to doubt, and when the first hints of sunlight began to blush in the eastern horizon, Cara piloted them beyond the atmosphere to the L'eihr transport.

She landed inside the docking bay, and they climbed out of the shuttle, taking a moment to stretch their stiff limbs and backs before making their way inside a small holding area, beyond which stretched the corridor to the main ship. Colonel Rutter was waiting there with a regretful grin on his face.

"You're doing the right thing," he told them.

Nobody in the group spoke, mostly because they hadn't slept in twenty-four hours. But to the casual observer, it would probably seem they were overcome by the sadness of parting ways. Cara's eyes were especially bloodshot and swollen, her skin blackened by her fight with the clone.

Rutter jerked his chin at Cara and her brother. "I'd like to pretend I never saw you here, but that'll be hard if we share a ride back to the States."

"I'm taking Aelyx's shuttle," Cara said, her voice cracking.

Emotion choked off the rest of her words, and she hid her face in her hands.

She was good.

Rutter fixed his gaze on his boots and began scratching his neck as though he'd developed an allergy to female tears. "Call your parents, Sweeney," he mumbled. "They're frantic." Then he wasted no time in returning to the docking bay.

As soon as Aelyx heard the rumble of Rutter's shuttle departing, he released a breath. They'd cleared their first hurdle. Now they needed as many L'eihr crew members as possible to witness his goodbye with Cara. Pictures were a must, too. Later Cara could upload them to her blog as proof that he'd returned home.

Someone hissed his name, and he turned to find Larish approaching from the main corridor to the ship. Larish already knew the plan. They'd spoken hours earlier via com-sphere.

"You're early," Aelyx said. "Is the ambassador in his room?"

Larish nodded. "Under heavy guard. Whatever Jaxen did to his mind, it hasn't worn off. But that's not why I'm here. There's something you should know."

"Hey, *Calyx*." Troy held up his phone. "I'm on half battery, so let's get this photo shoot started."

"One moment," Aelyx told Larish. He strode away and extended a hand to Cara. "Ready?"

Her fingers were cold when she laced them in his. "Not really."

He cradled her face between his palms, careful not to hurt her bruises, and reached out to her with his eyes. *Have faith. The universe hasn't been able to keep us apart yet. No matter what, I'll always find my way back to you.*

Instead of responding with words, Cara projected her love for him, an emotion so pure it made both their eyes water.

"That's perfect," Troy muttered, clicking pictures with his phone. "Extra mushy and gag-inducing."

"I think it's sweet," Elle said, and ended Troy's commentary.

The flight crew entered from the hangar and informed Cara it was time for her to leave, so Aelyx drew her body closer as she stood on tiptoe and twined both arms around his neck. He nuzzled the slope of her shoulder and closed his eyes to focus on the soft, warm curves pressed against him. Her breath hitched, and he had a feeling she wasn't faking this time. Before he lost his nerve, he released her and faced away, then strode quickly into the main ship.

He'd done it. He'd left her behind—in front of witnesses.

As he strode toward his quarters, Larish scrambled up from behind and tugged on his tunic. "I have to talk to you."

"What is it?"

Before Larish could answer, Syrine jogged in front of them and spun around, forcing them to stop. "Wait." She pressed a palm to Aelyx's chest. "I changed my mind. I want to stay with you."

Aelyx blinked. "Are you sure?"

She nodded while anxiously tugging on her pendant. "What's there to go home to? My friends are here, and *Cah*-ra was right. You need my help."

Aelyx didn't argue—he was glad she'd changed her mind—and yet something wriggled in the pit of his stomach,

110

a warning that Syrine needed his help more than he needed hers. "All right. You know what to do." He glanced at Larish. "What did you want to tell me?"

Twin lines appeared between Larish's eyes. "It can wait."

Elle caught up and asked Larish, "Did you bring my med-bag?"

"Oh." Syrine's brows jumped. "And my box?"

"Yes, it's all in my quarters," Larish said. "But we can't take everything. We should meet in my room and separate the bare necessities."

Aelyx had everything he needed—his com-sphere and the clothes on his back—so he continued to his quarters and waited for Cara's call. Alone in his room, he unclenched his jaw and took a seat on the bottom bunk. The reality of what they were about to do weighed on his shoulders until his muscles were in knots. He rotated his head in a stretch and mentally repeated his own advice: *have faith.*

When his sphere buzzed, he shot upright so quickly he hit his head on the upper bunk. Rubbing his skull, he spoke his passkey and waited for Cara's image to appear.

She flickered to life in miniature form, her head and shoulders visible from inside the shuttle. "Okay, it's done. I'm back in US airspace."

"Now enable the cloaking mode, like I showed you." To be safe, he talked her through the procedure. "If it's done right, you should see the icon displayed on the control panel."

"I see it."

"Good. You can come back now. The transport won't detect you."

"I'm on my way. I'll buzz you when I get there."

They disconnected, and Aelyx made his way to Larish's quarters.

"It's time," he told the group. Since none of them knew precisely when the transport would depart, they had to move quickly. He peered at the scattering of items on the floor, most of which were David's belongings—sports magazines, loose change, photographs, and assorted electronic devices. He didn't see the deck of trick cards, so he assumed Syrine had packed those in the bag slung over her shoulder. "Ready?" he asked her, using his tone to imply a deeper meaning: Was she sure about this?

"Almost." She scooped up David's dog tags, then looped the chain around her neck and stuffed the necklace under her shirt. "Now I'm ready."

Elle hugged her med-kit. "This is all I need."

Larish strapped a bag over his chest and tossed a small duffel toward Aelyx. It landed at his feet with a light crunch. "I liberated a week's worth of nutrient packets from the kitchen."

Aelyx slid open the door and darted a glance up and down the hallway. After finding it vacant, he and the others rushed to the stairwell, where they jogged up five flights of steps and continued to the washroom at the far end of the ship—the one with an oversize waste disposal hatch.

They were all panting for breath when they reached the washroom. Aelyx felt perspiration forming across his brow, and he snatched a microfiber cloth from the hand cleansing station. "Wipe off any traces of moisture," he told the others. "Or it'll freeze on your skin once we're beyond the hatch."

Elle nervously licked her lips, then caught herself and scrubbed her mouth with her shirtsleeve. "You're sure Cara

112

knows to meet us at the correct waste port? There are several different ones."

"I trust her completely," Aelyx said, though it *had* crossed his mind that she might not be in the right position when they expelled themselves from the ship. They could survive the exposure for as long as ninety seconds, but not without lasting consequences.

His com-sphere buzzed, and Cara announced, "I'm in position."

He brought the sphere close to his lips. "You're sure, right?"

"No boyfriend of mine is dying in space."

"Remember, the shuttle won't let you open the doors unless you use the manual override."

"I know," Cara said. "It's already done. And I set the ventilation controls so we won't lose too much pressure when I open the door. We're ready on this end."

More distantly from the shuttle, Troy called, "Jump. I won't let you fall."

Aelyx pocketed his sphere, and the group strode to a locked maintenance door at the rear of the washroom, beyond which stood the waste disposal unit—a closet-size chamber flanked by two doors. Larish had already programmed his handprint into the ship's system, so he pressed a palm to the keypad and the first door retracted into the wall. The air in the chamber was cold, indicating how close they were to the outside.

"This is where we'll stand," Larish explained. He pointed at a second door, the hatch itself. "It's a double airlock system, so the hatch won't open until the first door is closed.

Then someone has to push the release button from here in the washroom."

Aelyx frowned as something occurred to him. "Who's going to stay inside and press the button?" Originally Syrine had agreed to do it, but she was no longer staying behind.

"I'll go last," Larish said. "I might be able to trigger the release switch from the circuit panel inside the chamber. If that doesn't work, I'll stay on board and cover for the rest of you until the transport arrives home."

"Are you sure?" Aelyx asked, but then he heard the transport engines rumble to life, and he knew there wasn't time to argue. He stepped inside the waste chamber and waved Elle and Syrine forward.

They squeezed in together, shifting bags and stepping on toes until they were crammed far enough inside to allow the interior door to shut. Surrounded by utter blackness, Aelyx reminded them to link hands and close their eyes. He felt a small palm clasp his, and then the floor vanished from beneath his feet.

His body lurched backward as if he'd been sucked through a drinking straw. Cold enveloped him, a chill so acute it burned. His face swelled, and his tongue throbbed as moisture evaporated from his mouth. Panic rose inside his chest, and the next thing he knew, a hand tightened around his elbow, and he was dragged inside the shuttle, towing Elle and Syrine behind him.

At once, the pressurization released the vise at his temples. Warm air spewed from the surrounding vents, thawing his skin and returning him to his senses. He opened his eyes and helped Troy pull Elle and Syrine all the way inside. Once all four of them were in the backseat, the cabin doors sealed shut, and the vent blowers quieted to a gentle hiss.

"That'll wake you up," Cara said, shivering visibly in the pilot's seat. "Tell Larish we're ready for him next."

Aelyx noticed the waste chamber hatch had closed. He used his com-sphere to contact Larish, and in response, a hologram of pure shadow appeared.

"I'm inside the chamber," Larish said. "Can't talk. I have to trigger the hatch."

Then the connection ended.

"What was that about?" Cara asked. She seemed to notice Syrine for the first time, and a look of confusion crossed her face.

Aelyx explained the complication of the chute's double airlock system. He hadn't yet finished when he saw movement from his periphery, and he sat bolt upright. The transport was leaving.

Cara muttered a curse. "What do I do?"

"Follow it, just in case Larish releases the hatch."

Aelyx tried contacting Larish to tell him to stay on board, but his summons went unanswered. Ahead of them, the transport increased velocity. Soon the shuttle wouldn't be able to keep pace, and if Larish ejected at this speed, he might end up as a stain on the windshield.

"Keep going, but change your position." Aelyx calculated Larish's potential trajectory and leaned forward, pointing at the belly of the ship. "Follow from below, so we don't hit him."

Syrine gripped his arm. "He wouldn't eject now, would he?"

Until Larish answered his sphere, there was no way to know.

The transport picked up speed, and Cara accelerated. From their path beneath the ship, Aelyx could no longer see the waste hatch. He'd begun to assume Larish would stay inside when he saw something small and dark shoot out from the top of the ship's hull.

Aelyx pointed. "It's him!"

"Everyone strap in," Cara called while veering left. "Get ready to grab him."

When she neared Larish's somersaulting body, she slowed and engaged the override to open the doors. At once, the vents whooshed, pressurizing the craft with heated oxygen. Aelyx's door slid open, and frost skittered across his skin. He was closest to Larish, so he loosened his harness strap and leaned into the void, reaching out an arm. He clenched his teeth against the burn and gripped Larish's collar, then towed him inside, where he landed on several laps. The shuttle doors sealed shut, and Aelyx watched in amazement as Larish's bloated face returned to its normal proportions.

Larish shivered violently on their laps, his teeth clattering so hard it was difficult to understand when he spoke. "D-d-didn't go as p-p-planned."

Elle chafed her hand over his back to warm him. "It's all right. None of us died in the cold void of space."

"I call that a win," Troy said.

"So what now?" asked Syrine.

Cara steered the shuttle toward Earth and began a steady descent into the atmosphere. "Now I find a Wi-Fi connection and upload a new blog post. Once everyone thinks you're gone, it should take some of the pressure off. Then we'll hit

Jaxen and Aisly while their guards are down. Oh, and I need to call my mom and dad."

"Sleep," Troy interjected. "Let's squeeze that in."

"Okay, first sleep," Cara agreed. "Then we'll start saving the world."

# CHAPTER NINE

Cara paused with her fingertip suspended an inch from the smartphone screen. She stared at the *publish* button, unable to pull the trigger on her newest blog post. She knew she didn't have much time before the military tracked her signal, but despite that, her instincts told her something was wrong. And she had a pretty good idea what it was.

"I can't do it," she said. "I can't tell people about the Aribol. What if Colonel Rutter is right and it causes riots and hoarding, just like when the L'eihrs made contact?"

When no one inside the shuttle answered, she glanced around and found Aelyx asleep at the wheel and the entire backseat in a collective drool coma. Despite the weight pressing on her own eyelids, she couldn't help smiling. Larish slept with one cheek stuck to the window, the glass dragging his face into a comical grin. Beside him, Syrine's neck was tipped back and her mouth was hanging open like a flytrap.

Elle slumbered at the opposite end of the seat, her mile-long lashes settled atop her cheeks. Her head was propped on Troy's shoulder while his head rested atop hers.

*Adorable.*

Cara used the phone to snap a picture, figuring Troy would appreciate the memento. Not that she gave her brother's romantic life much thought—because *gross*—but this was probably the farthest he'd ever made it with his crush.

With time ticking, she let the others sleep and drafted a new blog post with a smaller dose of truth and a larger dash of emotion. If she wanted help from her readers, she would have to make them *feel*, to pluck at their heartstrings instead of exploit their darkest fears.

Subscribe [Archive] [Recent Entries] [About Me]

**United**

MAY THE SOURCE BE WITH YOU

FRIDAY, AUGUST 11
Save Calyx

This will be a short post, in part because the government is tracking me, but mostly because my heart is too broken for words. Yesterday the Earth Council expelled all L'eihrs from our world, including Aelyx, the boy I loved enough that I traded my human life for one as a colonist. Now his transport is gone, and for reasons I can't disclose, I was forced to stay here.

My insides are shattered, but I'm not ready to give up, and I hope you're not either. I'm sure the government will remove this post soon, so I encourage you to screen-shot it and plaster my message across the Internet. Which is this: The president and the Earth Council have been misled—I'm not a threat to anyone, and neither are the L'eihrs. We're a thousand times stronger together than we are apart.

Please make your voices heard. Contact your Council representative and demand the reinstatement of L'eihr visas. If my words won't convince you, then maybe these pictures will. I challenge anyone to look at my last moments with Aelyx and tell me that separating our people is the right thing to do.

Don't let hate win. Save Calyx.

*Posted by Cara Sweeney*

• • •

Cara didn't know how long she'd slept or where Aelyx had taken them, but she awoke with the sun beating down on her window and found herself alone in the shuttle, surrounded by an ocean of sand. She yawned and squinted, taking in the rolling dunes that stretched all the way to the blue horizon.

The view made her thirsty.

She searched for a bottle of water to unglue her tongue from the roof of her mouth, eventually finding one in the backseat. The liquid was warm, but so delicious she chugged the entire bottle in a few gulps. Wondering where the others had gone, she wiped a hand over her mouth and peered out the side windows.

The girls were nowhere in sight, but she spotted her brother talking with Aelyx and Larish beneath the shade of a canopy they'd built from a tarp and some retractable support poles from the shuttle's supply compartment. The cabin had

grown stuffy, so Cara opened her door and stepped outside
. . . right into a brick oven.

There was no other way to describe the intensity of the
desert heat. The air leached the moisture from her skin,
making her face itchy and tight. Her feet shifted on the
dunes, and in the time it took to circle the shuttle and duck
beneath the tarp, her ballet flats were half filled with sand.

Now she knew where Aelyx had brought them. To hell.

"Good morning." Aelyx greeted her with a smile,
his stunning face somehow enhanced by the sheen of
perspiration glistening on his brow. He had no right to look
so gorgeous under the circumstances. "Or rather afternoon,"
he added. "It's past three."

Cara mumbled hello and leaned against the shuttle,
emptying her shoes one at a time. She didn't want to know
what she looked like. Or smelled like. Her mouth was
starting to feel as though something had died inside it. "I
don't suppose anyone packed a spare toothbrush."

"I brought enzyme mouthwash," Larish said, making
him her new favorite person in the universe. "Elle and Syrine
have it at the moment."

Cara glanced around. "Where are they?"

Troy, apparently the only person as exhausted by the heat
as she was, flapped a hand listlessly toward the rear of the
shuttle. "Over there somewhere making a pit stop."

"Oh." Cara's bladder suddenly made its presence known.
"I'd better go, too."

She slogged down one dune and trudged up another as
sand filled her shoes again. The grains rubbed her bare feet
raw, and she grumbled to herself, wishing she'd stolen a pair
of flip-flops instead, or maybe some sturdy boots.

It turned out the girls had ventured farther than she'd thought. She heard them long before she saw them, but they definitely weren't engaged in friendly bathroom chitchat. Judging by their raised voices, they were arguing.

Cara paused, not wanting to eavesdrop but uncertain whether she'd walked far enough to cop a squat in privacy. She stood on tiptoe and couldn't see the shuttle, so she decided to risk it. She tried not to listen to the argument while she answered nature's call, but she couldn't stop snippets of L'eihr from reaching her on the breeze. She understood enough to know that Elle was upset because Syrine wouldn't use Silent Speech with anyone.

"What you're doing is unnatural," Elle said. "I can tell you need help."

"I don't want to share the contents of my head with you. There's nothing unnatural about that."

"But why? Your grief won't shock me. It's nothing I haven't felt before."

"Just leave me alone."

"Are you having another breakdown?"

Clearly Elle had plucked a nerve because the pitch of Syrine's voice climbed high enough to break glass. "No!" she screeched. Then she either called Elle a *h'ava* beast or told her to go fornicate with one; Cara couldn't tell.

Either way, she didn't want to be there when the girls came storming over the next sand dune, so she zipped up and returned to the shuttle as quickly as she could.

Troy tossed her a nutrient packet and muttered around a bite of food, "Breakfast is served."

"Unless you'd prefer pork rinds," Larish added. "I brought a bag of those as well. I find them oddly addictive."

122

"I'll stick with this, thanks." Cara devoured every last crumb and resisted the urge to ask for more. To take her mind off her hunger, she pressed a hand against her growling stomach and asked what she'd missed while she was sleeping.

"Quite a bit," Larish said. "Jaxen and Aisly have been busy."

"They hit six manufacturing plants in the last twelve hours," Troy added. "And guess what they all had in common."

"Fertilizer."

Aelyx used his com-sphere to display a map of the United States. The image floated in the air between them, each factory represented by a red dot. "Here's the interesting part," he said, pointing to the first few dots. "These factories were destroyed in the same approximate timeline as these." He indicated the second set of site markers. "Which can only mean—"

"They split up," Cara finished with a hopeful smile. The hybrids were weaker alone than together, and better yet, they'd never expect a group of six to come after them, not with Aelyx and the others supposedly expelled. "We have to take them down while they're still divided. Do we know their next move?"

"I predict Canada," Aelyx said. "There are two other plants there."

Larish blotted his forehead with his sleeve. "And a few more in Europe. That's where they'll probably go next."

As grateful as Cara was to discover a lead on the hybrids, she still found it odd that fertilizer plants were their targets. Why not military bases or armories? But she shrugged off her confusion and focused on what she knew: Jaxen and

Aisly were headed for the Great White North, and in order to ambush them, she had to get there first.

"So which plant do we go to?" She wanted both hybrids stopped, but Jaxen was her top priority. "Assuming they divide and conquer, we have a fifty percent chance of nailing Jaxen and finding his ship."

"That's what we can't decide," Aelyx said. The map vanished, and he pocketed his sphere. "I think we should split up into groups of three and cover both plants."

Cara couldn't disagree more. Much like the hybrids, their group was stronger together than they were apart. But before she had a chance to say so, Elle and Syrine returned from their bathroom break and brought a thick cloud of tension with them. Both girls were red in the face, their shoulders stiff and their arms folded, and neither would look within twelve inches of the other. Elle thrust a bottle of enzyme mouth rinse at Larish and snapped, "Here."

Larish plucked it delicately from Elle's grasp and handed it to Cara, who in turn shared a loaded glance with Aelyx. He lifted a dark brow as if to ask her what had happened, but he was too far away for Silent Speech, so she mouthed *Tell you later.*

Cara cleared her throat and flagrantly changed the subject. "I posted a new blog this morning. Any news on that?"

"Yeah, they shut you down," Troy said. "Your site's gone."

*"What?"* Cara almost lost her grip on the bottle. "The whole thing? I had three million followers."

Her brother's answering shrug said that didn't impress him. "Don't worry. People screen-capped it in plenty of time. It's all over the Internet."

That wasn't the point. Coding Web sites was a real pain,

and this was the second time someone had erased her blog. Syrine had deleted the first one.

At that moment, Syrine flinched and began patting down her pockets. There was no sound other than the light pelting of sand against the landing gear, but Cara recognized the look of urgency on Syrine's face. Her com-sphere was buzzing, a noise only the recipient could hear. Syrine found her sphere and spoke her passkey, and seconds later, the miniature image of Jake Winters appeared in her palm.

"Hey, I need to ask you something," he whispered in an urgent tone that implied the need for secrecy. So Cara perked up her ears. "Things are going well with Ayah. She helped me program the first group of drones, and we launched them into—"

"Did they work?" Syrine interrupted.

Jake blinked as if taken aback by the question. "Well, yes, but not the way I hoped. One of the probes detected brainwave activity, but when we investigated we found humanoids, not Aribol. It's probably one of the planets they seeded."

Cara's mouth dropped open. She stormed over to the hologram while picking sand grains off her tongue. "You found a new civilization, and you didn't think to tell me about it?"

Instead of answering, Jake glared at Syrine. "You didn't tell me we weren't alone."

Syrine turned up a palm. "You didn't ask."

"Excuse me," Cara interjected, dizzy from a rage-embarrassment cocktail she hadn't experienced since her run-in with Jake on the colony. She'd thought they had

125

reached an understanding, but here he was, undermining her authority again. "Why didn't you contact me?"

"I was going to."

"When? Tomorrow? Next week? I shouldn't be the last to know."

Syrine slid her a glance. "I imagine Alona would say the same thing about what we've just done."

"That's different, and you know it," Cara snapped. She'd withheld information from Alona to keep the team together—to fight harder against their enemies instead of giving up. By comparing the two, Syrine was just trying to stir up trouble.

"What's she talking about?" Jake asked.

"Nothing." Cara pulled a deep breath through her nose and counted backward from five to one—in Spanish—while exhaling. Her blood was still simmering, but the urge to tear out her hair had passed. "Did you make contact?"

"No," Jake said. "There was talk of reaching out to them to form a stronger alliance against the Aribol, but The Way discussed it and told us not to. I guess they thought it would open a can of worms. I can see their point . . ."

He prattled on, but Cara wasn't listening. Her mind had fixed on one small detail that changed everything. The Way had convened without her. That had never happened before. Did that mean they'd ejected her? And if so, why? Because she was a disappointment to them? Because she couldn't make people like Jake respect her? Or was it because she was a human, and The Way had already decided to meet the Aribols' demands?

The last possibility scared her the most.

"Did you hear me?"

"What?" she said, refocusing on Jake.

"We have one more day. If we can't find the Aribol by then, the L'eihrs are calling off the search."

Cara rubbed her temples. This was a disaster. She had to find Jaxen's flight log and relay the coordinates to the Voyagers. "Okay, keep looking and stay in touch." Then she clarified, "With *me*."

After rolling his eyes, Jake disconnected. His attitude left Cara with a few unspoken swears on her tongue, and Syrine didn't help matters when she sniffed in irritation.

"Why were you so harsh with him?" Syrine shook her com-sphere. "Now I don't know what he wanted to ask me."

For a few beats, Cara could only stare. "You know what? Elle was right." When Syrine's lips parted, Cara twirled a hand toward the sand dunes in the distance. "Yeah, I overheard all that. And I agree with her. There's something off about you now, and I think it's weird that you won't use Silent Speech."

Aelyx crossed through the center of the group, but to Cara's surprise, he didn't stop at her side. He continued past her and wrapped a protective arm around Syrine's shoulders. "Leave her alone. She needs our support, not our scrutiny."

Cara drew back as if she'd been slapped. She couldn't believe he was defending Syrine again. Had he forgotten all the times she'd crossed them? Did he think the girl was helpless? Because if so, he was delusional. Syrine had an independent streak and a wicked strong backhand—which she'd used on Cara in the past.

"She's not some delicate flower," Cara said. "I remember what she's capable of, even if you don't."

Aelyx released his best friend and stood close enough to

push a thought into Cara's mind. *I remember everything. That's why I'm trying to prevent her from having a nervous breakdown.*

*That's not what's happening here,* Cara told him. *She's hiding something, but you're too close to her to see it.*

*You don't know what she's been through. You weren't here last winter. Try to show some compassion. How would you feel if it were me who'd died instead of David?*

*I would feel crushed, but that's beside the point.* Cara tried to hold back the hurt and betrayal she felt, but she couldn't contain it. Aelyx was her *l'ihan*, her partner, and it stung that he'd sided against her.

*I'm not choosing sides,* he said. *We're all in this together.*

*It doesn't feel that way.*

*Maybe it would feel that way if you treated the rest of us like partners instead of making your own rash decisions.* He was referring to her choices to seek out Jaxen in the factory and to reassign Mary's job on the colony without talking to him first.

*I can't believe you brought that up.* That was fighting dirty.

He paused for a moment, breaking the connection as if to process the emotions she'd shared with him. Then he let loose a cold thought. *This isn't about Syrine. This is about your frustration with Jake Winters and The Way. You're projecting your anger onto the wrong person.*

Cara gaped at him. *This has nothing to do with Jake. Syrine has been acting sketchy since we left the colony. Ask your sister if you don't believe me.*

*She's no more objective than you are when it comes to Syrine.*

That was all Cara could take. She closed her eyes to sever the connection while hot tears prickled behind her lids. Until today, she and Aelyx had only used Silent Speech out of love, never anger, and now the whole thing felt tainted.

"I agree with you," she said aloud, and spun the other way so he couldn't see her blinking furiously to dry her eyes. "We should split up and cover both factories. You can go with Syrine, since she needs your support so much. I'll take Troy and Elle."

He didn't respond, so she charged away to the opposite side of the shuttle and left him to disassemble the tarp. In doing so she lost the shade, but gained privacy, which was worth a sunburn. She'd just stopped her breath from hitching when Larish shuffled up behind her, wearing an expression she couldn't quite read. It wasn't until he reached out to her with his eyes that she understood.

He had suspicions about Syrine, too.

*There's something I've been wanting to show Aelyx, but now I think you should see it instead.* Larish held up his com-sphere. *While I was at the safe house, I accessed video footage from the stairwell where Aisly escaped, and then uploaded it to my sphere because something about it bothered me.*

*What's on the video?*

*An interaction between Syrine and Aisly*, he said. *But it's not clear what they're doing. There was no audio component, and the video is rather open to interpretation. That's why I haven't shown anyone yet.*

"Let's see it," Cara whispered.

After checking over both shoulders to ensure they were alone, Larish spoke a command to his sphere, and a black-and-white image appeared of the stairwell interior. The landing was vacant at first, and then the door burst open and Aisly stumbled into view, locked in battle with Syrine. The girls struggled for a moment, and then as soon as the door shut behind them, Syrine released her grip and whirled around to face the other direction.

Larish paused the footage. "At first I assumed Syrine had turned her back on Aisly to avoid eye contact. So she wouldn't be entranced."

"But?" Cara prompted.

"But then I saw this."

The video played on, now showing Aisly escaping and fleeing down the stairs. She disappeared from sight, and Syrine collapsed to the floor and leaned against the stairwell door, either out of exhaustion or to make it look like she'd been attacked. It was hard to tell.

"Now watch closely," Larish said. "Right here."

Syrine opened one hand to reveal something tiny resting in her palm, and the footage paused. Larish zoomed in to enhance the object, but it was still too grainy to identify.

"It's a key," he whispered. "I think Aisly gave it to her during the struggle."

When the video continued, the door opened an inch and Syrine quickly shoved the key in her pocket. Then she moved aside and gripped her temples as if in pain. That was how Aelyx found her. He entered the frame, dragged her backward into the hall, and the door shut, leaving the stairwell vacant again.

Larish shut down the image. "Like I said, it's open to interpretation. But to me, it almost seems as if she intentionally allowed Aisly to escape."

Cara agreed. "I'd like to get my hands on that key."

"I already did." Sheepishly ducking his head, Larish produced a standard brass key, then replaced it in his pocket. "It was in her bag."

Cara grinned at the scholar. She'd always known Larish

had a brilliant mind, but clearly she'd underestimated him. "Well, look at you—a L'eihr of many talents."

His cheeks colored. "I did some research based on the coding engraved on the key. It belongs to a storage unit at a facility in New York, about ten miles from the site of the first explosion."

"Interesting." Cara wondered what was in there. Her instincts told her it was something important. A weapon, perhaps. If the key had belonged to Aisly, maybe she and Jaxen kept their Aribol gadgets in storage.

"Do you think we should show Aelyx?"

"No," Cara said. To her it was plain Syrine had let Aisly go on purpose, but Aelyx wouldn't interpret it that way. He'd watch the footage and see what he wanted to see— Syrine as the perpetual victim. "Let's keep this quiet for now. Whatever Syrine's hiding, I don't want to tip her off and give her a chance to have the storage unit emptied."

Suddenly, Cara knew exactly what she needed to do.

She strode to the front of the shuttle and crooked a finger at Troy and Elle. Then she hollered at Aelyx, "Change of plan. Elle's joining your group. Troy and Larish are coming with me."

## Chapter Ten

Cara had crossed multiple galaxies and lived on two different planets, but she'd never visited Canada before now. The instant she'd caught her first glimpse of its pristine white-capped mountains and its forests of rich pine, she mused there could be no greater contrast to the sand dunes she had left behind. Where the desert was dead, this place exuded life. Even in the industrial area where the shuttle had landed, the very air she breathed seemed fertile—ripe with cool moisture and buzzing with insects.

Unfortunately, the change in temperature had done nothing to soothe her temper. If anything, her hurt and anger had built like steam inside a pressure cooker. Each moment Aelyx refused eye contact, each time his hand rested beside hers but never connected, she felt another stab of rejection. She supposed she could apologize—be the bigger person— but she didn't want to. What she wanted was for him to choose her, to put his faith in her. Until that happened, she had nothing to say to him.

So she spoke to Elle instead. "Did you scan the building for explosives?"

Elle stood across from her in the empty factory parking lot. Their group was already divided: Aelyx and his team on one side, Cara and her crew on the other. If this were a teen movie, a dance-off would happen next. "I think—"

"Yes," Aelyx interrupted, lifting the *iphal* Troy had taken from the ambassador. He kept his gaze fixed on the empty space above Cara's head when he spoke. "Remember, shoot to kill, but only after you have a visual on Jaxen's ship. He'll probably cloak it, so we'll need to know exactly where it lands in order to access his flight log."

Troy checked his ammunition clip, then shoved it back inside his spare pistol and tucked the weapon beneath his waistband. "What about Cara's reboot? I've got no problem taking out the hybrids, but I don't think I can ice my own sister."

For the briefest of moments, Aelyx flicked a glance at her. "The replicate is not your sister. She's her own person. I was cloned from a L'eihr who lived two thousand years ago, but that doesn't make me him."

"Wait a minute," Cara said. She had no desire to swap friendship bracelets with her clone, but that didn't mean she wanted Rune dead. It was one thing to kill Jaxen and Aisly; they had once intended to purge half the human race. But Rune's only crime was being born to the wrong person. "She hasn't done anything wrong."

Aelyx used a hand to indicate the bruises on her face.

"Nothing serious enough to *die* for."

He heaved a sigh. "Then capture her if you want. Let's just get on with it. The next plant is fifty miles away, and for all we know the hybrids could be there by now."

Cara narrowed her eyes at him. "Excuse me for caring about a human life. I'll try to do better next time."

"Don't twist my words," he snapped. "I'm trying to save your entire race."

"*My* entire race? What about yours? I thought we were in this together."

He opened his mouth as if to argue, but clamped it shut again. Then he turned and began making his way toward the factory while Cara's shoulders sagged in disappointment. She didn't know what she'd expected from him, but a simple *goodbye* would've been nice.

To her surprise, Syrine ran after him and grabbed his shirt. She hissed something to him, which caused him to shake his head. Cara chewed the inside of her cheek and watched as the pair argued in hushed tones. She couldn't hear them at first, until Aelyx flung a frustrated hand in the air, and Syrine raised her voice loud enough to trip a probe in the next solar system.

"David said it to me over and over," she shouted in L'eihr. "But I never said it back because I thought we had more time. I was wrong. One minute he was there, and the next minute he was gone." She shoved Aelyx's chest. "So tell her. Then you can go back to being angry."

"Fine," Aelyx said, then spun to face Cara and spat, "I love you!"

Cara gasped, never imagining those words could sound so ugly. She gripped her hips and hurtled at him, "Yeah? Well, I love you *more*."

"Jesus, you two are weird," Troy muttered. He nudged her toward the shuttle. "Come on, let's go."

Face blazing, Cara clambered into the shuttle. The rest of her team joined her, Troy in the passenger seat and Larish in the back. They lifted off before Aelyx and his group had made it inside the factory building. As much as she hated to admit it, Aelyx was right. The hybrids could show up at any moment.

With the cloaking mode engaged, she zipped across fifty miles of airspace as if the shuttle were nothing more than a stone skipping over a pond. They arrived at the second factory so quickly Troy hadn't finished fastening his safety harness. Cara alighted in the parking lot and peered around, finding no signs of the hybrids. But that didn't mean anything. If Jaxen or Aisly were here, their crafts would be cloaked, too.

"Are you sure you're okay doing this without me?" she asked Troy. Maybe she should stay here and investigate the storage unit later. "Because Larish is a thinker, not a fighter." She glanced at Larish in the backseat. "No offense."

"None taken," Larish said absently while using a handheld electron tracker to scan the area. "You're right."

"I'll be fine." Troy cocked his pistol and surveyed the area though his window. "This is what the Marines trained me to do. It's actually better if you're not here. It'll be easier to focus if I'm not worried about keeping you safe."

"Hey." She objected to that. "I can hold my own, you know."

He smiled and tugged her braid, then stepped outside. "Yeah, I know. But still, go on. Find out what's in that storage unit. I'll call you when it's over."

"If you need me, buzz my sphere," she called to Troy as he and Larish strode across the parking lot. "I can be back here in just a few . . ."

She trailed off when it was clear they weren't listening. With her lower lip caught between her teeth, she sealed the doors and lifted into the air once again. But this time, she hovered there for a few beats, feeling as if her ankles were tethered to Troy's by an invisible rope. It wasn't until she watched him break into the building's rear entrance that she found the strength to veer south and punch the accelerator.

The flight to upstate New York didn't take long, but unlike the deserted fertilizer plants she'd left behind, Sherzinger Self Storage bustled with activity. She floated above a small city of storage sheds, arranged in dozens of rows across the fenced-in property, and watched movers unload furniture and boxes from trucks and U-Haul trailers.

Because she didn't have the luxury of waiting until closing time, she checked the inscription on the key Larish had given her—unit number 113—and landed at the end of the corresponding row, making sure to stay in the blind spot of the nearest security camera. After ensuring no one could see her exit the craft, she slipped out the door and used her fob to raise the cloaked shuttle ten feet into the air.

She kept her head down and the brass key in her hand as she jogged to unit 113. Up close, she found the shed was smaller than she'd expected, about half the size of a single garage, with a similar style sliding aluminum door. She unlocked the door and slid it up just high enough to duck beneath it, and once inside, let the door fall to the ground.

Darkness surrounded her, and a chill brushed her skin, raising the hair on her arms. She knew some of the units offered air conditioning, but this one seemed too frigid, like the inside of a meat locker. She felt along the wall for a light switch, and as she did so, her fingers slid along the surface as if frost had formed there. She grew colder and colder, and by the time she found the switch, her body was trembling.

She flipped on the lights and blinked her eyes to adjust to the brightness. At once, she noticed tendrils of smoke curling and rising around the room, obstructing her view of the floor. Her heart jumped, and for an instant she thought a fire had broken out. But then she realized the substance was more of a water vapor, the kind produced by dry ice.

She didn't see any ice. In fact, she didn't see much of anything at all. The entire space was vacant except for one large, rectangular box at the far end of the room, near the wall. Dark and metallic, it was raised off the floor by two wooden supports, and when she looked more closely, she saw an attached power cord that stretched to the middle of the floor and disappeared into the fog.

Curious, she crept forward, careful not to kick anything hidden by the swirling vapors. Her breaths clouded into fog in front of her face. The icy puffs came more rapidly as her pulse ticked in anticipation of what lay ahead. Something heavy congealed in the pit of her stomach. Her instincts told her to turn back, but her feet refused to obey. More than ever, she wanted to know what was in that box.

She reached the spot in the center of the room where the power cord disappeared and crouched down, waving her hand. The fog parted and revealed a volleyball-size chrome sphere that Cara recognized. She'd seen others like it at the colony. It was a L'eihr energy sphere, a battery pack designed to provide months of power.

She stood and glanced at the rectangular box. A hint of familiarity tingled at the back of her skull, as if her subconscious had already made the connection but the rest of her mind hadn't caught up yet. She inched across the smoky floor until she stood close enough to the box to make out the tiny temperature gauges and pressurization readings displayed along its side. Then a new shiver rolled over her, one that had nothing to do with the temperature.

She knew the purpose of this box.

A layer of frost had covered the small window located on the lid. Using the hem of her shirt, Cara scrubbed away the ice. There, beneath the thick glass pane, lay Private David Sharpe, frozen in the eternal slumber of his cryogenic tomb.

Aelyx crouched in the bushes outside the factory's northern-facing wall, trying to listen for the approach of an overhead engine but instead hearing the mental echo of Cara's furious final words to him. *I love you more.* There had certainly been no love in her voice, though in all fairness, he hadn't showered her in affection either.

He hated fighting with her. Such occurrences were rare, but they always left him feeling disoriented, as though he'd misplaced something very important, but he couldn't remember what he was supposed to be searching for. It was a horrible sensation.

Before meeting Cara, he'd had no experience with love. It never failed to amaze him how many unexpected tortures the emotion could generate. Missing her caused a suffocating pain directly behind his breastbone; wanting her created an ache low in his core; the fear of losing her was so acute it manifested in every one of his nightmares. And then there was jealousy, a phenomenon that defied logic but tormented him nonetheless each time he caught another male admiring her.

Make no mistake, the suffering was worth it. He would sacrifice his sanity on a thousand separate occasions for one night in Cara's arms, but that was no comfort to him now. He thought back to what Syrine had told him earlier about running out of time. What if the worst truly came to pass and his last exchange with Cara was one of anger?

Maybe he should call her . . .

Except he couldn't. He'd used his sphere to create a three-way connection with Elle and Syrine. They had to keep it open to communicate from their various stations along the building's perimeter.

"Anything?" called Syrine's voice.

"Nothing on my end," Elle said.

Aelyx shifted aside to take the pressure off his knees. In doing so, he earned himself a shrubbery-poke to the eye. "It's better that we arrived too soon than too late. They'll be here. I'm sure of it."

"Maybe one of us should go inside," Elle suggested again.

"There's no reason to," Aelyx reminded her. He prayed to the Sacred Mother, the gods of L'eihr, and even a handful of Cara's earthly saints that Jaxen came to this plant and not the other one. He'd waited a long time for a second chance to put that *fasher* in the ground. "They won't make it that far."

"Are you sure we should kill them?" asked Syrine. "Maybe it would be smarter to interrogate them and learn more about the Aribol."

Aelyx scoffed. "You wouldn't say that if you knew—"
*how David died.* He cut off just in time.

"If I knew what?"

"Nothing. I'll tell you another time."

"Tell me now."

"It's not the right—"

"I know it's about David," she interrupted, "because you're treating me like an infant. So stop it. Whatever this is, I have a right to know."

Aelyx hesitated. It was only Syrine's refusal to use Silent Speech that had allowed him to hide the truth for this long. Perhaps he should tell her. She would find out eventually.

"All right," he began. Then he told her everything—how David had been diagnosed with a fatal degenerative disease, and Jaxen had offered him L'eihr drugs. The medication had worked temporarily. But instead of providing the entire cure at once, Jaxen had doled out small doses according to his whims. Next he'd required David to perform tasks for him, sabotaging alliance efforts. Then he'd given David an ultimatum: In order to receive the final lifesaving dose, he would have to kill Aelyx. "He didn't want to do it, but by that time, he'd fallen in love with you. He said you'd given him a reason to live."

Syrine didn't respond.

"In the end, he couldn't go through with it," Aelyx went on. "There was another man with us who was working for Jaxen. David turned on the man to save me, and they shot each other. His last words were begging me not to tell you—I don't think he understood how Silent Speech works—but you deserve to know what happened." Aelyx ran a thumb over the *iphal* holstered at his hip. "And why Jaxen deserves to die."

There was a long pause, followed by, "What about Aisly? Did she know?"

"Yes. But I don't think she was involved directly, if that matters."

"It doesn't," Syrine said in a flat voice. Aelyx worried he'd overwhelmed her, until she finished her statement. "But my opinion still stands. They might have information we can use. We should question them first. Then kill them."

"She has a point," Elle added. "The Aribol are a mystery. We can't fight an enemy we don't know."

Aelyx scratched his jaw and weighed their logic against his own. On the surface, capturing the hybrids might seem like a good idea, but interrogating the pair wouldn't necessarily yield the truth. "I think it's too much of a risk to let them live. If I get a clean shot at either of them, I'm going to—"

A low rumble interrupted him, originating from somewhere high above. Aelyx flattened his back against the wall and nestled into the bushes for more concealment. "This is it," he called through the sphere. "As soon as the ship lands, report its position. Then disconnect and go silent."

But as it turned out, they never had the chance.

The ship remained cloaked and didn't land, instead hovering above the factory for several long seconds. Aelyx heard light plinking noises, like hail falling onto the roof, and then Jaxen's amplified voice called out over the whirring engine.

"I'm disappointed, but I can't say I'm surprised." The voice boomed from all around, menacing and almost godlike in its effect. Aelyx's stomach clenched because he realized what this meant. Jaxen knew. Somehow he knew they were waiting for him. "I gave you a chance to return where you belong, so don't let it be said that I'm not reasonable. This is the outcome you deserve."

Still invisible, the ship's engines roared, and it jetted into the distance, leaving a warm gust of wind in its wake. Aelyx jumped to his feet as understanding dawned. He yelled, "Run!" at the top of his lungs and sprinted away from the building, pumping his legs as fast as they could carry him. He'd barely made it halfway across the parking lot when a surge of blistering energy came from behind and swept his boots off the ground.

He was flying, hurtling through the air with dizzying speed toward the wooded acreage beyond the lot. He flailed his arms and watched in horror as a thicket of tree limbs rose up to meet him. He saw bark, rough and patchy, and shut his eyes. In his last moment, there was no reflection or regret, only fear of impact as he tensed his muscles for the blow. Then his body collided with unmoving timber, and the earth went dark.

Cara was already in the shuttle when her brother called. "I'm on my way," she told him.

"No rush. The ambush was a bust." As if anticipating her next question, Troy quickly added, "Don't freak out. I'm fine and so is Larish."

"What happened?"

"Aisly was here," he muttered darkly. "I fired on her as soon as she stepped out of her shuttle. Hit her too, but she's slippery as sin. She ran around the other side and climbed back in before I could catch her; then she was gone. She didn't have a chance to blow up the factory, though, so there's that. Maybe she'll come back."

Cara slouched in her seat. They'd lost the element of surprise. "Not alone, she won't. Any word from the other group?"

"No. They're not answering their spheres. I don't like it."

Cara didn't need to hear any more. She veered east toward Aelyx's location. "I'm going to check it out. Find someplace to lie low until I can come and get you."

"Hey, Pepper?"

"Yeah?"

"I know you can hold your own, but promise you'll be careful, okay?"

"Promise," she said absently, and disconnected.

Her mind was already reeling with terrifying explanations for why Aelyx hadn't answered his sphere, and it didn't help to see a turret of smoke rising in the distance where his factory stood . . . or had once stood. She'd seen smoke like that before, and she knew what it meant.

She pushed the accelerator to the limit, occasionally glancing at the roads below for emergency response vehicles. She didn't see any, which told her the explosion had just happened. As she approached, her fingers trembled on the controls, her grip so sweaty that she overshot the destination and had to turn around.

The demolition was noticeably different from the site in upstate New York. Instead of a pile of rubble, half the factory walls remained standing, as if the building had been detonated from above. The ruins were engulfed in flames, so she hovered close to the ground, below the smoke, and scanned the rubble for Aelyx.

She had to keep wiping her clammy palms on her jeans and reminding herself to breathe. Each time she came up empty, she fanned farther and farther out from the building. As she continued searching without any sign of him, it began to occur to her that his group might've been inside when the structure collapsed. Her eyes watered, and she roughly scrubbed them clear.

She couldn't afford to think that way.

Movement from her periphery caught her eye, and she whipped her gaze to a line of broken trees adjoining the property. A petite body rolled over to face her. It was Elle. Cara landed the shuttle so abruptly her skull rattled. In an instant she was by Elle's side, shouting in a rush, "Are you all right? Where're the others? Where's Aelyx?"

Panic had tunneled Cara's vision, so it took a moment before she noticed the blood seeping down the side of Elle's shirt. She searched for the source of the wound and discovered a six-inch sliver of wood protruding from Elle's shoulder.

Elle used her other arm to push into a sitting position. Half her face was blackened. "Is my med-kit in the shuttle?"

Cara nodded. "I'll get it."

"No." Elle gripped her sleeve. "Help me inside. I'll start treating my wounds while you look for the others."

Cara wrapped an arm around Elle's waist and gently lifted her to her feet. Soon the shuttle was airborne again. While Elle rummaged through her medical kit, she told Cara that each of them had been stationed at a different wall before the explosion. Cara glided south, and soon afterward, she spotted Syrine rocking back and forth on the ground, cradling a broken ankle. Cara helped her into the shuttle, too. As she returned to the pilot's seat, she detected the distant wail of sirens and knew it wouldn't be long before the authorities arrived and proceeded to blame her for this, assuming they didn't shoot her on sight.

She had to find Aelyx, fast.

While scanning the area for him, she remembered an advanced function in their com-spheres that allowed one user to track another. She called over her shoulder into the backseat, "Someone track Aelyx's sphere."

Syrine whimpered in pain but did as she was asked. She pointed a trembling finger north. "Go that way for three hundred yards."

The signal led to a dense expanse of trees, the tops of which had been blown off during the blast. Below the scorched tips, enough leafy branches remained intact to block Cara's view of the ground, so she landed as close to the woods as possible and hit the grass running. She followed the tracker to Aelyx's sphere, buried beneath a pile of leaves, but he was nowhere to be found.

"Aelyx!" she shouted, turning in a clumsy circle.

The only reply was a chorus of sirens, growing louder by the second.

She ran deep into the trees and called out to him. Her eyes burned from the haze of smoke in the air, but she forced them open as she pushed a trail through the underbrush. She grunted in frustration, slowed by low branches that slapped her arms and face, until a familiar gray shirt came into view, and her heart turned over in her chest.

She'd found him, crumpled on the ground in an

unnatural position that sent a surge of panic through her veins. She skidded to a stop beside him and dropped to her knees, instantly checking his face for color. He seemed to be breathing, but her hands shook too violently to check for a pulse. She lightly slapped his cheek and said his name.

He moaned and slurred something she couldn't understand.

Instincts took over. As if operating independently of her brain, her eyes scanned the lacerations on his face and the angle of his limbs to assess his injuries while her fingers gently probed his spine to determine whether it was safe to move him. She didn't feel any irregularities, but she was no expert. "Can you move your legs?"

He answered with a groan and shifted his feet.

That was good enough for her. She stood up, grabbed him beneath the arms, and began hauling him back the way she'd come. He struggled to maintain consciousness, lifting his head and then letting it fall back. At one point, he opened his eyes and asked in his native language if she was real.

"I'm real," she panted, stumbling across the scorched, littered landscape. "Try to wake up. Keep talking to me."

"I don't want to fight anymore," he slurred in L'eihr.

Neither did she. She couldn't believe she had ever cared who was right and who was wrong. She didn't want to be right. She only wanted him to be okay.

Elle was waiting outside the shuttle, having already removed the jagged splinter from her shoulder. Together she and Cara hoisted Aelyx onto the backseat. Then, as the first fire engines and squad cars pulled into the lot, Cara raised the shuttle and piloted them away from the smoking ruins.

This place didn't seem so fertile anymore.

## Chapter Eleven

Human scientists claimed that pain couldn't be felt in dreams, but Aelyx knew better. On a regular basis he experienced pain while he slept, either because he wasn't human or simply because the scientists were wrong. Regardless, his mind had been replaying the events of the attack, forcing him to relive every detail of his suffering: the sick sensation of falling, the crunch of his bones upon impact, the dull, pulsating throb of his organs as he lay on the ground unable to move. He watched it happen in a detached sort of way, but his nerve endings screamed just as loudly as they had in real life. When the dream began to falter, interrupted by fingers of reality, his agony faded by gradual degrees until the only discomfort that remained was a slight ache between his temples.

He groaned in immense relief.

Someone whispered, "He's waking up." It sounded like Syrine.

The first thing Aelyx detected was a mildew scent, not the kind found in nature, but the concentrated dampness of an old, neglected home. He was aware that he lay on his back, stretched out with a pillow supporting his head. As he shifted his limbs, he felt the cool brush of linen on his bare skin. He knew this sensation. He was naked between bedsheets.

His eyes flew open. Where was he, and why was he naked?

He darted a glance at his surroundings and found himself lying on a thin mattress situated on the floor of what appeared to be a formal living room. Right away he could tell the house had been abandoned. There were no furnishings in the room other than a dilapidated wingback chair missing its seat cushion and a broken, upended coffee table resting beside an empty fireplace. The wood floors were dirty, and someone had defaced the walls with red spray paint. With no electricity, the only illumination came from between the slats of a boarded-up window. Judging by the dim orangey glow outside, dusk had fallen.

He didn't see Cara, but he noticed her brother leaning against the open doorframe, his arms folded and his face concealed by shadows. In the opposite corner, Syrine sat on the floor wearing an expectant smile. One of her feet was propped up on the chair's missing seat cushion. Elle knelt at the foot of the mattress. As soon as his eyes met hers, she crawled across the sheets and sat beside him.

"Hello, brother." Her mouth curved in a triumphant grin, as if she'd beaten him in a game of sticks and couldn't wait to gloat about it. "Feeling better, are you?"

Aelyx cleared the thickness from his throat and pushed slowly to his elbows. His muscles protested against the movement, but only with the slight soreness that followed

148

an intense workout. He noted the med-kit lying open on the floor. Half its contents were missing.

"Remember the other day," Elle said, "when you wanted me to use the healing accelerant to fix your *l'ihan*'s bruises, but I insisted on saving the medicine for an emergency?" Her teeth flashed. "Well, your spleen can thank me for that. And your ribs. And your concussed head, which isn't nearly as hard as I thought it would be."

"And my ankle," Syrine added, pointing at her elevated foot.

At these words, Elle lost her smile, and her posture stiffened visibly. Aelyx noticed a reaction from Troy as well, who clenched his shoulders and released a loud breath through his nose. Syrine seemed to detect the abrupt change in them too, because she quickly turned her eyes to her lap. In the time it took to blink, the tension in the room had grown heavy enough to carpet the floor.

"Yes." Elle forced a grin that didn't fool him. "We were lucky. There was barely enough accelerant to go around."

Troy announced, "I'll go tell Cara you're awake," and then he walked away without a backward glance.

Sacred Mother. What had happened inside this house?

"Cara went to find you some clothes," Elle prattled on. "We had to cut off your old ones before I could treat you."

For the first time, Aelyx noticed his sister wasn't wearing her L'eihr uniform, and neither was Syrine. They'd both changed into oversize sweatpants, rolled up at the ankles, and mismatched, loose-fitting T-shirts. But that didn't matter. He wanted to know what they weren't telling him. "Where are we?" he croaked, and cleared his throat again.

"How long have I been asleep? And why is everyone acting so strangely?"

Elle flicked a lightning glance at Syrine and then seemed to make a concerted effort not to look at her again. Aelyx might assume the pair had been fighting if it weren't for the way Syrine curled against the wall, pressing herself to the plaster as if wishing she could disappear inside it. He knew his best friend well enough to see she felt guilty about something.

Elle smoothed a wrinkle on the top sheet. "It's been about four hours since the explosion. Cara picked us up in the shuttle, and then we went to fetch Troy and Larish. Jaxen bombed their factory, too."

Aelyx gasped, suddenly realizing Larish wasn't in the room.

"Larish is fine," Elle said, and pushed him back down on the pillow. "He's making some calls from the shuttle."

"He and Troy left the property before Jaxen arrived," Syrine added, talking mostly to her lap. "We're still in Canada, but in a different province. Larish researched a list of foreclosures while we were airborne. That's how we found this house."

That answered his first two questions, but it didn't escape Aelyx's notice that they'd avoided the third. He was about to press them for information when he heard the rapid tapping of shoes descending a staircase, and Cara ran into the room, where she skidded on the gritty wooden floor and waved her arms for balance. She righted herself and looked at him with a smile so wide and pure it lit up her face like a solar flare.

In response, an automatic grin formed on his lips. Somewhere deep inside, a small piece of him he hadn't known was missing clicked into place, and just like that, he was whole again. "Hi," he told her, because he couldn't think of anything more fitting to say.

"Hi," she echoed. He wanted her to come sit by him, but she stayed in place, nervously wiping her palms on her pants. An awkward tension rose between them, and his heart sank as he remembered their fight. There was damage to mend. "I found some clothes for you, but I left them upstairs."

"It's all right." He hoped she knew he was talking about more than the clothes. When Troy reentered the room looking more somber than before, Aelyx asked, "What happened? How did Jaxen and Aisly know we were waiting for them?"

"Aisly didn't know," Troy said. "I caught her by surprise, but not fast enough to kill her. As for Jaxen . . ." He trailed off and glanced at Syrine. "We have a theory about who tipped him off."

The room went silent.

Aelyx looked from Troy to Cara to Syrine, hoping for clarification but receiving none. Then Cara flinched and retrieved her com-sphere from her pocket. Instead of speaking her passkey, she held the sphere at a distance as if it might detonate in her face.

"It's Alona," she said.

"You might as well answer," Aelyx told her. She couldn't deny a summons from The Way. No one could. Her sphere would only continue to buzz inside her head until she accepted the transmission.

Cara strode to the middle of the room and sat cross-legged on the floor. She set the sphere in front of her, then took a deep breath and spoke her passkey.

Alona's image appeared directly below a beam of fading sunlight from the window. The effect was almost angelic, an odd contrast to the burning fury in her gaze. "Miss Sweeney, please explain to me why the quarters of Aelyx, Larish, Syrine, and Elyx'a were found vacant, and why no trace of them exists on the inbound transport."

Cara lifted her chin in a show of confidence, but negated it by wringing her hands in her lap. "Because they never left Earth. They're here with me."

Aelyx had never seen the head Elder speechless before. Alona couldn't seem to operate her mouth, but the force with which she gripped her chair arms spoke volumes. She finally growled, "By what authority do they seek to defy The Way?"

"By mine," Cara answered smoothly. "I ordered them to stay. And because I'm still a member of The Way—or at least I was yesterday—they were bound by law to obey me. If you want to punish someone, it'll have to be me."

"Not so brave a statement when you're beyond my reach."

Cara's lips parted. She seemed wounded by the implication that Alona would lash her if given the opportunity. Her voice was less bold when she answered. "I'll gladly take the *iphet* if it means defeating the Aribol and keeping our people together."

"And that's what you believe you're doing?"

"I'm trying."

"Trying," Alona repeated coldly. "Naïve girl! Your efforts will be the death of us all. The Aribol are the most powerful force in the charted universe."

Cara held up an index finger. "Exactly. So why are they threatened by an alliance between two insignificant worlds?

Why did they send hybrids to display their power on Earth and on L'eihr instead of doing it themselves?"

"L'eihr?" asked Alona. "No hybrids have breached our borders other than the ones we've bred ourselves."

"That's not true. There's something you don't know." Cara delivered a quick sideways glance at Syrine. "It wasn't Zane who destroyed the Voyager fleet and the spaceport that night. It was Aisly, using detonators the Aribol gave her."

Aelyx felt his eyebrows jerk toward his scalp.

"Syrine has something to tell you," Cara said, and indicated the spot beside her.

All eyes shifted to Syrine, who used the wall to push herself to standing. Aelyx moved to help her, but she thrust a palm forward and told him to stay in bed. Keeping her weight on her uninjured foot, she gripped the wall like a crutch and limped along its length until she'd reached the other end of the room. Then she lowered herself to the floor and inched her way to Cara's side.

"Go ahead," Cara prompted.

Syrine fidgeted with her pear-seed pendant and then seemed to catch herself. She tucked both hands beneath her legs before she spoke. "It happened on the continent, the night before the spaceport was destroyed. I had just finished therapy with my sister healers. They said I was free to join the colony, but the next shuttle didn't leave until morning." She swallowed. "It was a nice evening, so I decided to take one last walk around the grounds. That's when I saw her."

"Aisly?" asked Alona.

Syrine nodded, eyes fixed on her sweatpants. "I think she was on her way to see the other hybrids in their prison. Maybe to release them, I don't know. I was faster than she was—stronger, too—and I knew not to look her in the eyes. So when I caught her, I turned her face down on the ground and held her there while I found my sphere. I was going to call the capital guards to come and fetch her. But then . . ." She paused until Cara elbowed her. "But then she said something that made me hesitate."

"What did she say?"

"That she knew about my *l'ihan*, David, and how he had died on Earth. She knew instead of cremating him, I'd asked permission to have his body brought to the colony for burial."

"A request I granted," Cara interjected.

"So then—" Syrine's voice cracked, and she began again. "So then she asked me if he'd been buried yet. I told her no, and she said if David stayed well preserved, there was a way to bring him back."

The whites of Alona's eyes flashed. "From the dead?"

"Yes," Syrine said. "At first I didn't believe her. But then she said she'd been to visit the Aribol, and they had created technology beyond anything I could comprehend—an elixir full of enzymes to regenerate dead or damaged cells. She promised that as long as enough of David's remains were intact, he could be fully restored."

Alona sat back against her chair as a look of understanding crossed her face. "And in exchange for your cooperation, she agreed to provide this elixir."

Syrine bowed her spine. Though her features were hidden by locks of wayward hair, Aelyx saw tears drop to the floor. He found himself shaking his head. He wanted her to deny it. But the clues rose to the front of his mind— her unwillingness to hold a burial, her refusal to use Silent

154

Speech, her decision to stay on Earth, Jaxen's knowledge of their whereabouts, David's missing body, which obviously had not been cremated.

Cara had been right. Syrine had betrayed them.

"I didn't know she was going to hurt anyone," Syrine said, dragging a hand beneath her nose. "I just wanted David back. When he died, an invisible blade wedged itself right here"—she clutched her chest—"between my ribs, and all these months later I still can't remove it."

"After destroying the fleet, Aisly stole David's body and brought it to Earth," Cara said. "I found it today in a storage unit."

"But I swear I wasn't in league with the hybrids," Syrine insisted. "I didn't know their plans. I've never spoken to Jaxen. All I did was let Aisly go, and I haven't talked to her since that day in the stairwell, to ask where she'd hidden David. I didn't tell her about the ambush. I would never put my friends in danger like that."

"You already did," Aelyx told her. His voice sounded every bit as hurt as he felt inside. "When you trusted Aisly's word. She's a liar and a manipulator. You know that."

With her face still averted, Syrine gave a small nod. "As soon as you told me what Jaxen had done to David, I knew Aisly was doing the same thing to me. Even if the elixir is real, she never had any intention of using it. She only brought his body here so she can hold it over my head."

"So anyway," Cara said to Alona, "the Aribol aren't the ones who destroyed our fleet, at least not directly. I think this proves they're not as mighty as everyone believes."

"Or they simply don't wish to dirty their hands," Alona pointed out.

"Maybe, but something's not right," Cara argued. "Jaxen didn't say so, but I know the Aribol promised him and Aisly some kind of control over us when this is done. Once they have us separated and we can't travel beyond our own worlds, we won't be able to fight back. They'll rule us for generations to come."

Alona's mouth formed a hard line.

"I know it's a risk to ignore the deadline," Cara went on. "But I think it's an even bigger risk to call off the search. The Aribol must have a weakness. Let's keep looking until we find it."

Alona steepled her fingers and appeared to consider the request. Aelyx watched her intently, holding his breath as the seconds ticked by in silence. Finally she said, "Very well. I'll allow the last Voyager ship to continue its search."

"Thank you."

Alona dismissed Cara with a wave. "Don't thank me, girl. I might have just damned us all."

"Am I still part of The Way?" Cara asked. "Because I want to be, but I understand if you don't trust me anymore."

Alona's face softened by a fraction. "We will include you the next time we convene. There simply wasn't a moment to spare last time."

The transmission ended, and everyone in the room released a collective breath. If nothing else, at least they'd earned another day or two.

"So what do we do about *her*?" Troy asked, jutting his chin at Syrine.

In response, Syrine drew both knees to her chest, and Aelyx had to fight the urge to defend her. "I didn't tell anyone about the ambush," she said. "I would never let Jaxen hurt any of you."

"Then how did he find out?" Aelyx asked.

"I don't know, but I'm telling the truth." She swiveled her gaze to him, wide-eyed as if to use Silent Speech. "I can prove it."

He turned away. He didn't want her inside his mind.

"Just because she's telling the truth doesn't mean we can trust her," Troy said. "Her loyalty's divided. She's proven that."

Aelyx had to agree. How many L'eihrs had died inside the spaceport when it was destroyed? How many Voyagers had gone down with their ships? Innocent lives had been lost, all because Syrine had allowed Aisly to escape.

He couldn't believe he'd stood up for her.

Elle strode across the room to where Cara and Syrine sat on the floor. She stopped directly in front of them and announced, "This is what we're going to do about *her*." She reached down with one hand. "We're going to forgive her. And then we're going to move David's body someplace Aisly will never find it. After that, we're going to forget this happened and focus on the real enemy."

Aelyx stared at his sister. He hadn't expected this from her.

"Don't look so shocked," Elle chided him. "You should know better than anyone that feelings and logic are mutually exclusive. Didn't I defend you to Cara last year when you made a similar mistake?"

He and Cara shared a glance.

"Remember how you struggled?" Elle asked him. "Remember how unprepared our generation was when The

Way removed our hormone regulators? We knew nothing of love and even less of heartbreak. I felt that same knife in my ribs when Eron died, and if Aisly had made me a similar offer then, I can't say I would have refused it. Does that make me unworthy of your trust?"

Aelyx turned his focus to his top sheet, rubbing it between his fingers.

"Now imagine Syrine, even more unprepared for her *l'ihan*'s death because of the gift she possesses," Elle said. "Emotional healers feel differently than we do. They love more deeply, and their grief has no limits."

"I know that," he mumbled.

"Of course you do." Elle waited for him to meet her eyes. "That's why you supported her before. And why you'll do it again."

Maybe he would. But right now the wound was too fresh.

It seemed Cara felt the same way. "I think we should take some time to calm down and process what happened before we decide."

Troy released an angry huff. "I don't need time."

"Well, I do. And I'm not going to make another snap decision, not for something this important." Cara dug in her pocket and pulled out a brass key, which she handed to Elle. "Now's a good time to move David's body. You know how to fly the shuttle, right?"

"I can manage."

"Take my brother and Larish with you. Syrine, too. She should see that his remains are safe. Then we'll meet back here and put it to a vote."

"Come on," Elle said, extending one hand to a teary-eyed Syrine. "You can prop up your ankle on the backseat."

Troy made a noise of disgust and left the room. His combat boots clunked loudly toward the front of the house, and then a door slammed hard enough to rattle the windows. Cara chewed her bottom lip and watched the empty doorway, but she didn't follow her brother.

Aelyx remained in bed while Cara walked the others to the shuttle. After the engine whirred and faded into the distance, she returned to the living room and paused in the doorway. For a while, neither of them spoke. A wall of complete silence stood between them, not even the faint hum of a refrigerator filling the background. Aelyx couldn't read her face in the near darkness, and he didn't know what to say, or if he should speak at all.

"How do you feel?" she finally asked.

"Okay," he said. But that wasn't fully true, so he added, "Physically."

"And emotionally?"

He extended a hand to her. "Why don't you come sit down?"

She left the doorway and settled beside him on the mattress, close enough for him to smell the smoke and citrus on her hair, but not touching him. She didn't seem to know what to do with her hands, so he took one of them and held it between both of his. She responded by scooting over until their legs met through the sheet.

"Today was scary," she whispered, looking down. "I thought I'd lost you."

He squeezed her hand and tried to lighten the mood. "It would take more than death for you to lose me. I meant it when I said I'll always find my way back." When that didn't help, he tipped her chin until their eyes met. *I'm sorry about before. I was wrong about Syrine. I should have listened—*

*It doesn't matter who was wrong,* she interrupted. But in contrast to her words, a jumble of emotions and memories from the day's events leaked from her mind into his.

Aelyx felt a pang of shame when he understood how deeply his actions had hurt her. But at the same time, he was glad the argument had affected her as deeply as it had him. Oddly, that left him feeling even more ashamed because he shouldn't be grateful for her pain, and he realized how right his sister had been. In some ways, he was still unprepared to experience love.

The connection closed with Cara's eyes. "No matter how hard I try, sometimes it feels like I can't do anything right. Your opinion matters the most to me, so when you brought up my mistakes on the colony, it really stung."

"I shouldn't have done that." He could see how unfair he'd been. He had accused her of projecting her anger onto the wrong person, but he'd done nearly the same. "Sometimes your position in The Way makes me feel like we're not partners. I should've admitted that instead of criticizing you."

"We *are* partners. I can't do this alone."

"It would help if you included me more. I know we won't always agree on what to do, but I can respect that if we talk about it first." He offered her an encouraging smile. "I like the way you handled the issue with Syrine. The old Cara might have made that decision on her own."

She returned the grin, though shyly. "So we're okay?"

"Only okay?" he teased. "Haven't we already proven we're highly gifted?"

Her grin gave way to a small laugh, and then she leaned over his pillow to kiss him. Their lips had barely met when their com-spheres buzzed. Aelyx didn't know where his sphere was, so he waited for Cara to answer hers.

Larish's image barely had time to form before he blurted in a rush, "Quick! Find Syrine's old clothes and get them out of the house."

"*What?*" Cara asked. "Why?"

"Because I think I know how Jaxen did it," Larish said. "And if I'm right, he could be on his way there now."

# Chapter Twelve

Cara bolted into the night, her shoes slapping the pavement as she sprinted down the middle of the street with Syrine's clothes balled under one arm. She tried to keep her pace steady while activating the electron tracker she'd grabbed on her way out the door. The device beeped as soon as she passed it over Syrine's tunic, telling her Larish had been right. Aisly had planted a beacon on Syrine during the struggle in the stairwell. That's how Jaxen had found them.

Cara heard the churn of rushing water and glanced to her right, where runoff from the street poured into an open sewer grate. She slowed to a jog and considered shoving the tunic into the sewer, but after thinking it through, she changed her mind. Jaxen had every reason to believe he'd killed half the group. If she put the tracker in the right place, he might keep believing it. So she ran on until she reached an old church bordered by a sprawling graveyard.

*Perfect.*

She used a rock to break the sod between two headstones and dug a shallow hole. She'd just finished burying the clothes when Larish contacted her again.

"Jaxen and Aisly were spotted in Europe," he said. "So no need to panic."

Cara sat back on her heels, wiping a hand across her forehead. "Now you tell me."

"We're done relocating David's remains."

"All right. Meet you back at the house."

An hour later, everyone reconvened around Aelyx's mattress in the living room to plan their next move. Midnight was approaching, bringing an end to the longest day of Cara's life. She couldn't believe just that morning she'd shuttled Aelyx to the transport to fake his departure. It felt like a week had passed since then.

She fought back a yawn and glanced at the others by the light of a single candle resting on the floor. "All right, then. The vote carries four to one. Syrine can stay."

"This is a mistake," Troy said, not caring that Syrine sat a few feet away. "War is risky enough when everyone's on the same side. Any commander would tell you—"

"But we're not the Marines and she isn't a soldier," Cara reminded him. "She made a mistake any one of us could've made. She knows it was wrong to let Aisly go, and she's sorry. Now we have to put it behind us so we can regroup. Jaxen thinks he won. This could be our last chance to catch him off guard." She turned to Larish. "Where is he now?"

Larish used his sphere to project a map of Europe into the air above the candle. He'd already marked a variety of sites on the map with pulsating red dots. "There's been an interesting change in the pattern. After destroying two manufacturing plants in Canada and another two in Europe, the hybrids began targeting phosphorus mines."

"Phosphorus mines?" Cara scrunched her forehead. "Why?"

"Aside from their role in nourishing plant growth, I can't say. But whatever the reason, it was urgent enough for them to kill the security personnel at each site."

Cara looked at her brother. "This seals it. I don't know why the hybrids are blowing up fertilizer plants, but it has nothing to do with cutting off our food supply."

Troy merely sucked his teeth in silence.

"I'm inclined to agree," Larish said. "And there's one mine they haven't destroyed—the largest remaining. It's in the western Sahara."

Cara groaned. "Great, another desert."

"And nowhere near here," Aelyx pointed out. He glanced at the wall, where his sister sat with Syrine's head resting on her lap. "How soon can we travel?"

Elle pursed her lips in consideration while stroking Syrine's hair. Cara's heart ached at the sight. It was hard to hold a grudge against Syrine when she lay curled on her side, crying without sound. In a way she'd lost David all over again. Aisly had committed some heinous crimes in her lifetime, but giving Syrine false hope might've been the cruelest thing she'd ever done.

"It's not the travel that concerns me," Elle said. "It's the exertion once we arrive. Bones heal quickly, but for internal injuries the accelerant needs twelve hours to restore organs to peak condition."

Larish shut down the map and rolled his sphere between

two fingers. "It makes the most sense to leave now and rest once we're there."

"Then let me fly," Aelyx said. He pushed into a sitting position and threw off the top sheet, revealing the faded jeans and tank top Cara had brought him. "I've had more sleep than the rest of you combined."

"You were *unconscious*," Cara argued. "Not sure that counts."

Troy grumbled from the doorway. "How about we quit wasting time and do our talking in the shuttle? Unless you'd like to override me on that, too."

Cara shot her brother a withering look. He wasn't helping.

"Aelyx is safe to pilot the craft," Elle said. "His concussion should've healed by now."

With that decided, Troy spun on his boot and exited the room, leaving the rest of them to gather their things, which didn't amount to much—one half-empty medical kit, a satchel of protein packets, half a bag of pork rinds, and a duffel filled with David's possessions.

Syrine's fractured ankle had healed well enough to allow her to limp independently, but she leaned against Elle as they crossed the floor. Cara slung a bag over each shoulder and supported Syrine from the other side. Syrine turned to her with a watery grin, and for the first time in months, she opened her thoughts to Cara.

No words were exchanged, but in that brief moment, Syrine shared more than either of their languages could express—sorrow and shame for her perceived weakness, determination to make up for her mistakes, and rising above it all, gratitude for a second chance. She considered Cara a friend, nearly as dear to her as Aelyx, and she'd hated herself for driving a wedge between them.

The connection closed before Cara could apologize for judging Syrine so harshly, or say how touched she was to be ranked among her closest friends. She hadn't known Syrine thought of her that way, and it cast their relationship in a new light.

When everyone was seated in the shuttle and the miles passed beneath them in a dark blur, Cara chewed on her thumbnail and tried to figure out the reason for the new heaviness in her chest. It took a while, but by the time they'd chased the setting sun to the northeastern tip of Africa, she realized the cause of her unease.

The Aribol hadn't simply threatened her race and her future with Aelyx. They wanted to rip her away from Syrine, Elle, and Larish, too—three people she'd come to care for during the last few trying days together. The time they'd spent on Earth, both good and bad, had shown her what was at stake. She didn't want to lose any of them, but she would if they failed to find a solution before the deadline.

Suddenly, the shuttle came to an abrupt midair halt, flinging her against her harness straps. She turned to Aelyx in the pilot's seat, but before she could ask him what was wrong, he pointed out the front shield. "Look. They're here."

At first glance, all Cara noticed was the mine—an enormous canyon at least three hundred feet deep and a quarter of a mile wide, scooped out of the middle of the desert. The quarry walls were striped in alternating layers of golden sand and powdery white phosphorus. All around the cliffs at ground level sat mountainous heaps of discarded earth. The setting sun cast shade behind the dirt mounds, and there, half concealed by the nearest shadows were two unmistakable spacecraft, neither of them cloaked. The first was a shuttle slightly smaller than their own, and the second was a midsize cruiser, perfect for interstellar travel. The hybrids were nowhere in sight, but that didn't stop Cara's heart from leaping with joy.

They'd done it. They'd found Jaxen's ship.

Aelyx held his position, well outside detection. "It's an X-class vessel, a L'eihr craft. I can't fly it, but I can access its log."

"And disable it?" asked Troy from the backseat.

Aelyx smiled. "Easily. The shuttle, too."

"Then do it now, and let's deal with the hybrids later," Troy said. "Jaxen can wave his staff all he wants, but it won't fly him out of this desert."

Cara squinted through the front shield, wishing she could spot Jaxen and see if he had his staff with him. Tinkering with an engine wouldn't reopen Aelyx's wounds, but being knocked ten yards across the sand would. "How close can we get without tipping them off?"

"Depends on where they are," Aelyx said.

"I assume they're inside the mine," Larish told them. "In order to collapse it, they'll first need to drill deep into the cliff walls and place explosives within the holes. The fact that they're not in view leads me to believe they're not ready to detonate."

"How about this," Cara suggested. "We'll drop off Aelyx and Larish at the ships. Then while they're pulling the coordinates from the flight log and disabling the engines, I'll fly the rest of us over the quarry to get a visual on Jaxen and Aisly."

Syrine finally spoke. "Who has the *iphal*?"

"It's gone," Aelyx said. "I lost it in the blast."

Troy removed his rifle clip and inspected it. "I've still got twenty rounds." He snapped the clip back into place. "That's eighteen more than I need."

Syrine shook her head. "I still think we should take them alive."

"Of course *you* would say that," Troy muttered under his breath.

"What's that supposed to mean?" Elle demanded.

"It means her loyalty's divided, just like I said before."

Aelyx landed the shuttle purposefully hard on the sand, jarring them into silence. "This chance may never come again, so let's make the most of it." He stepped out the side door, and Cara scooted into the pilot's seat while Larish exited through the back.

"Careful," she whispered to Aelyx. "Be kind to your spleen."

He patted his abdomen. "Promise."

After agreeing to use their spheres to check in, they shared a quick kiss, and Cara left him to his work. She lifted off gradually, so as not to sandblast Aelyx and Larish with the thrusters. When she reached the top of the dirt mound, she engaged the cloaking mode and accelerated past the cliff ledge to the valley beyond.

The low angle of the sun cast the mine in darkness, making it difficult to pick out anything except gargantuan dump trucks and towering piles of white powder. But then something shimmered in her periphery, and she glanced at the opposite end of the gorge to find sunlight glinting off the metallic edge of Jaxen's hovercraft, which was rising slowly from the depths of the mine.

Jaxen stood in between Rune and Aisly on the skateboard-style craft. Each girl clung to his waist while he wrapped an arm around their shoulders, making him the cream filling in the world's most bizarre cookie sandwich. Even from this distance, Cara could see the Nova Staff tucked beneath one of his arms.

She used her sphere to send Aelyx and Larish a message. "They must've set the explosives, because they're on their way up."

"I need more time," Aelyx said.

Troy scooted up from the backseat. "I have three words for you, Sis: *hit and run.*"

Cara couldn't help smiling. "Knock them out of the sky?"

"Problem solved."

But she would have to be delicate about it. She agreed with Syrine. The hybrids were more useful alive. So she waited until the hovercraft had cleared the cliff ledge, where the drop wouldn't kill them. Then she gripped the wheel and warned, "Hold on. I've never run over anyone before."

She punched the accelerator and zoomed across the canyon toward the hovercraft, prepared to bump it with her starboard wing. She approached so quickly Jaxen didn't have time to react. His head snapped in her direction, his eyes wide. But too late, Cara realized she'd left the cloaking mode engaged. Without a visual of the wing, she could easily chop Jaxen in half instead of knocking him to the ground. She swerved around the craft and disabled the cloaking device, then came around for another pass.

This time Jaxen was ready. He raised his staff while Aisly

and the clone crouched low to give him more freedom of movement. The staff headpiece glowed alive, and Jaxen aimed it at the shuttle. Cara dodged the invisible force with a sharp right, and then came at him again. She was closer now, close enough to see the fear etched onto her clone's face. Rune had changed visibly since their last encounter. She'd lost weight, making her cheekbones more pronounced and her jaw sharp. She must've known what was coming, because she released Jaxen and jumped to the ground. Cara was only a few yards from connecting with the hovercraft when Jaxen raised his staff and struck out again.

There was a loud buzz, and instantly, the shuttle engine died.

As her stomach dipped in a freefall, Cara tipped the shuttle aside, just enough to tap the hovercraft with her port wing. It connected with a resounding *thunk* that tossed Jaxen and Aisly overboard.

Cara barely had time to brace for impact. The shuttle sailed toward the sand, where it hit with a bone-rattling jolt and skidded on its belly until it met the resistance of a dirt mound and jerked to a stop. Cara's neck snapped forward and back. She opened her eyes to find the shuttle nose embedded in the landfill. The controls were silent, the whole system dead, but a quick glance in the backseat revealed everyone alive.

Troy had already started unfastening his harness, reminding Cara to do the same. She rubbed her aching neck with one hand while using the other to free herself. Elle and Syrine followed suit, and soon they all filed outside into the sweltering desert.

Dusk had fallen, the sun a mere glow on the horizon, but

it was enough for Cara to make out Rune in the distance, hurt and limping toward Jaxen and Aisly, who were near the cliff ledge, struggling to stand up.

Troy didn't hesitate. He dropped to one knee and extended his pistol, squinting to take aim. Before Cara could tell him to stop, he squeezed off four deafening shots. The hybrids flinched and ducked. Cara thought she saw Jaxen stumble backward a pace, but it was hard to tell.

"I hit him," Troy said, standing. "I need a closer shot."

And with that, he took off at a sprint, kicking up dust in his wake. Elle followed, yelling for him to wait. Cara started after them, then remembered Syrine's broken ankle. The healing accelerant must've done its job, because Syrine sped past her.

The dusty air dulled Cara's sight as she followed the others. By the time she caught up, she found the hybrids divided. Aisly sat alone at the cliff's edge, cradling an injured foot, while about ten yards away, Jaxen stood protectively in front of Rune. A patch of blood blossomed out from his stomach. It seemed to be spreading quickly. When Troy fired another shot, Jaxen absorbed the bullet's velocity with his staff and rebounded that energy in a bolt that sent Troy hurtling backward. His pistol landed on the sand, and Syrine dove for it. Once she had the weapon in her grasp, Jaxen knocked her into a violent roll.

"It's over," Cara called to Jaxen. "Aelyx disabled both of your ships. You'll die if that wound isn't treated, but if you lay down your staff and—" A force slammed into her, and she landed hard on the dirt.

She brushed herself off and watched Jaxen summon his hovercraft. Once it reached him, he scooped Rune into his arms and stepped onto the narrow board. "A generous offer, *Cah*-ra," he hollered with a grin, "but I'm afraid I'll have to decline."

*Decline?* Had he lost his mind? There was nowhere to go. He would bleed out before the hovercraft carried him beyond the desert.

Aisly managed to stand on one wobbly leg, raising a hand toward Jaxen as if hailing a cab. He rose higher and higher into the air, then began motoring in the other direction. Aisly let out a sob of panic and shouted to him in L'eihr. "Jaxen! Don't leave me!"

But that was exactly what he did. It appeared Rune had replaced more than just Cara in his brittle excuse for a heart. All alone, Aisly screamed obscenities at him, until she noticed Troy and Syrine approaching. She glanced behind her, but there was nowhere to go but down.

Wiping the dirt from her face, Aisly tried to appeal to Syrine, who held the gun trained on her chest. "You need me. I'm the only one who can bring back your *l'ihan*. If I die, he dies, too."

"He's already dead," Syrine replied in an eerie calm. "But don't worry. I'm not going to kill you." She added, *"Yet."*

"Give me the gun," Troy ordered, but Syrine waved him off. The pistol began to tremble in her fist. If she didn't calm down, she'd shoot Aisly whether she meant to or not.

Cara wedged herself between the two, holding out a hand for the pistol. "It's okay, Syrine. You can give me the gun. I promise I won't let Troy shoot her."

After that, everything happened in a rush.

Aisly called Troy's name, and he made the mistake of looking her in the eyes. An instant later, he rounded on Cara and grabbed her by the throat. Cara clawed at his fingers as her airway closed. She kicked and sputtered, but nothing fazed him. He dragged her toward Syrine, using his free hand to snatch at the pistol.

Elle stepped in, throwing a handful of sand in Aisly's face. Then she picked up a smooth stone and struck Troy in the head. At once, the fingers around Cara's throat loosened, and her brother collapsed.

Blinded, Aisly fought to maintain her balance while clearing the grit from her eyes. She began to stumble backward, dangerously close to the ledge. Cara lunged out to grab her. The tips of her fingers skimmed Aisly's tunic, but before she could get a better grip, the arid soil crumbled beneath Aisly's feet, and she fell backward into the abyss.

Cara's breath caught in horror. Aisly's screams echoed through the night and then abruptly cut off, replaced by a macabre silence. Goose bumps raised on Cara's forearms. She remembered her brother and dropped to her knees by his side.

"Will he be okay?" she asked Elle.

"I'm sure there are healing accelerants in Aisly's shuttle. She would have needed them after Troy shot—" Elle cut off with a gasp, pointing back the way they'd come. "Jaxen!"

Cara leaned around Elle, squinting in the growing darkness at their shuttle, which was still partially embedded in a pile of dirt. Jaxen pointed his staff at the engine, and it hummed to life, restored of the energy he'd stolen from it.

Cara jumped to her feet. "He's stealing our shuttle."

"All of our things are in there," Syrine said, then drew a sharp breath. "*David's* things are in there!"

But they were powerless to stop him. Jaxen and Rune

boarded the shuttle, and the engine revved in reverse, freeing its nose from the dirt. Moments later the craft ascended, and then it was gone.

Cara's com-sphere buzzed. Aelyx asked, "Where are you going? Come back."

"That's not me." She explained what had happened. "I hope you didn't ruin Aisly's shuttle, because we're going to need it."

Larish's face popped into view. "I only removed her cables. I can reinstall them."

"How about the Aribols' coordinates?" Cara asked. "Did you find them?"

Aelyx answered with a smile, his teeth glowing white in the darkness.

"I'll take that as a yes."

His grin fell. "I thought you'd be happier."

"I'll take a celebratory rain check. Right now I need to restrain my brother before he wakes up and tries to kill me again."

"Stay where you are," Aelyx said. "I'll come to you."


Ten minutes later, an unconscious Troy was tied to the front passenger seat in Aisly's shuttle while the rest of the group stood outside his open door, trying to figure out how to undo the effects of Aisly's brainwashing. Cara had a feeling the girl's death hadn't magically erased whatever orders she'd given Troy. The hybrids had a way of permanently altering minds when they wanted to.

"I was right," Elle said. She knelt on the ground, using a

flashlight to sort through the medical kit she'd found in the shuttle. "There's some healing accelerant left."

Elle filled a syringe with milky fluid and injected it into the side of Troy's neck. He began to stir, and Elle hopped back just in time. Fully awake, Troy thrashed wildly against his bindings with the kind of fury that made Cara worry he might hurt himself.

"Can we sedate him?" she asked.

"I'm already working on it." Elle used another syringe to inject Troy with something that caused his muscles to relax. He didn't fall asleep, but his eyelids slid to half-mast and he rested his head against the seatback.

Cara massaged her temples. What was she supposed to do now? She couldn't take her brother to the hospital. The Marines would arrest him, and regardless, there was no cure for this sort of thing in the medical handbook.

Syrine made her way to the front of the group. "I'd like to try something."

Cara moved aside.

"I've never seen into the minds of Aisly's victims," Syrine said. She situated herself in front of Troy and took his head between both hands. "I'm curious whether I can remove her influence the way I can remove negative emotions."

She peered deeply into Troy's eyes and fell silent while Cara held her breath in anticipation. The seconds ticked by and turned into minutes. Syrine's hands began to shake. She strained to hold the connection until she abruptly broke away and slouched over, panting for breath. Cara was about to ask if it worked when Troy blinked sleepily and slurred, "Shouldn't have looked her in the eyes. I told you that bitch has skills."

Cara sighed with relief. "*Had* skills. Aisly's dead."

"Good," he mumbled. "She told me to kill all of you, then shoot myself." He yawned widely and flinched. "Why does my head hurt?"

Elle extended a hand to touch him and then pulled back. "I'm sorry. I hit you harder than I meant to."

Syrine grinned at her friend. "I'm fairly certain you'll earn his forgiveness," she said in L'eihr. "He's in love with you. I felt it."

Elle's mouth flew open in perfect sync with her eyes. She snapped her gaze to Troy, but he didn't notice. His lids had drifted shut, and he'd begun snoring lightly.

Cara shared an amused glance with Aelyx and then cleared her throat. "Do you think you can do that again?" she asked Syrine. "To a whole group of people?"

Syrine blotted her forehead with her shirt hem. "Yes, one at a time. I'd have to rest in between sessions, though."

"Perfect." Cara smiled, cashing in her celebratory rain check. "Let's see if we can book you an appointment with the president."

## Chapter Thirteen

"I'll pass the coordinates on to the navigator team." Jake swallowed hard enough to shift his Adam's apple. His hologram paled visibly, which was saying a lot, as his blond-haired, blue-eyed software geek complexion was fair to begin with. "I can't believe you found them."

Neither could Cara. But now that her adrenaline had worn off and the night breeze cooled her flushed skin, she understood Jake's reaction. She felt a prickle of sympathy for him. She'd been so focused on pinpointing the location of the Aribols' home planet that she hadn't given much thought to what the Voyagers would have to do with those coordinates. Soon they would go knocking on hell's door to face an enemy they knew nothing about.

They had to be terrified.

"Will you pass along something else for me, too?" she asked.

"What is it?"

"My gratitude. I want all the colonists on board, yourself included, to know how proud I am of you. None of you had to join the search. You volunteered. And what you're about to do is the bravest thing I can imagine." She smiled at him. "I'm glad to have you on my team, Jake."

The praise seemed to make him uncomfortable. He scratched the back of his neck and inspected his shoes while mumbling something vaguely resembling a thank you. He peeked up through his lashes. "If that's it, will you hand me to Syrine? I want to ask her something before I go."

Cara bit the inside of her cheek and glanced at the shuttle, where Syrine and the others were catching a few hours of much needed shuteye. "Now's not a good time."

"Oh. I'll try her later, then."

Cara was pretty sure what Jake wanted to ask Syrine, and *later* wasn't a good time for that discussion either. "There's something you should know. I don't want this getting out, so keep it between us." After Jake nodded, she told him how Aisly had manipulated Syrine with the false promise of reanimating the love of her life. "Now she's grieving for him all over again, so you can probably imagine why it's a bad idea to ask her for romantic advice."

Jake's whole face melted into a frown. "The poor girl. That's awful."

"Yes, it is," Cara agreed. "So why don't you ask me instead?"

His blond brows shot up.

"Oh, come on, I'm totally qualified for this. I fell for a L'eihr, too, remember? I know better than anyone what you're going through. The whole 'culture clash' thing was a nightmare at first."

"At first?" That piqued his interest. "So it got easier?"

"Sure, but there was a lot of trial and error along the way." Cara thought back to those first awkward weeks with Aelyx. Neither of them had understood anything about the other. She'd tried to force-feed him pizza, which he'd hated, and he'd offended her with his clinical honesty regarding her waist-to-hip ratio. Even their first kiss had happened because of a competition to see whose method of expressing affection was best. (She'd won.) "So why don't you tell me what's going on between you and . . ." She tried to remember the L'eihr girl's name. "Arah?"

"Ayah."

"Right. Ayah."

"Nothing's going on," Jake said. "That's the problem. We finished the project, and now it's business as usual. Sometimes I catch her looking at me in the cafeteria, but she only talks to me if I ask her a direct question. I can't get a read on her signals."

"Ah, signals." Cara understood all too well what he meant. "Here's the thing. Humans and L'eihrs have different social cues. Our signals don't match. She probably has no idea you like her." That'd been the case with Elle and Troy. "Your best bet is to be direct."

Jake cringed. "To come right out and say *Hey, I like you*?"

"Maybe not in those exact words. You could tell her how much you enjoyed her company when you two were working together, and then invite her to a game of dice in the common room so you can get to know each other better. Make it clear you want to find out if the two of you are compatible. That's what most clones care about."

179

The suggestion seemed to scare him more than his impending invasion of Planet Aribol.

"Look at it this way," Cara said. "Both our species might be dead in a week. What have you got to lose?"

He tipped his head. "You know, that's not a bad pickup line."

"On that uplifting note, I should go. I need to schedule an appointment to deprogram the president."

Jake cracked a grin. "As one does."

"I know, right? Just another day in the life of Cara Sweeney."

"Hey, by the way," Jake said right before they disconnected, "thanks."

"Anytime, Jake. Good luck to you." She shut down the call and whispered, "Good luck to us both."

The worst side effect of supersonic globetrotting was losing track of the days, closely followed by a level of exhaustion Cara liked to call "stupid tired," in which she caught herself spreading cream cheese on her napkin instead of the bagel Larish had bought for her from the corner deli.

They were back in Manhattan, safely cloaked inside Aisly's shuttle, while Syrine and Colonel Rutter met with the president and the Earth Council inside the United Nations building. The pair had only been gone for an hour, and though Syrine had successfully removed Aisly's influence from three Council members, she had a long way to go before it was safe for Cara to go inside and meet with them.

So now there was nothing to do but wait.

"Ugh." She found a smudge of cream cheese on her wrist

and licked it off before remembering she hadn't had a shower in two days. Or was it three? God, it hadn't been four, had it? "I can't eat this," she said, holding up her naked bagel. "I'm too tired to chew." She turned around and handed it to her brother in the backseat. "Want the rest?"

Troy had already eaten, but he never refused good food. He tore the bagel in half and offered part of it to Elle, who sat beside him rifling through a duffel bag she'd found in the rear hatch. Though Troy was only being polite, Elle gaped at him as if he'd dropped to one knee and thrust a diamond ring in her face.

"What?" he asked. "I didn't lick it or anything."

Elle scooted an inch toward the window. "I'm not hungry."

Troy made a *suit-yourself* gesture and tore off a bite. He chewed contentedly for a few moments until he noticed Elle staring at him, and then he glanced at her, lowering one black brow.

"What?" he asked a second time.

"Nothing."

"Why are you looking at me like that?"

She dropped her gaze to the duffel. "I'm not looking at you."

He shook his head, muttering to himself about women.

Cara tried not to laugh. Ever since Elle had learned about Troy's crush, she'd been studying him like he was a statue on display at the Louvre. Cara didn't know if that was a good sign, but she figured it was her sisterly duty to give her brother a hand.

She winked at Aelyx and then said to Larish in the back, "Hey, do you mind switching seats with me? I need a nap, and there's more room back there."

"Certainly."

They took turns climbing in between the front seats. Cara sat on the opposite end from Elle, putting Troy in the middle. She kicked off her flats and curled up on the seat, then pointed at her brother's lap. "Can I use you as a pillow?" When the corners of his mouth pulled down, she added, "You *did* try to choke me today. Or yesterday. I can't remember."

He pushed her head down.

"And scoot over," she said.

He moved an inch toward Elle.

"More."

Another inch.

"A little more."

"Keep it up, Pepper," he grumbled, "and I'll finish what I started."

Since she'd already accomplished her goal, Cara didn't press her luck. She rested her cheek on Troy's lap and snuggled down a little farther into the seat cushion. Almost as soon as she closed her eyes, she felt herself drifting toward sleep, and then she was out.

"The president sends her deepest apologies for attacking you," Colonel Rutter said later that afternoon when he escorted Cara inside the United Nations building and to the Earth Council headquarters on the thirtieth floor. "And for issuing the order to shoot you on sight."

Cara scoffed. She'd expected an invitation to the White House for a weekend of groveling, but whatever.

"And," the colonel continued, "she would appreciate

it if you kept the details of the incident to yourself." He whispered behind his hand, "She's up for reelection."

"My lips are sealed," Cara promised. "As long as she calls a press conference to tell everyone I'm not a threat to national security."

"It's already in the works. We're blaming the mistake on bad intel."

Of course they were. *Politicians.* "Oh, and I want my blog fully restored—every single post, follower, and comment."

"I'll see to it personally."

Rutter held the door open for her, and she preceded him into the Earth Council lobby. From what he'd said, a conference was already in session between Alona and the Council. Now that the world's leaders had their marbles restored, there was a lot of catching up to do.

When Cara opened the conference room door, she found Alona's hologram at the head of the table, but not in miniature form. Somehow she'd magnified her image to life-size, so she blended seamlessly with the dozens of other leaders seated around the long table. It was a wise strategy that demonstrated her understanding of human culture. Despite what people claimed, size mattered.

Alona noticed Cara, though her face remained impassive. "Welcome, Miss Sweeney. I've finished recounting the most recent events for the Council. They're now aware that the last transport has arrived, and the L'eihr ambassador has been returned home. If Syrine, Aelyx, Larish, and Elyx'a remain hidden on Earth, the Aribol will have no reason to doubt we've complied with their demands."

*Unless Jaxen tells on us,* Cara thought. She doubted he would, because it wasn't in his best interests. If the Aribol destroyed mankind, he'd have no one to rule. But despite that, she couldn't deny his behavior had grown harder to predict. She never would've expected him to abandon Aisly.

The representative for the European Union raised his hand. "They'll know when your Voyager ship arrives at their planet."

"Irrelevant," Alona dismissed. "As long as the Voyagers arrive before the deadline, we're in no violation of the terms. The Aribol demanded the surrender of all intergalactic travel technology by a specific date. They didn't expressly forbid exploration in the meantime. The official Voyager directive is to engage in peaceful negotiation with Aribol leaders. If the commander is unsuccessful, his orders are to surrender the ship."

"But what about the crew?" Cara asked, thinking of Jake and the other human colonists she'd encouraged to volunteer for the mission. She'd had no idea about this. "They'll be trapped there."

"Assuming they're not executed," added the representative from China.

"Perhaps," Alona droned. "They may die, they may be returned home, or the Aribol may use them to seed a new race. Regardless, I consider it a worthy risk."

Cara was still trying to process the news when Alona added, "Now that you understand what has occurred during your . . . mental absence . . . I invite you to join me in conferring with the Aribol representative, Zane. The transmission will begin momentarily."

Alona was full of surprises today.

"I ask you to remain silent while I lead the discussion. The less information we reveal, the better." After scanning all the faces in the room as if to ensure their cooperation, Alona tapped a set of controls out of view, and Zane appeared, his head and shoulders floating above the middle of the table.

His image looked the same as Cara remembered, a masklike porcelain façade that loosely resembled a human face. She wished her Noven brain was capable of seeing his true form, because the curiosity was killing her.

Once again, his mouth remained sealed when he spoke. "Greetings, children."

Cara fought back a shiver. His computerized voice was eerie.

"And to you," Alona replied. She swept a hand toward the opposite end of the table, where Cara stood, not having found a vacant chair. "As you can see, my Chief Human Consultant has returned to her home planet. The colony is vacant, and the last intergalactic transport has returned to L'eihr. Once it is destroyed, your demands will have been met."

"Not quite," Zane told her. "We've discovered an error in our original calculations. When we destroyed your Voyager fleet, there was one ship unaccounted for. Where is it?"

Everyone in the room went collectively still, Alona included. The head Elder didn't respond. She had to know that if she told Zane the truth, he would order the Voyagers to return home at once.

Cara thought fast for a way to dodge the question. On a whim, she employed a tactic she'd used countless times on her parents—deflection.

"The fleet *you* destroyed?" she asked Zane. "Don't you mean Aisly? Because I know your secret. She was the one who blew up the spaceport. Oh, she's dead, by the way.

Whatever technology you gave her, it didn't save her from the laws of physics. She fell into the phosphorus mine she was trying to destroy—on your orders, I assume. But you'll be glad to know Jaxen's still alive, wreaking havoc with the clone you made for him." She narrowed her gaze. "A clone of *me*, which, for your information, I don't appreciate very much."

"None of this is relevant, young human."

"It's relevant to me," Cara argued. "Me and everyone else on Earth. You call us your children, but look how you behave. You tear us away from our loved ones on L'eihr, and deny us the wonder of exploring new worlds. You send hybrids to our planet with the unchecked power to kill and destroy, the same hybrids who wanted to enslave mankind and use our people as an infantry against *you* in a preemptive attack. Are those the actions of a benevolent parent?"

Zane stared at her with shadowy eyes. "It is our wish to preserve the worlds we've seeded, but do not mistake our investment for paternal kindness. Not all gods are benevolent."

*Gods?*

Cara drew back, struck by the weight of that word. Maybe she couldn't remember the last time she'd confessed her sins or attended mass, but that didn't make her beliefs any less sacred. Her faith had never wavered, not even when she'd learned of mankind's Noven origins. She believed in a Creator for all living things, including the Aribol. She pointed at Zane and told him, "You are not my God."

"As you wish. We do not require worship, only obedience." His veneer swiveled to face Alona. "The next time we speak, you will account for the missing craft."

Then he vanished.

● ● ●

The setting sun painted the sky in a kaleidoscope of pastels, but Aelyx didn't stop to admire the view. He towed Cara by the hand up the front steps of the safe house porch, eager to claim one of the two existing showers before Elle, Syrine, and Larish beat him to it. He was so filthy he could scratch his name into the grit on his forearm.

The colonel had returned them to the woods in the interest of hiding the L'eihrs from view, and to ensure that news of their presence on Earth didn't leak to the media, he'd reduced the security detail to a handful of guards with top-level government clearance. Bill and Eileen Sweeney were also on their way to join them, and if Aelyx hurried, he might be able to share a shower with Cara before her parents arrived . . . the kind that involved more than bathing.

But the instant he and Cara crossed the threshold, two pairs of arms pulled them into a hug and the questions began flying. *Are you okay? Where have you been? Why haven't you called? We've been worried sick!* Then Eileen pulled back to inspect her daughter's face and gasped in alarm. "Oh, Pepper. What happened to your face?"

This was why Aelyx had wanted to use the healing accelerant on Cara's bruises. Her fight with the clone had blackened one eye, and her brother's recent attack had left a purple, hand-shaped ring around her throat. The damage was only cosmetic, but it wouldn't appear that way in the eyes of a parent.

"I'm fine," Cara insisted. "Believe me, it could've been worse. In the last two days, I've been attacked by the president, punched by my clone, and strangled by my own br"—she cut off before saying *brother* and finished smoothly—"bracelet." She held up her bare wrist. "It fell off in the desert and the clone tried to choke me with it."

"That settles it, young lady," Bill declared, folding his thick arms over his chest. "You're not leaving this house again."

Cara didn't argue, likely because they'd achieved their goal of finding Jaxen's ship, and now there was nothing to do until they heard from the Voyagers.

Troy and the others came bounding through the door. Larish made a beeline for the computer, Eileen snagged Troy in an embrace, and Elle and Syrine darted up the stairs to the bathrooms. Aelyx groaned. The girls would use all the hot water.

Bill clapped Troy on the shoulder. "I'm glad you looked out for your sister, son."

Cara slid a look at her brother while coyly fingering her bruised neck, and Troy admitted, "We looked out for each other, really."

Larish called to them from the computer desk in the living room. "The phosphorus mine was destroyed an hour ago. Jaxen must have returned and detonated the explosives."

"Rune could've done it," Aelyx pointed out.

"Either way, Jaxen's probably alive," Troy grumbled. "Those hybrids don't go down easy."

Eileen slashed a hand through the air. "No more talk about hybrids, or alien invasions, or secret plots. Let the authorities handle it."

"Your mother's right," Bill said. "I want you all to clean up, and then we're going to have a nice dinner in front of the idiot box"—he thumbed toward the television—"just like a normal family. I think the twenty-eighth Batman movie is on."

"Sounds perfect," Cara said, and smiled a bit too sweetly for Aelyx to believe. She led him and Troy up the stairs under the pretense of finding a change of clothes, then tugged them into a vacant room and whispered, "I figured out what our next move should be."

Troy snorted. "I'll bet it doesn't involve the Dark Knight and a bowl of popcorn."

"I want to find Jaxen and talk to him," she said. "Face to face."

Aelyx was so shocked by the absurdity of the idea he could only laugh. He and Troy told her, "No," at the same time.

She held both palms forward. "Hear me out. Zane made it clear that he cares for the human race about as much as I cared for the sea monkeys I ordered off the Internet in third grade. Assuming the Aribol don't blow our Voyager ship out of the sky, odds are they'll capture the crew before they can tell us anything useful. That leaves one person with the information we need, one person who doesn't want to see Earth destroyed."

Aelyx didn't know what a sea monkey was, but he imagined Jaxen saw humans in much the same way. "One person who's part Aribol and has no regard for human life."

"Except for my life," Cara said. "Jaxen's always liked me."

Aelyx scoffed. *Liked* was putting it mildly.

"He could've killed me at the factory and the mine," she pressed, "but he didn't. He said the universe is a better place with me in it."

Troy pointed back and forth between himself and Aelyx.

"But he'll whack both of us without batting an eye, which means you'd have to go alone."

"Which is out of the question," Aelyx added.

"Syrine and Elle can—"

"He would kill them, too." Aelyx shook his head. "You're asking me to risk my *l'ihan*, my sister, and my best friend. I won't agree to it."

Stubborn as ever, Cara propped a hand on her hip. "I promised I would talk to you about things like this, but I didn't say I'd ask permission."

"Oh, yeah?" Troy grinned. "Then I'll tell Mom and Dad your plan. Should make for interesting dinner conversation, don't you think?"

She glared at him. "You wouldn't."

"You have a short memory, Pepper. Let's review all the times I've snitched on you." He began ticking off items on his fingers. "There was sophomore year, when I saw that douche Eric sneaking through your bedroom window. And then the night you came home smelling like a distillery and yakked in Mom's begonia bushes . . ."

"Fine," Cara spat. "Never mind. It was just an idea."

Troy patted her on the head. "I'm glad we understand each other." The noise of running water stopped, and he pointed to the nearest bathroom. "I'm calling dibs on this one."

"Whatever. I'll take the master bathroom." She jabbed a finger toward Aelyx and clarified, "*Alone*," before charging away, angry because he didn't want to send her unprotected into the arms of a genocidal sociopath.

He rolled his eyes. *Females.*

"Hey," Troy said while peeling off his shirt. He pointed

the garment in Cara's direction. "Keep an eye on her. She can be sneaky when she wants someth—"

Just then, the bathroom door opened, releasing a cloud of steam, and Elle stepped out wearing a towel wrapped around her waist. Troy went mute at the sight of her bare chest, and in turn, Elle froze at the sight of his. There was much blushing and stammering from Troy until he blocked his view with one hand. "You can't walk around like that. This isn't the Aegis."

"I forgot." Elle adjusted her towel to cover herself. She backed away but couldn't seem to tear her gaze away from Troy's navel. "It won't happen again."

Aelyx bit back a laugh. He considered giving the two their privacy, but the exchange was too entertaining to miss.

"Listen," Troy said, and twisted his shirt nervously between both hands. "I already thanked Syrine, but I didn't get a chance to thank you for what you did at the mine."

"For giving you a concussion?"

"For saving me from myself." Troy glanced at the floor, then up again. "If I had hurt Cara, it would've ruined me— my whole family. You don't know what she means to us. I hope I can pay you back someday."

Elle didn't appear to like the idea of Troy in her debt. She mumbled, "You don't owe me anything," and then she turned and darted down the hall. The slamming of her bedroom door soon followed.

Troy shook his head and shifted his glance to Aelyx. "Girls confuse the hell out of me sometimes."

In a human gesture of solidarity, Aelyx extended a fist, which Troy then bumped lightly with his own. "For once, you and I have something in common."

## Chapter Fourteen

Though her brother didn't know it, Cara would've chosen the master bathroom anyway, because it was the best place on the second floor for sneaking out. A sturdy pine tree grew right outside the window, close enough to allow her to climb down. Her tree-scaling skills left much to be desired—her tailbone could testify to that—but as perfectly as these branches were spaced, not even she could botch it.

The real trick was returning before anyone noticed her absence.

She got right to work, locking the bathroom door and turning on the shower. She found an old clock radio beneath the sink and cranked up the volume to a pop rock station. The blaring music would give her an excuse for not responding if someone knocked on the door.

With the gears of her ruse in motion, she raised the window and removed the screen. A few precarious moments later, she stood on the adjacent tree limb, surveying the backyard for security personnel while the night breeze tossed her hair behind her shoulders.

The moon glowed full and bright in a cloudless sky, allowing her to pick out each soldier in the skeleton crew Colonel Rutter had left behind. Once the men finished their sweep of the backyard and strode to the front of the house, Cara descended the tree branches as if they were rungs on a ladder and jumped to the ground.

She wiped her sap-sticky palms on her pants while jogging across the lawn to where the shuttle was parked. She had no intention of taking the craft; the engine's noise would give her away. Instead she rooted around the backseat until she found what she was looking for, then stuffed the object in her pocket and sprinted toward the woods at the rear of the lot.

She didn't know how long she ran, but she stopped when the glassy bay came into view between the trees. She scanned the area until she found the best spot for what she had planned, a wide clearing in the woods bordered by thick oaks and maples. Then before she could change her mind, she scrolled through the list of contacts in her com-sphere and selected the frequency to the shuttle Jaxen had stolen.

She couldn't see him with the hologram function switched off, but he answered with a smile in his voice that was easy to picture. "Why, *Cah*-ra Sweeney. What a nice surprise."

"How'd you know it was me?"

"Your frequency is programmed into the system here. I imagine the same is true for your companions. If I cared enough to make the effort, I could track all of your spheres and pay the group a surprise visit tonight."

Cara felt a pinch in her stomach. She hadn't thought of that.

"Perhaps I should," he added. "After all, you did kill Aisly."

"That was an accident. She fell off the ledge . . . after *you* ditched her."

"Semantics."

From beside him, Rune demanded in L'eihr, "What does she want?"

"Rune makes an excellent point," Jaxen said. "To what do I owe the pleasure, *Cah*-ra?"

Cara drew a deep breath and hoped she wouldn't regret this later. "I want to meet with you. I'm unarmed and I'm alone. If you don't believe me, track my sphere and compare it with the others."

"That only proves where their spheres are located, not their bodies."

"I give you my word. Nobody knows I'm here. But if you don't feel safe meeting me in person, we can talk like this. All I want is information. If something doesn't change soon, the Aribol will destroy both our worlds. I know that's not what you want." When he didn't respond, she told him what he doubtlessly wanted to hear. "I need you, Jaxen. Please help me."

There was a brief pause. "I'm locked on your signal. I'll be there soon."

By the time he touched down in the shuttle, Cara had positioned herself at the opposite end of the clearing, in front of a massive tree trunk at least four feet thick. Jaxen and Rune exited through the front doors and took a moment to sweep the area with a handheld device, likely scanning for weapons.

During their inspection, Cara noticed a shift in the dynamic between the two, a mutual intimacy that hadn't been there before. Jaxen curled his arm around Rune's waist, protective as ever, but now the clone reciprocated with casual touches to his chest and along the nape of his neck. At times she grew distracted from the scan and stood on tiptoe to whisper in his ear. Whatever she said made him smile, and he responded by lowering his hand and squeezing her bottom.

Cara hitched her upper lip in disgust. But then she noticed something that made her take a closer look at Rune. The clone hadn't simply lost weight in her face. The chiseled angles of her jaw line made it seem as though she'd aged—significantly so—by at least ten or fifteen years. Jaxen had said he'd used Aribol technology to speed up her development. Maybe it had backfired.

He pocketed his scanner, and the pair strode forward.

"Stop." Cara lifted both palms. "That's far enough."

Jaxen took another step. "I thought we were going to trust each other."

Cara jutted her chin at the clone. "She's got a mean right hook, and it'll be hard to pretend I was never here if I go home with another black eye."

"Fair enough."

Rune stuck out her bottom lip, which looked oddly childish on her thirty-year-old face. "I can't understand what you're saying," she whined in L'eihr.

"It's nothing, my darling," he told her. "She's afraid of you, that's all."

While Rune gloated with a triumphant smile, Cara turned

her attention to Jaxen. "There's something wrong with her, isn't there? She's aging too fast. A few days ago, she and I could've passed for twins, but now—"

"It's nothing I can't handle," he interrupted. But in contrast to his words, his gaze faltered and his voice grew terse. "Now tell me what you'd like to discuss."

"The Aribol," Cara said. "What do they really want from us?"

"You're a smart girl, *Cah*-ra. What do you think they want?"

"Control."

"See? You don't need me for this."

"But why are they threatened by the alliance? If the Aribol are as powerful as they claim, they shouldn't care about humans and L'eihrs teaming up to share our resources."

Jaxen quirked his head as if upset by something she'd said. "*If* the Aribol are as powerful as they claim? I assure you they're more powerful than you have the ability to fathom." He picked up a handful of dried foliage and threw it into the air. As the debris spiraled to the forest floor, he explained, "You and I are leaves at the mercy of the wind . . . and the Aribol are a tornado, capable of scattering us into oblivion."

Chills raised on Cara's arms.

"Would you like to know how it will happen?" he asked. "How they will destroy your world, if it comes to that?" He didn't wait for her to respond. "It will start with a global blackout—not simply of the electrical grid. Anything powered by generators or batteries will cease to operate. Humans will be trapped in their communities, helpless to resist, with nothing to do but wait for the fleet to arrive."

"The fleet?" Cara whispered.

"Yes, small ships that deliver concentrated shockwave pulses to liquefy soft tissue, like organs and skin and eyes. People will simply melt to the ground in a puddle of flesh and bones."

He painted a vivid picture, one that stopped Cara's breath.

"It may seem macabre," Jaxen went on, "but the Aribol won't harm the planet itself with radiation or fissionable explosives. Despite the vastness of the universe, worlds that support our kind are in short supply. They'll cleanse the Earth of mankind and start over, seeding a new, more compliant race in your place."

What he described was too horrible to process. A cosmic do-over at the expense of billions of lives? The Aribol couldn't be that cold . . . could they?

"If any humans survive the initial attack, the Aribol will simply don their suits and find them during a ground invasion."

"Suits?" Cara repeated. "Why would they need suits?"

"Irrelevant," Jaxen dismissed. "The point is there will be nowhere to hide. They have the means to dispose of the bodies as well—microscopic nanites that transform organic remains into carbon and then die, so as not to affect the ecosystem for the following society." He wrinkled his nose. "I've seen the nanites used on the Aribols' home world. It's an efficient process, though unpleasant to watch."

Cara imagined tiny organisms rendering bodies into dust. Was that how the Aribol would dispose of Jake and the other members of the Voyager crew? She caught herself shaking her head. She didn't want to believe it. "But I thought . . ."

"What?" Jaxen interrupted. "That there was hope? No,

*Cah*-ra. While I usually admire your tenacity, in this case it will lead to your downfall."

But there were still unanswered questions, things that didn't make sense. "What about the phosphorus mines and the fertilizer plants? If Zane sent you here to pave the way for an invasion, why haven't you targeted our armories?"

"Because there's no reason to. You've seen what my Nova Staff can do. Now imagine that technology on a larger scale. There's no weapon on Earth or on L'eihr that can penetrate the hull of an Aribol Destroyer. Your only hope is to pray you never see one."

"You didn't answer my first question."

At that, Jaxen's lips curled in a sly smile. He advanced a pace. "You didn't offer me anything in exchange for the answers I've already provided. That's rather rude, isn't it?"

Cara swallowed a lump and stood her ground. "Stay back."

He took another step and paused while Rune peered up at him as if to gauge his intentions. The clone glanced back and forth between Jaxen and Cara, the wheels clearly turning in her mind. Then her gaze turned frosty in a way Cara recognized from firsthand experience.

Rune was jealous.

"What do you want from her?" Rune demanded of Jaxen. "Why do you allow this girl to live when she's an inferior copy of me? Kill her, and let's leave this place."

Jaxen's whole face transformed in rapture. "You see?" he told Cara while gazing at the clone and cupping her cheek in one hand. "Such passion. She's a gift to me, everything I could ever want in a *l'ihan*."

Cara didn't know who he was trying harder to convince—

her or himself. As he bent to kiss his lab-made partner, Cara said, "Too bad she'll be dead soon."

Jaxen froze with his brows pinched together.

"How long do you expect her to last when she's aging a decade every other day?" As Cara spoke, something else occurred to her. Rune was young and only knew the things Jaxen had taught her. The clone might think her rapid aging was normal. "Have you told her what's wrong? Does she realize what's happening to her body?"

Rune, who could obviously see the exchange had upset her master, spun on Cara and raised a threatening fist. "Shut your filthy mouth, or I'll shut it for you."

Ignoring her, Cara extended a wrist to Jaxen. "Is this the prize you want in exchange for your answers? More of my blood, so you can make a second copy of me when this one expires? Or a third? How many innocent clones are you willing to kill before you realize I can't be replaced?"

In that moment, she knew she'd pushed him too far. Jaxen's eyes turned to slits and his nostrils flared. "Perhaps I was wrong," he growled, stalking forward. "I believe the universe will do perfectly well without you in it."

Cara's heart hammered, but she stood in place and tucked both hands behind her back. She reached into her pocket and retrieved the syringe she'd hidden there earlier. As Jaxen closed the distance between them with murder burning in his gaze, she placed her thumb on the plunger and held still, listening to the sound of his boots crunching over dead leaves.

When he reached her, he stretched a hand toward her throat. But instead of connecting with flesh and bone, his hand passed through her and struck tree bark. He blinked in confusion. Before he had time to realize he'd been talking to a magnified hologram, Cara darted out from behind the tree and plunged her needle into the side of his neck, flooding his veins with enough sedatives to drop an elephant.

She didn't wait to see him fall.

While Rune screamed and rushed to Jaxen's aid, Cara sprinted to the shuttle and prayed that it still recognized her handprint. The keypad responded to her touch, and the pilot side door opened. She jumped inside and started the engine, then lifted off the ground before her door had fully closed. With Jaxen and Rune beneath her, she turned the craft west and piloted it to the safe house lawn.

Judging by the chaos in the backyard when she arrived, her absence had been noticed. Floodlights cut wide paths across the lawn and illuminated her entire family and half a dozen soldiers, each with an assault rifle trained on the shuttle. She knew the bullets wouldn't pierce the hull, but she couldn't say the same about the windows, so she used her com-sphere to contact Aelyx and tell him she was alone inside the craft.

After landing, she exited to the clamor of shouts and accusations. The words blended together and drifted to her mind's periphery, but she couldn't escape the look of disappointment on the faces of everyone she loved. Aelyx, especially. He was so furious he could only stare at her boot tips while his throat worked visibly to form words that wouldn't come. Cara held up both hands in surrender and started to apologize, but just when her mouth opened, she closed it again as her spirits sank.

Jaxen's warning chose that exact moment to hit home.

She'd tried telling herself he was wrong about the Aribol,

but deep down, she knew better. A slow sensation of despair settled around her, blanketing her shoulders in a weight so heavy it rounded her posture. There was no hope, no grand scheme to outwit the enemy. The only thing left to do was surrender the last Voyager ship and pray that Jaxen wasn't angry enough to tell Zane about the group of L'eihrs hiding on Earth.

But after tonight, that was probably what he'd do.

Her breath hitched and her vision blurred. Through a veil of tears, she noticed Aelyx watching her. Concern softened the angle of his brow, and he asked if she was all right.

"No," she told him in a hollow voice. "I was wrong about everything. We can't stop them. We should've done what Zane told us from the very beginning. I kept pushing everyone to fight back. Now I think it's too late."

She covered her face, but she couldn't stop images from filling her head, flashes of the extinction she'd brought upon her people. Now she knew how the world would end: not with a bang or a whimper, but in puddles of flesh.


Later that night, when her throat was raw and she'd cried herself dry, Cara showered and plaited her hair in a low braid. She dressed in a L'eihr uniform she'd found in one of the bedroom drawers and steeled herself for what she had to do next.

Break the news to Alona.

"I believe he's telling the truth," she said to Alona, after relaying the details of her conversation with Jaxen. She sat on her bedroom floor beside Aelyx, resting her head on his shoulder while he held her hand. She'd requested permission for him to join the meeting so she wouldn't have to tell her story twice. Once was painful enough. "We went back and looked for Jaxen, but he was gone. I don't know if he'll keep our secret anymore. I think we should tell Zane about the Voyager ship and do what he says."

"Agreed." Alona drew a long breath. "I wish we'd spoken before you sought out Jaxen alone. You don't know the danger you were in. A few hours ago I received a response to my inquiry regarding the hybrids in captivity."

Cara had almost forgotten about that. "Are they acting strangely, too?"

"Yes, but the changes were subtle. My inquiry prompted their caretakers to perform a medical scan. They found abnormal tissue growths in the hybrids' bodies and brains. It seems the DNA used in their creation was too old to be properly repaired. The growths are quite small at this stage, but because Jaxen is older than the others, his tumors have likely grown large enough to impact his cognitive function."

No wonder his behavior was so erratic. If Cara had known, she never would have engaged him. She paused to swallow a marble of emotion. "I'm sorry. I should have listened to you and sent the L'eihrs home on the transport."

Alona dismissed the apology with a wave. "The responsibility rests with me. I will contact Zane and—" A high-pitched whine interrupted her, the same alert Zane had used during their first conference call on L'eihr. "Let me do the talking," Alona told Cara. Then her eyes shifted to Aelyx, who wasn't supposed to be on Earth. "Send your *l'ihan* out of the room."

Aelyx quickly made his way into the hall. As soon as

the door closed behind him, Alona accepted the incoming transmission.

Zane's image appeared. "Greetings, children."

"Also to you," Alona said. "In keeping with your demands, I can now account for the missing Voyager craft."

"The craft is no longer the issue," Zane told her. His digitized voice sounded heavier than usual—sad, if such a thing were possible. "Both of you have conspired to subvert our terms. At least four L'eihr citizens remain on Earth in direct violation of our command to segregate your kind."

Cara clenched a fist. Jaxen had tattled faster than she'd expected.

"Therefore a Destroyer has been dispatched to each of your worlds. The ships were already in stasis nearby, so they will arrive soon." Zane paused. "Please know this gives me no pleasure. I have enjoyed watching your societies develop over the millennia. I'd hoped you could be saved."

"I've not yet disposed of the intergalactic transport," Alona said. "I'll return it to Earth at once to retrieve my citizens."

"I'm afraid the time for that is past."

"Please," Cara begged. "Give us one more chance."

Zane's façade swiveled to look at her. "I wish I could, but the decision is not mine. Much like you, I am a representative of my race."

"But this is my fault. Most humans don't know what's happening. They would've obeyed your orders if I'd given them a choice. Tell your leaders to punish *me*. I'm the problem."

Zane tilted his face in what appeared to be a sympathetic gesture. "No, you are not the problem, young human, and the decision will not be reversed. Typically I provide no advance warning of neutralization, but in this case it gives me solace to allow you to prepare yourself for death. When the end comes, I hope you will be at peace."

"How long?" Cara asked.

"One solar day. Perhaps two."

"Is there anything we can do? Anything at all?"

Silence was his only answer.

An odd sense of calm settled over her, and Cara folded both hands in her lap. "Then I have a request. When I'm gone, don't clone me again. I know Jaxen will ask you to, but I don't want him to have any part of me, even if it's a reproduction."

"I will present your request for consideration," Zane replied. Then he told her something he'd never said before. "Goodbye."

His image vanished.

Cara and Alona remained, but for a while, neither of them spoke. They stared into the empty space between their holograms until Alona lifted her chin and broke the silence.

"Well, as the Aribol have resolved to terminate us, and nothing I say or do can worsen the outcome, I see no reason to destroy the remaining transport. I will give the evacuation order and fit as many of my people on board as I can. We'll depart before daybreak and travel until we deplete our fuel reserves."

Cara thought that was wise. Even if the Aribol caught up with the transport, dying in space was no worse than dying planet-side. "Good luck."

"I wish you were here so I could take you with me."

That made Cara tear up. After all the mistakes she'd

made, Alona still wanted her there. She wiped her eyes. "What about the Voyagers? They should know the truth. They have more than enough fuel to go back to that planet of humanoids. Maybe they can live there."

"Yes, I agree. If the planet were closer to L'eihr, I would do the same. Will you inform the commander on my behalf? I'll be busy overseeing the evacuation. Tell him he has permission to do as he pleases."

"I will." Cara knew Alona had to go, so she didn't drag out their final goodbye. "Thank you for welcoming me into your world and making me one of your own. It's been my honor to serve as your Chief Human Consultant."

"The privilege has been mine, Miss Sweeney." Alona extended two fingers toward Cara's throat in a L'eihr greeting that also served as a farewell. "May the Sacred Mother be with you until we meet again by Her side."

Cara lifted two fingers in return, and the transmission ended.

In the silence, she cradled her dormant com-sphere and thought back to the colony apartment she'd shared with Aelyx, how she'd resisted the impulse to bring her seashell collection with her as a souvenir of home. Leaving the shells behind had been an act of faith, certainty of her return to the blissful life she'd made there for herself. She'd fought so hard to protect that future, and in doing so, she'd lost it all—for everyone.

Zane was a fool if he thought she would ever make peace with that.

## Chapter Fifteen

Someone had found a bottle of brandy hidden behind the cooking oil in the pantry. Since then, that bottle had made a dozen passes around the living room, where the group sat in front of a crackling fireplace, chilled despite the summer heat. The brandy came to Aelyx again, and he took a swig. The amber liquid went down as smoothly as broken glass, but each mouthful softened the edges of his fear. He offered the bottle to Cara, who was curled up on his lap with her cheek nestled against his chest. She shook her head, so he handed it to her brother.

"There's only one logical thing to do," Troy said, and paused to take a long drink. He wiped the back of his hand across his mouth and passed the bottle to his parents. "The same thing they're doing on L'eihr. We cram as many people as we can into our shuttles, and we make a run for it."

"That reminds me." Larish raised an index finger and hiccupped. "I removed the cables from both crafts and hid them under my bed, so Jaxen can't steal either of them. If the human race dies, he should stay here and share their fate."

Bill Sweeney clapped Larish on the shoulder and offered him the brandy. "Good man. I like the way you think."

Elle and Syrine sat on the hearthrug in front of the fire. They shared a somber glance with Aelyx, and he knew they were all thinking the same thing. Shuttles were built for short-range travel, not intergalactic journeys. The passengers would die long before reaching the nearest inhabitable planet.

"It won't work," Cara said into his shirt. "The shuttle life support system will only last a few days—less than that if there are extra people on board breathing the air. We won't even make it to the closest wormhole."

"So what?" Troy argued. "That's three days more than we'll have if we stay here."

"You could cloak the shuttles and anchor them to the moon," Larish suggested. He held the brandy toward Elle and Syrine, and when they shook their heads, he finished the last of it. "And wait for the Aribol to . . . well . . . *finish* . . . before you return to Earth."

Cara threw him a disbelieving look. "Among billions of rotting corpses?"

"If you hide in an uninhabited location or a bunker, you might be able to blend in with the new inhabitants once they're seeded. If nothing else, the human race would live on."

"What does it matter?" Cara said. "Humans, L'eihrs, whatever the new arrivals will be called—all of us are Noven. It's not like we're really going extinct. Besides, I can't leave everyone behind to pay for my mistakes. It wouldn't be fair."

Aelyx hugged her close and placed a kiss atop her head.

He hated that she blamed herself for this. "It's not your fault. It was my idea to sneak away from the transport, remember?"

"Yeah, but if I hadn't provoked Jaxen, maybe he wouldn't have told on us."

"The truth would've come out eventually. It always does."

She peered up at him and reached out with her eyes. *I want to stay. It's the right thing to do.* There was so much guilt inside her it hurt.

He smoothed a hand over her hair. *Then I'll stay, too. Whatever happens, we'll face it together.*

A tear slid down her cheek, and she closed her eyes.

"Well, we can't give up." Troy glanced around the living room as if seeking support. "We can get at least fifteen people off this planet. We might make not make it far, but we have to try."

Eileen Sweeney spoke softly from within her husband's arms. "But which fifteen people, love? That's a terrible choice to make, one that'll haunt you."

"Better fifteen than zero," Troy muttered, but in a dark tone that said his mother's message had resonated with him.

Syrine raised her hand. "I'll offer my seat to someone else. I want to stay here with David." Her lips curved in a hesitant grin. "I never believed in the afterlife, but I hope I'm wrong. I know the first thing I'll say if I see him again."

That made Aelyx smile, and when he looked at Cara, he saw the same reaction on her face. Cara lifted her head from his chest. "I bet I can guess."

"Me, too," Aelyx said. Syrine had always regretted failing to tell David that she loved him. "But he already knows."

Syrine blushed. "Still, he deserves to hear the words. Everyone deserves that."

"You're right," Cara agreed. "I wish I could tell the world what's happening, so people can skip work and spend their last days with the ones they love. I hate the idea of anyone missing their chance to make up, or apologize, or confess their feelings. Now's the time to throw caution to the wind and live without regrets, not to sit in an office."

At those words, Troy and Elle shared a charged glance from across the room. While Elle stared at Troy with her lower lip caught between her teeth, Troy fidgeted with his dog tags and cleared his throat. After hesitating twice, Troy stood from the sofa and extended a hand to her. "Someone should inspect the shuttles. To, uh, you know, see how . . . roomy they are. Want to come with me?"

Elle peeked at Syrine as if seeking her approval, and when Syrine answered with a gentle nudge, Elle took Troy's outstretched hand. He pulled her up from the floor, and within seconds, they were gone. Aelyx smiled after them. By his guess, the *roomy* shuttle interior was about to be put to good use.

"It's about time," Cara said, leaning aside to watch the back door close. "He's had the hots for her for ages. He told me she was the medic on his transport to L'eihr last fall. She gave him an injection for speed sickness, and just like that, he was sprung."

Bill chuckled to himself. "Well, if the shuttle's a-rockin', don't go a-knockin'."

"Bill!" Eileen chided, delivering a light smack to his chest while trying not to laugh. She composed herself and stood up to massage her lower back. "It's late," she told the rest of them. "And we've had a shock today. Let's turn in and talk about it in the morning. A good night's sleep will clear our heads, and maybe tomorrow we'll see a solution we missed."

Everyone nodded, and before Bill and Eileen retired to the second floor bedrooms, Cara gave each of them a long hug. But instead of following them upstairs, she strode into the kitchen and began making a pot of coffee.

Aelyx joined her, leaning one hip against the counter while she sprinkled coffee grounds into a reusable filter. "What are you doing? Aren't you tired?"

Cara set the machine to brew and turned to wrap her arms around his waist. She propped her chin on his chest and peered up at him with weary eyes. "I don't want to sleep. I can sleep when I'm dead."

She'd used that expression before, but this time he didn't like her choice of words. He couldn't tell if she was joking or if she really believed her life was over. "For what it's worth, I agree with your mother. There might be a way to block the shockwave pulses with manmade shields or to evacuate people below ground. Didn't you say the Earth Council is experimenting with that right now?"

"Sure, until the power dies."

"So for at least another day, every developed nation in the world has its top scientists working on a solution," he pointed out. "Don't you think we should do the same?"

"Don't *you* think the Aribol will have a backup plan? As smart as they are, they won't be fooled by shields, and if we ferret our way underground, they'll only follow us."

Aelyx frowned. His beautiful warrior wasn't living up to her nickname. He expected her to be afraid—he certainly was—but not to surrender before the fight had begun.

"What do you want to do, then? Cry and grieve? Pretend we're already dead?"

"Not at all." Something in her gaze shifted, and she skimmed a hand down the curve of his backside while settling her fingertips at the base of his throat to measure the hitch in his pulse. "I want to live. I want to seize every last minute and fill it with so much fire there's nothing left. And when the Aribol come, I'll greet them with two middle fingers and a smile, because I will have experienced more in one day than they will in a thousand years of playing god with people like me."

Aelyx wanted to form a reply, but Cara stood on tiptoe to kiss his neck, and in doing so, she diverted all the blood flow away from his brain.

"They're only spectators," she murmured, and licked a teasing trail to his ear. "We're the stars. So let's do what stars do best and burn this place down."

He groaned when she exhaled into his ear, and gently pressed on her head to encourage her to do it again. "This doesn't mean I'm giving up."

She sucked his earlobe, causing his eyes to roll back. "You know," she whispered, guiding his hand to the pulse point at her clavicle. "You never topped my high score. I'd love to see you try."

*Challenge accepted.*

He gripped her by the thighs and lifted her up until she locked both legs around his waist. As he bent to kiss her, Syrine and Larish strolled into the kitchen and froze at the sight of them. Larish snatched a bag of pork rinds from the counter, then turned on the ball of his foot and returned to the living room while Syrine, nonplussed, simply pointed behind them.

"We smelled the coffee and thought it might help us brainstorm. If you'll move out of the way, I'll fill two mugs and let you get back to"—she quirked a brow—"copulating in the room where we prepare our meals."

Cara unlocked her ankles and lowered both feet to the floor. "You can have the kitchen. We'll take this party somewhere else." Her gaze darted between the bedrooms upstairs and the shuttles in the backyard. Neither option seemed to appeal to her.

Aelyx had an idea. "Let's walk to the bay. If the water's warm, we can swim. And if it's cold . . ." They could find creative ways to generate heat.

One corner of her mouth lifted. "I'll get the towels. You fill a thermos with coffee."

"Deal."

A few minutes later, they snuck past the guard detail and jogged into the woods. Once they cleared the property line, they slowed to a stroll and passed the thermos back and forth between them, sipping the bitter coffee and waiting for the energy rush. At first they didn't talk as they picked a path through the trees, but when Aelyx noticed Cara's hand growing cold and clammy within his, he knew her thoughts had strayed into dark territory. So he distracted her with a question that had lingered at the back of his mind for nearly a year.

"When was the first time you knew you loved me?"

She smiled, the moonlight glinting against her teeth. "I don't know. It's hard to say because it happened so gradually." She pursed her lips and thought for a moment. "Maybe the day after our first kiss. Remember how you wouldn't talk to me?"

Aelyx scoffed. "I had just learned the alliance I'd sabotaged was the key to mankind's survival. Believe me, I wish I could forget."

"Well, that's when I knew for sure," she said. "It hurt too badly to be anything less than love." She squeezed his palm, and he noticed she was no longer cold. "How about you? When did you fall victim to my charms?" She playfully bumped his shoulder. "I'll bet it was after I baked *l'arun* for you, wasn't it?"

He laughed remembering the burnt shards of flatbread she'd made in an effort to recreate his favorite breakfast from home. "That's how it began. I saw you differently after then." But the real turning point had been when she'd stood beside him during the organized shun. Her loyalty had stolen his heart. "The day I knew I loved you was when I held your hand for the first time. At that moment, there was no doubt for me."

Her smile widened, and she peered up at him with enough warmth to make him forget—for just a moment—that their world might end. "I remember that. It was in the school parking lot, in front of all those protesters. That was the first time you really touched me, and I went all gooey inside."

"Gooey?"

"It's a good thing."

He lifted their linked hands and kissed hers. "I'm glad, because I enjoyed touching you, too. Maybe too much. After that, I made the mistake of researching human mating rituals, and I drove myself out of my mind thinking about doing those things with you."

She laughed, and when the bay came into view, she spread the towels on the ground. "If it makes you feel better, you had a steady role in my daydreams, too." She set down the thermos and winked. "You still do."

"Come here." He took her hand and drew her to him, then softened his gaze to connect with her mind. He wanted to show how much he loved her, and to feel the comfort of her affection in return.

She faced away. "No Silent Speech."

"Why not?"

She tapped a finger against her temple. "Because there's a lot going on up here. I want to live in the moment with you, but if I slip up and start feeling guilty or afraid, I don't want you to feel it, too."

"But I like knowing how you feel."

"Not tonight, okay? Let's use our words." She peeled off her shirt. "Or not talk at all."

He knew she was trying to distract him—and that it would work if she removed any more of her clothing. So before she finished unfastening her jeans, he gathered her against his chest and spoke softly in her ear.

"All right, then, here are my words. I told you I would never stop fighting for us, and I meant it. No one will take you from me while I have breath in my body. I'll use every weapon I can find, even if I'm flinging pebbles from the street, because you are the very heart of me, and what we have is worth clawing and scratching to hold on to."

She sniffled and tried to push away. "I don't want to think about that."

"You need to hear me," he said, holding her close. "Whatever we do here after we take off our clothes isn't a distraction, and it isn't surrender. Not for me. This is a reminder of what I'm fighting for." He cupped her face and tipped it toward his. "And that's you. For twenty thousand more nights with you. For more arguments and making up, for burnt flatbread and chess games and holding you in the dark. I want it all with you, and no one else."

Tears welled in her eyes. "You think I don't want that?"

"Then show me. Say you'll fight for me, too."

"Even if we don't stand a chance?"

"Even if we're flinging pebbles from the street." He brushed a thumb over her freckled cheek. "Promise you won't quit."

"I love you."

"Then promise."

She drew a stuttered breath and nodded. "Okay, I won't give up."

"Thank you." He dropped a gentle kiss on her lips before turning his attention to the sensitive bend of her neck, where he knew from experience a single nibble would buckle her knees. He brushed his mouth back and forth over the spot. "And what are we doing here tonight? Living our final moments?"

"No." She tilted her head aside to give him better access, and when he bit down, her legs went slack. He held her by the waist and did it again, and then she hooked a leg around his hip, and it was his turn to go weak in the knees. She knew what she was doing. With a coy look in her eyes, she said, "We're here to prove you can't beat my high score."

He grinned and settled a palm over her chest to count its frenzied thumps. "One twenty-five, and I'm just getting started."

"Oh, yeah?" She pressed a thumb to his neck and smirked. "One thirty, and I haven't laid a hand on you yet."

"I hope you've got an iron heart," he taunted while peeling off his shirt, "because tonight I'm not holding back."

"You talk a big game, buddy. Show me what you've got."

So he did.

They never made it as far as the water, which was probably for the best, as their activities would have scandalized the fish. Aelyx was surprised the moon itself didn't blush. There was nothing he and Cara didn't do in their quest to outperform the other. He used every move in his arsenal, every secret technique Google had taught him to unravel her control, but just when he thought he'd won, she slowed her hips, and he was at her mercy.

But despite the wild heat between them, he missed the emotional connection of Silent Speech. Without it the experience seemed one-dimensional. He wanted to share everything with her, both the good and the bad, so he tilted their foreheads together and peered deeply into her eyes.

"Open to me," he whispered.

She did, and then they were linked to the very blood cells careening through their veins. As they each gave themselves up to the other, the outside realm ceased to exist. There was only one love, one rush. They were perfect and whole together.

They were everything.

Later they lay on a blanket of rumpled terrycloth and leaves, their bodies slicked with sweat and their hearts racing too fiercely to count. "Let's call it a draw," Aelyx suggested, in part from exhaustion but also because he was certain he'd lost.

"A tie," she agreed, panting. "You really brought your A-game. My heart's about to explode."

"Mine, too." He glanced at the moonlit bay. "Forget swimming. I'm so weak I could drown in six inches of water."

"What happened to all your stamina from the colony?" she teased.

"Well, you have to remember this planet is slightly larger than L'eihr. The gravitational pull is a greater strain on my body."

"Uh-huh, nice try." She patted his chest and sat up. "Come on. I've never been skinny-dipping on Earth, and neither have you." Before he could ask, she clarified, "This isn't a 'bucket list' kind of thing, so don't think I'm quitting. I just want to cool off."

He forced his rubbery limbs into motion, and together they waded into the shallow water, which was freakishly cold. For that reason the skinny-dipping session lasted only long enough to wet their flushed skin, and then they ran back to shore, where they toweled dry and put their clothes back on. After slinging the towels around their necks and collecting the thermos, they started back through the woods the way they'd come.

Cara swung their linked hands between them, her mood lighter than before, so Aelyx didn't feel the need to fill the silence with distracting small talk. They listened to the summer symphony of crickets and bullfrogs, occasionally stopping to share a kiss, until he heard a noise that made him pause.

"Listen." He cocked an ear toward the sound. From somewhere nearby, a woman's voice carried on the breeze.

She was crying. More than crying. The despair in her hoarse, choking sobs told Aelyx she might be injured.

Cara patted herself down as if looking for a weapon. "What if Jaxen's out there? I *did* steal his shuttle, and we never found him."

She made a valid point. The smart thing to do was continue to the safe house and ask the soldiers to check on the woman. But then another series of muffled sobs broke out. "We'll be careful," Aelyx said, and he led the way toward the sound.

They tiptoed over fallen branches and logs, cringing every time a twig snapped beneath their shoes, until they reached a clearing in the woods. The woman, who had gone temporarily silent, made a wet sniffle and drew their attention to where she knelt at the opposite end of the clearing, wiping her eyes with the hem of her shirt. Her gray clothes had camouflaged her into the nearby underbrush, but now that Aelyx could see her outline, he knew he'd made the right choice in coming here.

She reminded him of Cara's mother, but rail thin and lacking the matronly curves that made Eileen's hugs so comforting. The full moon highlighted streaks of silver woven throughout the woman's braid, and even from a distance, he noticed the signature slackening of her jowls that came with age. She covered her face and began crying again, and her whole body shook with the intensity of her grief. Aelyx rubbed a palm over his chest to dispel a sympathy pain. He glanced at Cara expecting to find her features softened as well, but instead she stared at the woman with her mouth frozen in a perfect oval.

"Oh, my god," Cara breathed. "It's Rune."

Aelyx whipped his gaze back to the woman, seeing her with new eyes. She looked nothing at all like Cara. "Your clone? But you said she'd aged to her midthirties."

"She had." As if entranced, Cara stepped out from their hiding place behind a cluster of trees and advanced into the clearing. "I thought she was aging a decade every two days, but she must be aging exponentially."

A twig snapped, and Rune gasped, turning toward them with a hopeful expression lifting her brow, as if she'd been waiting for someone. But when her eyes found Cara, they widened in panic, and she scrambled backward until she met the resistance of a bramble bush.

Cara flashed both palms and spoke in L'eihr. "I won't hurt you."

Unconvinced, Rune tugged her tunic free from the thorny bush and pushed to her feet. She swiped at her wet eyes and then crouched with both arms outspread, prepared for battle. She reminded Aelyx of a wounded predator. Any sympathy he'd felt for her promptly died. This woman was dangerous, regardless of her age.

He glanced around the clearing in case this was a trap. When he didn't see anyone else, he demanded, "Where's Jaxen?"

It was obvious the clone had understood him, but instead of answering, she picked up a rotten branch and broke it in half. With her stubborn chin lifted, she waved the stick back and forth in a warning to stay back.

"He left you, didn't he?" Cara asked the clone. "Just like he did to Aisly."

"No," Rune yelled in a voice raw from crying. "He'll

come back for me. I'm his perfect match—not you. Me! We were made for each other. He said so."

The tender way Cara looked at Rune reminded Aelyx of the time she'd found a stray puppy on their walk home from school during the student exchange last fall. Even though she was allergic to dogs, she'd wrapped the animal in her sweater and carried it from door to door until she'd found it a home. Then she'd broken out in itchy, red welts that'd lasted a week.

All of a sudden Aelyx knew exactly what she was thinking. "No. Absolutely not. We can't take her with us."

"I didn't say we should."

"But you're thinking it." He pointed at the clone. "Elire, you can't trust her. She's dangerous. Jaxen trained her to fight. To *kill*. Even if this isn't a trap, which it very well may be, she'll murder us the minute we let our guard down."

Cara bit the inside of her cheek and made that pouty face, the one that told him her heart had taken command of her brain. "Have some compassion."

*"Compassion?"* He indicated the bruises on her face. "She attacked you!"

Cara folded both arms and turned to study the clone. "Try to see it from her point of view. All she knows are the lies Jaxen told her. He created her to be his partner, and to make sure she loved him, he filled every single role in her life—father, teacher, lover, friend. Jaxen is her whole world, and he abandoned her in the middle of nowhere. She probably has no idea why he left, or what's happening to her body. All she knows is she's alone and afraid." Cara sighed, and her eyes misted over. "Try to imagine how she feels."

Aelyx pinched his temples and tossed aside the thermos,

because he was going to need both hands to catch the clone and relocate her to the safe house. He knew Cara wouldn't be swayed by logic, and truth be told, her speech had stirred an inkling of sorrow within his chest.

A very small inkling.

"Fine, we'll bring her with us. But only if you agree to keep her under watch."

Cara smiled, eyes glittering. It was like the puppy all over again. "She'll never leave our sight. I promise." She kissed his cheek. "Thank you. You won't regret this."

Groaning inwardly, Aelyx stalked toward the feral replicate of his *l'ihan* and prepared to take a beating with the stick in her hand. "I already do."

## Chapter Sixteen

"Be careful not to break her hip," Cara told Aelyx as he readjusted his hold on the clone, who was slung over his shoulder, kicking and thrashing like a rabid wolverine. "She's almost sixty, I think."

Aelyx slid her a glare while Rune used both fists to hammer his lower back. "My bruised kidneys say she doesn't feel a day over twenty-five."

"I love you for this by the way." Cara gave him an encouraging thumbs up and winced at the six-inch gash Rune had opened on his cheek. "Remind me to disinfect that. The rotten branch she stabbed you with was probably crawling with bacteria."

"Will do," he said tersely.

All of Rune's grunts and swears brought the safe house security team to the backyard, where Cara had to explain to a red-faced sergeant why she'd pulled a second Houdini act in one night. She omitted the R-rated details from her story, focusing instead on the clone. "She's been working with Jaxen," Cara said in English, which Rune didn't understand. "But he dumped her. If I can convince her to trust me, maybe she'll give us some intel about him."

The sergeant ducked down just in time to dodge a boot to the face. He pointed at the ground while retrieving a pair of cuffs from his utility belt. "Drop her there," he told Aelyx.

"Gently," Cara interjected.

The sergeant threw her a sharp glance. "I'll contact Colonel Rutter and see how he wants to proceed. Until then, tell her if she makes a move against any of my men, they have orders to shoot her."

Cara took one look at the fury in the upside-down blue eyes staring at her from over Aelyx's shoulder and decided she'd better stay to help. "You go ahead and disinfect your cut," she said to Aelyx after he'd set Rune on the lawn. "I'll wait here with her."

He charged away, mumbling something about a puppy.

Once Rune's wrists and ankles were shackled together, Cara sat down beside her. The restraints didn't subdue Rune's spirit. If anything, she fought harder, tugging against the metal cuffs until she fell sideways in the grass and couldn't right herself. Cara took her clone by the shoulders and heaved her into a sitting position, then yanked her hand back when Rune snapped at her with her teeth.

"Enough," Cara shouted in L'eihr. "If you don't calm down, I'm going to give you a shot of the same drug I used on Jaxen. Is that what you want?"

Panic flashed in Rune's gaze, and she curled up against the wood siding, shaking her head. Cara realized with a tug of guilt how traumatic it must've been for Rune when Jaxen had awoken and reacted to the drastic changes in her face. Knowing him, he had probably run away without a word. Telling Rune the truth would've made it too real for him, and Jaxen always took stellar care of number one.

"I'm sorry he abandoned you," Cara said, more gently. "He's a terrible person."

Rune narrowed her eyes. "He told me you'd say that."

"Because it's true. Have you ever seen him do anything kind?"

"He was kind to *me*."

"To anyone else, though? Even Aisly?"

Rune let the silence answer for her.

"Did he say why he left?" Cara asked.

More silence.

"Because I'll tell you if you want to know."

That piqued Rune's interest. She flicked her gaze down and up again, hesitating for several beats before she finally nodded.

"It has to do with how you were created," Cara said, and she explained how the cloning process worked. She used Aelyx as an example, describing his gestation in the artificial wombs and his upbringing in the Aegis, a sort of boarding school on L'eihr. Then she defined the meaning of a year and did her best to clarify the natural progression of time. "But Jaxen didn't want to wait eighteen years for you to grow, so he used something to make you develop faster. But it worked too well, and now the aging won't stop."

A look of horrified comprehension crossed Rune's face, and she glanced at her wrinkled hands.

"You didn't do anything wrong," Cara quickly added.

"Jaxen ran away because he knows he made a mistake and he doesn't want to face it. Plus his thinking is impaired by—"

"He'll come back for me," Rune interrupted, but her gaze faltered when she spoke. She tucked her hands into her lap, out of sight. "I won't tell you anything about him, so leave me alone."

Cara's first instinct was to press the argument, but then she remembered how she'd felt after her worst breakups—the embarrassment and the hurt, and, more than anything, the need to keep it private. The only friends she'd wanted around were Ben & Jerry. "All right," she said. "I'll come back and check on you later."

Inside the house, news of Rune's arrival had caused quite a stir. Aside from Mom and Dad, who were asleep upstairs, the group huddled around Aelyx and listened to him recount the same story Cara had told the soldiers.

Elle dabbed at Aelyx's injured cheek with a cotton ball soaked in antiseptic. As Cara entered the living room, Elle noticed her and said, "You did the right thing. That poor girl."

Troy snorted and gave Cara a look that made his feelings clear. Then Elle caught him, and he quickly transformed his sneer into a grin. "Yeah, that poor, poor girl. You're a saint, Pepper."

Elle wasn't fooled by Troy's innocent act. She chided him with a glare, but she followed it with a wink that made his whole face turn scarlet, which was so adorable Cara couldn't bring herself to be angry with him.

"Whether you agree with me or not," Cara told him, "Rune is here now, and we're going to treat her with compassion."

"While keeping her in shackles," Aelyx said out of the

corner of his mouth as his sister affixed a Band-Aid to his cheek.

"Right now she's a hundred percent Team Jaxen, but if I can change that, maybe she'll tell us what he was up to in all those fertilizer plants and why the Aribol want to separate us. I think that's the key to saving ourselves."

Larish yawned and peered into his empty coffee mug. "I'd also be interested to learn where he keeps his Nova Staff, because it's not in the shuttle you stole from him."

During the chaos, Cara had forgotten about the staff. "He still has his hovercraft, too."

"But it won't fly him off this planet," Syrine pointed out. "If he wants to escape the Aribol fleet, he'll have to come for one of the shuttles."

Since Cara had taken Jaxen's shuttle before he'd tattled on her to Zane, she doubted that was the case. "He probably arranged a pick-up point for when the Aribol arrive." The bigger question was whether he'd done it before or after abandoning Rune. "I have to find out what the clone knows."

"Before she ages into dust," Aelyx added.

"Right. I should probably make another pot of coffee."


Two lattes later, Cara sat at the kitchen table brainstorming ways to befriend her clone while Aelyx and the others snored from the living room. She'd already visited Rune twice, once to ensure she didn't need a sedative, and again to relocate her to a cot in the basement after Colonel Rutter had given the all-clear to hold her prisoner inside the house. Both times, Rune had fixed her gaze on the floor and refused to say a word, even when Cara had offered to bring her something to eat. Rune had simply curled up on the cot and faced the wall.

She was heartbroken. Cara saw it written all over the face they shared.

And because they were identical right down to the taste buds, Cara also knew the only thing that had the power to distract Rune from her grief—the culinary wonder of pizza. Luckily, there was one in the freezer, along with a pint of cookies 'n' cream. So she preheated the oven and prepared a dinner filled with the breakup food of champions.

She didn't say anything when she carried the tray into the basement. She set the meal at the foot of Rune's cot and stepped back to let the rich, spicy aroma of pepperoni do the talking.

It worked.

Rune peeked over her shoulder at the food. Her stomach growled. Though she turned away and rested her head on the pillow, her resistance only lasted another minute or two. Then she pushed into a sitting position and inspected the tray while Cara sat down on a stool and surveyed the dingy basement. Empty concrete floors stretched into the darkness, illuminated by a single hanging bulb. The only finished portion of the area was a half bathroom located within walking distance of Rune's ankle tether.

"What's this?" Rune poked the mozzarella with an index finger.

Cara flapped a hand. "Just pizza." She faked a yawn, pretending she couldn't care less whether Rune ate it or not. "It's common dinner food. The dessert in the bowl is called ice cream, and the brown liquid is Coke." She shrugged. "In case you're thirsty, or whatever."

Cara stared into the corner and used her periphery to watch Rune lift the pizza slice from the plate and hold it to her lips. She hesitated twice before nibbling the very tip, testing it, and then her eyes flew wide and she sank her teeth in for a massive bite.

*Success.*

It turned out that Rune's love of pizza was rivaled only by her passion for Coke, which she slurped with a childish gusto that contrasted oddly with her motherly features. By the time she drained the glass and finished the last bite of crust, her chin was smeared with marinara sauce and soda. Then she tried the ice cream and *really* lost her mind.

"Ouch," Rune said after she'd devoured the entire bowl. She gripped her forehead and sucked a breath through her teeth.

Cara grinned. She knew that pain. "Brain freeze. You ate it too fast."

Groaning, Rune rubbed her belly and lay back against the pillow.

"I'm surprised you never tried it before. What have you been eating all this time?"

"Basic foods," Rune told her. "Lean proteins, whole grains, vegetables. Jaxen taught me we should eat for nourishment, never for pleasure."

"See? A terrible person."

Rune's lips twitched in a smile. She shut it down at once, but instead of facing the wall she shifted onto her back and stared at the ceiling.

"Can I ask you something?"

Rune answered with a grunt.

"Jaxen told me he used his mental abilities to transfer

concepts to your mind, and that's how you learned to walk and talk and fight so quickly. Does that mean you can use Silent Speech, too?"

Rune cast her a sideways glance. "What's Silent Speech?"

"It's a L'eihr way of communicating without talking. You lock eyes with someone and relax your mind. A connection forms, and then you can share thoughts and feelings. Some human brains are capable of it, too."

"Like yours?"

Cara nodded. "It took a long time for me to learn."

"No. I didn't communicate with Jaxen that way."

"The reason I ask," Cara said tentatively, "is because it's impossible to lie when you share your consciousness. You can block your thoughts, but you can't project something that isn't true."

"So what?"

"So I could use Silent Speech to prove I'm telling the truth about Jaxen."

Rune didn't respond, but the prospect of facing the truth must've scared her, because she turned toward the wall. Just like that, the lighthearted banter was over.

"Jaxen was created in a lab, too," Cara went on, "with ancient DNA that's causing him to go mad. He's a hybrid—part L'eihr, part Aribol. He can manipulate minds, but there's a girl here who's an emotional healer. She can remove his influence and allow you to think clearly."

"He didn't manipulate my mind. I love him."

"I know you do, and I know how strong that feeling is. That's why I'm asking you to be even stronger. Maybe he didn't tell you, but the Aribol are coming. We don't have much time."

"I know that and I still won't help you."

"But billions of people will die. *Your* people."

"They're not my people, and I'll die soon anyway."

"That's true," Cara admitted, "but only because Jaxen altered your development."

Rune snatched the pillow and pulled it over her head. "Go away! My stomach hurts. He was right about your food, and he was right about you. I won't tell you anything, so leave me alone."

Cara slouched on the stool. She should've remembered who she was dealing with—a stubborn, passionate girl with the legendary temper of the Sweeneys and the loyal heart of the O'Sheas. But unlike Midtown High's two-time state debate champion, Cara 2.0 was dying, confused, shackled to a cot, and in love with the enemy.

Cara collected the dinner tray and gave her clone some privacy. As she climbed the stairs toward the kitchen, she thought she heard the light sniffle of crying behind her. Moisture welled in her eyes, but she blinked it away and clenched her jaw.

There wasn't time for tears.

The next thing Cara knew, it was full daylight. She gasped and sat up at the kitchen table, where she must've fallen asleep making a list of things to do before the power grid went out. That list was now stuck to her cheek. She ripped it free while glancing at the stove's digital clock, and what she saw made her stomach hit the floor.

She'd slept until noon!

She stood so quickly black spots danced in her vision,

and she gripped the table ledge for balance. Someone had tucked a blanket around her shoulders, which she let fall to the floor as she stumbled into the living room to find her parents tidying the scattered mugs and discarded food wrappers from the night before.

The three of them were alone, the house silent. Mom bent over the sofa to fluff the seat cushions, and in true form, Dad moved in behind her, admiring her caboose while a devious grin broke out on his face. Cara rolled her eyes. Nothing short of Armageddon could stop those two. She cleared her throat before the cleaning session turned raunchy.

Both her parents' gazes snapped up. Mom flashed an ordinary smile, as if a legion of ships weren't on their way to annihilate the human race. "Good afternoon, Sleeping Beauty." She pursed her lips and chided, "Someone didn't go to bed when I told her to."

Cara laughed dryly. After the countless all-nighters she'd pulled in high school, Mom chose *now* to put her foot down? "Where is everyone? What's going on?"

"You didn't miss anything." Dad lifted an empty mug toward the backyard. "They're taking inventory of the shuttle supplies."

Cara spun toward the back door and stopped, then swiveled toward the basement door and stopped again. There was so little time. What should she do first: visit the clone, check in with Aelyx, contact the Earth Council, or brush her teeth?

Hygiene won. While she ran up the stairs two at a time, her stomach rumbled and she added *eat brunch* to the list. On her way back through the living room, she snagged an apple from the fruit bowl and jogged to the shuttles in the backyard.

Shielding her eyes from the high sun, she bit a chunk out of the apple and cringed as its sweetness clashed with the leftover toothpaste in her mouth. She noticed her brother and Elle kneeling on the lawn, where dozens of gadgets were arranged in tidy rows. They held a clipboard between them and inspected each item to catalog it. Syrine sat cross-legged nearby, taking stock of David's things, and Aelyx and Larish were scouring the rear hatches, probably searching for hidden compartments.

When Cara reached them, Aelyx poked his head out of the hatch and greeted her with a genuine smile that crinkled the skin around his eyes. At once, the tension unwound from her jaw, and all was right in her world.

"Before you yell at me for not waking you up," he said, and paused to kiss her cheek, "let me mention how breathtaking you are when you're asleep."

Cara laughed, remembering the drool that'd glued a sheet of paper to her face. "Stunning, I'm sure."

"Any progress with the clone?"

"Well, I progressed in making her hate me more. Does that count?"

He didn't say *I told you so,* which was one of the reasons she loved him. "Want to help us identify some foreign objects from Aisly's shuttle?"

"Sure, I'll give it a shot."

But when she knelt on the lawn and studied the gadgets, she couldn't make heads or tails of them. There were six items, presumably of Aribol origin, all cast from the same strange material that felt like plastic, but with the patina of aged metal. They ranged in shape from spheres to cubes and even one thin baton the size of a riding crop. Each was lightweight and cool to the touch with no visible buttons or hinges.

Cara tapped the rod against her palm and then gave it a gentle shake. Nothing rattled inside. "Add this to the list of things the clone could explain . . . if she didn't want all of us to die in a fire."

"Have you seen her today?" Elle asked.

"Not since the sun came up. I didn't want to start my day with failure." Cara tossed the baton into the grass. "So much for that."

Syrine placed the lid on her box, having repacked her mementos. "Want me to come with you?"

"No. She'll think we're ganging up on her." Cara recalled the items she needed to accomplish before the power grid failed. "Will you call the Earth Council for an update? I'm going back inside to have another crack at her shell."

Ten minutes later, she descended the basement steps with a bowl of steel-cut oatmeal in one hand and a bottled water in the other. Her stomach dipped when she spotted Rune's empty cot, but then a toilet flushed, and she noticed the thin chain leading from the cot to the bathroom door. Cara placed her offerings on the floor as Rune shuffled out from the bathroom, dragging her chain behind her.

Their gazes met, and Cara stopped breathing.

Rune had aged again, but that wasn't what paralyzed Cara's lungs. It was *how* she'd aged. The hard press of her mouth had softened, and her upper eyelids rested sleepily atop vivid, blue irises, giving her a peaceful expression that Cara recognized from her most treasured childhood memories.

Emotion thickened her airway, and she could almost smell the perfume of gingersnaps and arthritis ointment.

"What?" Rune demanded.

Cara cleared her throat. "You remind me of someone I used to know."

But it was more than that. While the logical side of her brain understood Rune was an individual, unique, with a spirit all her own, they shared the same DNA, and that connected them in a way that transcended science. Warmth swelled inside Cara's ribs, and in that moment, she knew what she had to do.

"I'll be right back. There's something I want you to see."

She ran upstairs and returned with Mom and Dad. Both of them had confessed to sneaking a peek at the clone, but neither had spoken to her, or more important, given her an opportunity to know them. Rune tensed when she noticed them approaching, so Cara encouraged her parents to hang back while she sat beside Rune on the cot.

"This is what I wanted to show you." Holding Mom's phone between them, Cara swiped through the photo album and tapped a picture of her grandmother in front of a Christmas tree, toasting the camera with a cup of eggnog. The image was grainy, but the gleam in Gram's eyes shone loud and clear. "You have her eyes."

Rune leaned in only far enough to glimpse the screen. "Who is she?"

"Your grandmother on the O'Shea side. But there's a lot of Sweeney in you, too." She scrolled through the album and enlarged a picture of her dad's mother when she was a twenty-year-old fiery redhead with a siren's smile. "I don't remember her. She died when I was a baby. But I can tell she had a fierce spirit."

"She was a force of nature, all right," Dad said.

"Just like both of you." Mom pointed at him and Cara.

As Cara translated, Rune scooted an inch closer. Her gaze moved over the screen for a long while, until she caught herself and her walls went up again. "Why are you showing me this? It doesn't matter."

"It does matter." Cara selected another photo, a three-generational shot of herself as a little girl, wrapped in the arms of her mother and her grandma. "I don't care how you were created or what Jaxen put inside your head. We have the same DNA. That might sound clinical, but it's not when you put a face with the genetics." She pointed at Dad. "Your temper comes from him, and he inherited it from his mom."

"My granny was a fireball, too," Dad said.

"And the loyalty you feel for Jaxen, even though he abandoned you," Cara went on, "that comes from our mother's side of the family. The O'Sheas have always loved blindly. One of them left her country behind and moved halfway across the world to be with the man who stole her heart. That's how we ended up here instead of Ireland."

Rune chewed the inside of her cheek and stared into her bowl of oats.

"That thing you're doing right now," Cara said, pointing at Rune's cheek. "I've done that ever since I can remember. By the way, you have two baby molars on the left side of your mouth with no adult teeth under them. You inherited that from Mom, too."

When Rune flicked a confused glance at Mom and Dad, Cara reached into her pocket and pulled out the key she'd liberated from the guard station. She knelt on the floor and unlocked the shackle around Rune's ankle. "You're not an animal on a leash, or a nut that needs to be cracked. You're one of us, and it's time to start acting like it."

Cara stood and extended her hand. "Want to meet our brother? Sometimes his brain gives him the silent treatment, but he's got a good heart."

Rune tipped her head at Cara as if trying to decipher a line of hieroglyphics. In the end, she didn't take the hand offered to her, but she stood up from the cot and let Mom and Dad lead her to the stairs. Together their bizarre, dysfunctional family moved out of the dark basement and into the light.

## Chapter Seventeen

Through the living room window, Aelyx watched the last point of sunlight wink above the horizon and descend into darkness. He closed his eyes and held on to the image for a while, replaying the spectacular blood-orange brushstrokes that had painted the sky moments earlier. Ordinarily, he didn't notice the transition from day into night, but this sunset was special.

It might be his last.

The others felt it, too. He could tell from the holes in their conversations. No one had vocalized their fading hope, not once during the entire day, but it had shadowed each of their failed experiments and punctured theories. The truth was they'd run out of ideas. Aelyx would fight to the end—that hadn't changed—but at this rate, his metaphor of flinging pebbles from the street was bound to turn prophetic.

Eileen called out from the kitchen and drew him from

his thoughts. "Anyone who expects to eat this dinner had better come help put it on the table."

The scent of braised meat and buttered potatoes lifted Aelyx's spirit as he filed behind the group into the kitchen. She'd made his favorite—pot roast.

Flanked by an assortment of covered dishes on the counter, Eileen pointed at Cara, Syrine, and Elle and delegated, "You girls fix a plate for the soldiers outside." She handed Larish a pitcher of iced tea. "You can fill the glasses while Bill sets the table." Wiping her hands on her apron, she peered around the kitchen until her gaze landed on a cutting board by the sink. "Aelyx, hon, why don't you finish dicing the tomatoes for the salad?"

Everyone set to work, except for the clone, who sat on a chair she'd dragged to the corner of the kitchen, as far from human contact as possible. She hadn't spoken a word since her liberation from the basement, but her body language said enough. She folded both arms in a shield across her chest while casting a mistrustful glare over the group.

Let her stay there. Aelyx didn't want her help.

He moved to the cutting board, which was piled high with neatly-chopped tomatoes, and picked up the remaining fruit to dice it. He couldn't find the paring knife Eileen had used, so he pulled a new one from the drawer and finished the task.

When the group gathered at the table, Eileen insisted they join hands and observe the human custom of blessing the meal. Aelyx waited patiently to hear *amen*, and then he speared a chunk of beef and eagerly lifted it to his mouth. An automatic smile formed as he chewed. The roast tasted like *l'ina*, a staple from home.

"What'd the Earth Council have to say?" Bill asked Cara while extending a plate toward the clone. Rune refused to budge, so he set the plate at her feet and returned his attention to his daughter.

Cara used her fork to push a potato across her plate, focusing on the Aribol gadgets Larish had brought to the table. "Not much. The government bigwigs are underground. I guess it's every man for himself now."

What she failed to mention was that every nation in possession of nuclear missiles had agreed to launch a simultaneous attack on the Destroyer, ensuring that any pockets of humanity fortunate enough to survive the shockwave pulses and the ground invasion would later die from radiation poisoning. The Council claimed it would be illogical not to use every available defense, but the decision reminded Aelyx of a child intentionally breaking his favorite toy so no one else could have it.

Cara lifted one of the Aribol cubes and tilted it to and fro. "If this is anything like the probes that landed on L'eihr, maybe it responds to language." She brought it to her lips and spoke a series of commands. "Power. On. Go. Open. Obey."

The cube remained quiet, but a husky giggle broke out from the corner. Rune balanced her plate on one hand, struggling not to laugh, while using the other to point at Cara. "You're wasting your time. All of those are accessories to the Nova Staff. They're useless without it."

"Of course. God forbid we catch a break for once." Cara tossed the cube onto the table, and Rune flinched so hard she spilled food on her lap. Cara noticed the clone's reaction and pointed at the square. "This one's a weapon, isn't it? I scared you when I dropped it."

Instead of replying, Rune shoved a carrot in her mouth.

Troy reached across Elle and picked up a sphere. "I wonder what this one—"

The lights abruptly died, enveloping the room in total blackness. Everyone held their breath. No one moved. In an instant, the air thickened with the most absolute silence Aelyx had ever heard. No motors droned, no watches ticked, no fans whirred, no vehicles hummed.

If death had a sound, this would be it.

There was a rustle of fabric nearby, followed by a scraping noise, and a flame appeared in Bill Sweeney's hand. "Already planned for this." With a smile that didn't reach his eyes, he extended the lighter to a pair of candlesticks in the center of the table. "Now we can dine in style."

"Maybe it's a normal outage. A downed power line." Cara dug her cell phone from her pocket and swiped the screen. It failed to wake. "Could be the battery. Try yours," she told her brother.

Troy and Bill each pressed the buttons on their phones while Eileen stood quietly from the table and checked the landline for a connection. All three of them shook their heads to communicate what nobody wanted to say. This wasn't a normal power outage.

Fear quickened Aelyx's heart. He shared a sideways glance with Cara.

*It will start with a global blackout,* Jaxen had told her. *Anything powered by generators or batteries will cease to operate. Humans will be trapped in their communities with nothing to do but wait for the fleet to arrive.*

Cara swallowed audibly. She had to be thinking about it, too. Aelyx shifted his gaze to the kitchen window. Part of him wanted to check for a massive ship blocking the moon, but his legs seemed glued to his seat.

"So what now?" Troy asked.

They all knew the answer. Now they waited.

Eileen raised her glass to propose a toast, but her hand shook, and she set down the tea. "Now we finish eating. I worked too hard on this meal to let it go to waste. Bill, pass the butter, please."

Aelyx couldn't eat. His stomach had turned to ice, and he wasn't the only one. Knives and forks scraped against porcelain, but nobody raised a bite of food to their lips. At least nobody at the table. From the corner, Rune nibbled on a dinner roll while watching the rest of them with the rapt attention of a moviegoer. When her gaze settled on him, he shot her a burning look, which she reciprocated before glancing away to study another waxen face.

They should've left her in the basement.

Each minute that passed felt like an hour. Eileen tried to enliven the table with news of a recent sporting event—a team called the Yankees had lost a game, which typically brought Bill and Troy great joy—but their answering smiles were wooden, and the conversation died as soon as it began. It went on like this, awkward silence punctuated by clinking ice cubes and occasional coughs, until Cara jumped in her seat as if stung by a wasp.

Nine sets of gazes jerked in her direction. The whites of her eyes grew, and she frantically patted down her pockets. "My com-sphere works. Someone's calling me."

A thread of hope lifted Aelyx's heart. If the blackout hadn't affected their com-spheres, maybe the rest of their L'eihr technology was operational, too. Maybe even the shuttles.

"The outage targeted electricity, batteries, and generators." Larish's face brightened. "But L'eihr technology is powered by—"

"XE-2," Aelyx finished with a grin. The element was so powerful a single grain of it energized a com-sphere for years. "The same element that fuels our transports."

Elle gripped Troy's forearm, leaning forward. "What about the shuttle engines? Are there battery components inside?"

"I'm not sure." Larish stood up so quickly he knocked back his chair. "I'll reinstall the cables and find out."

He bolted from the room at the same time Jake Winters appeared on the table in miniature holograph form, standing between the salt and pepper shakers. "We made it," he told Cara. "We're on the Aribols' home world."

While Cara blinked in shock, Aelyx searched the hologram background for a glimpse of enemy territory. There wasn't much to see. The ground beneath Jake's boots and all around him seemed scorched.

"I thought you were going back to the planet of humanoids," Cara said.

"We almost did. I told the commander we had permission to do whatever we wanted, so he called a ship-wide meeting and presented our options. He said he would listen to our concerns and weigh them before making his decision." A distant voice called to Jake, and he waved the person over. "Most of the crew wanted to turn back, but I argued for finishing the mission. I said if there was the smallest hope of saving our people, we owed it to them to try." A young

242

L'eihr female moved into the image and clasped Jake's hand, causing his cheeks to redden. "Ayah agreed with me, and then others followed. I can be persuasive sometimes."

"So I've heard," Cara said with a grin. "What've you learned?"

"The oxygen saturation here is comparable to Earth's, but it's crazy humid. It's like breathing soup. And it's hot here, ninety-six degrees where I'm standing. The planet's sandwiched between two suns."

"What are the Aribol like?"

"That's the thing." Jake mopped his forehead with one sleeve. "We can't find any. The whole place is deserted."

Ayah spoke to Cara in L'eihr. "There was a society here, but most of it has been destroyed. I can't tell if it was caused by weaponry or a natural disaster, but it must've happened a long time ago, because there are no bodies. We can't find a single trace of bones or other organic remains."

"Wait a minute." Cara lifted a hand. "Jaxen told me the Aribol use nanites to dispose of their dead. He said he'd seen them in use on their home world. Whatever this big disaster was, it could've been recent."

Aelyx followed her logic trail. "Recent enough to coincide with alliance negotiations between Earth and L'eihr?"

"I'll bet that's it," Cara said. "That's why they insisted on separating us. Their numbers are low, and they're afraid the combined power of two Noven races might threaten their hold on the universe. If we team up against them, they won't be able to play god anymore."

Just then Aelyx remembered something Alona had said weeks ago; that the Voyagers had already discovered the

Aribols' home galaxy but hadn't begun exploring it yet. "Our Voyagers came too close for comfort. . . ."

"So the Aribol decided to clip our wings," Cara finished. "That's why they wanted the surrender of our interstellar travel technology."

"He should be careful." Troy pointed his faux-wood knife handle at Jake. "No matter how many crew members the Aribol need to fly a Destroyer—"

"Two Destroyers," Cara interjected. "There's one headed to L'eihr, too."

"—they wouldn't leave their home base undefended."

"Something else to consider," Syrine said. "The Aribol have powerful minds. Some say they can project what they want you to see. There's a chance none of what you're experiencing is real."

Aelyx hadn't considered that. He hoped she was wrong.

"We have mechanical probes scouring the planet," Jake told them. "If anything's alive out there, we'll find it."

"Keep me posted," Cara said. "And see if you can find a link to phosphorus. Jaxen's been destroying fertilizer plants, but he wouldn't say why. There has to be a reason."

"I'm on it."

The transmission ended, and Larish ran in through the back door, waving the cables in his hand. "They work! Both shuttles work!" He held the cords forward. "I removed these for now. We don't want anyone stealing the last two operational vehicles on the planet."

Fresh resolve burned behind Aelyx's ribs. "According to Jaxen, no weapon on Earth can penetrate the hull of an Aribol Destroyer." He lifted one of the Nova Staff accessories to the flickering candlelight. "No weapon on *Earth*."

Troy smacked a palm on the table. "We need Jaxen's staff."

"Before the Aribol retrieve him," Cara muttered. She spun in her seat toward Rune, who'd been watching the exchange with the corners of her mouth sinking into her jowls. "I know you love Jaxen, and I won't ask you to betray him. All we want is his staff. If I promise we won't kill him—" Aelyx and Troy objected, and Cara shushed them with a backward wave. "If I give you my word that we'll let him live, will you tell us where he is?"

Rune bit into a potato and chewed thoughtfully for a long minute, her jaw working while her gaze simmered with calculation. Aelyx could practically see a plan forming in her mind. Whatever location she might give them, he knew better than to trust it.

Finally she swallowed and made a counteroffer. "I'll tell you exactly where to find him." She lifted a bony finger. "If you'll take me with you."

"*This* is his retrieval point?" Cara asked when the shuttle arrived at the coordinates Rune had provided from the rear seat. "The top of the Empire State Building? I didn't realize Jaxen had such a flare for the dramatic."

"Really?" Aelyx thumbed at the clone. "It's always been clear to me."

"Point taken."

He maneuvered the craft south of the building's high-rise observation deck in hopes that the blustery wind from the north would drown out the sound of the engine. For a city so teeming with life, the blackout had rendered Manhattan eerily quiet and dark. There was just enough moonlight for him to make out Jaxen's silhouette on the walkway below, and more important, the staff glowing in his hand. But there seemed to be no good place to land the shuttle. The observation deck formed a square path around an interior room, and surrounding that path were waist-high concrete walls topped with crisscrossing metal bars. The design was perfect for protecting viewers from falling, but it presented a challenge to anyone wishing to access the walkway from above. He would have to dock the shuttle in midair and jump down.

Syrine spoke from where she sat in between Rune and the door, in case the clone tried to make a premature exit. "It makes sense. This is an easy landmark for an Aribol pilot to identify, and without power, human authorities would have to scale more than a hundred flights of stairs to reach Jaxen. He chose a strategic spot."

"Uh-huh," Troy said. "Or the clone's leading us into a trap."

Aelyx quirked a brow. That was twice he and Troy had agreed on something. "We can't take him by surprise. Right now he's at the north-facing wall. If I dock the shuttle here"—he pointed out the windshield—"above the south-facing wall, he won't see us but he'll hear the engine."

"Not to mention our feet hitting the floor when we drop," Cara added. "He could be on us in seconds."

"And he has the Nova Staff, so pistols won't work against him."

"Whose brilliant idea was this?" Troy quipped.

"Yours, I think," Elle told him.

"None of that matters." Aelyx craned his neck to peer up at the night sky for a sign of the Destroyer. For now, he didn't see anything other than a blanket of stars. "Our only chance is to attack the Destroyer while its ships are still inside. Once they release the fleet, all we can do is run."

"Then let's get on with it," Troy said. "The fact that Jaxen's waiting for his ride means they'll be here soon." He thumbed at the clone. "What about her? She might sabotage the shuttle if we leave her alone."

"She'll have to come with us."

Aelyx waited for Larish, Troy, Elle, and Syrine to unfasten their safety harnesses. The clone was ready, having never fastened hers to begin with. When he and Cara had unbuckled their straps, he moved into position directly above the outer wall's metal safety bars and docked the craft.

He opened his door and jumped ten feet down to the brick walkway, where his boots connected with a loud stomp. Troy landed beside him from the rear starboard exit, followed by Cara and Syrine on the port side. Larish and Elle stayed on board to assist the clone, each holding one of her arms until she dangled within Aelyx's reach. Once he gripped her waist, they let go of her arms and jumped out the opposite door.

Aelyx noticed how fragile Rune had become. She felt skeletal in his grasp, aged to at least eighty. But as soon as her feet touched the floor, she smacked his hands and glared at him with more loathing than ever, eliminating any empathy he felt for her.

"Let's split up," he told the group, and pointed left and right. The path formed a closed square, so if they hurried they could trap Jaxen in the middle. "First person to reach him, tackle him and grab the staff."

Troy, Elle, and Syrine ran left while Aelyx led the way to

the right. He turned the first corner and saw nothing but a row of coin-operated telescopes, so he kept going without waiting for Cara and Larish. Around the next corner he found Jaxen, braced and prepared for an attack from either direction. The instant Jaxen noticed him, he used his staff to fling a bolt of energy that connected with Aelyx's chest and knocked him backward into the concrete wall. His lungs emptied and pain exploded along his spine.

Troy approached from the opposite corner, followed closely by Elle and Syrine. Jaxen was ready for them, too. In a flash, all three of them lay in a tangle of limbs. Aelyx pushed up and tried again, but he only made it a few lumbering steps before he was flat on his back, staring at the night sky. The clatter of footsteps and the thud of falling bodies told him Troy and the girls had made another failed attempt. When Cara and Larish caught up, Aelyx lifted a palm to halt them. If they stayed out of sight, they might be able to catch Jaxen off guard.

From the other end of the walkway, Troy stood up to make another charge, and Aelyx did the same. They ran at Jaxen simultaneously, but with nothing more than a flick of his staff, he sent them both flying back the way they'd come. This time Aelyx landed on his side. He heard a pop, and the nerves inside his shoulder screamed. He gritted his teeth and gripped his shoulder, using his eyes to tell Cara and Larish to stay put. But Rune crept up behind them and called in her crone's voice, "Two more are hiding back here."

She turned the corner and Jaxen caught a glimpse of his once-stunning *l'ihan*, now hunchbacked and frail, her dull, gray hair whipping in the wind. His eyes bulged, and

248

he swayed visibly on his feet as if the sight of her had wounded him.

"You said you would come back for me," she called over the whistling wind. "I waited for you all night. Why did you leave me?"

Jaxen nervously licked his lips before recovering with a charlatan's smile. He extended one hand to her while every other muscle in his body tensed to run. "I was detained, my love. But I never truly left. I was only waiting for my shuttle to arrive, and then I was going to return for you."

His lie wouldn't fool a child, but Rune quickened her steps and stretched out her arms to him. "Do you promise?"

"Of course, my darling." He closed the distance between them and hesitated for the briefest of moments before wrapping her in an embrace. With her face buried in Jaxen's chest, the clone couldn't see the revulsion contorting his features. "You're my perfect partner, my only love."

"Forever?"

"Until death." Jaxen glared over the clone's silvery head and shouted, "You can come out, *Cah*-ra, I'm not going to kill you."

Cara signaled for Larish to stay hidden, then strode around the corner. "I'm glad I could reunite you with your *perfect partner*. I know how much you missed her."

"You know nothing," Jaxen spat. "But let me enlighten you. The reason I'm not going to kill you is because that's more mercy than you deserve. When death comes, you'll spend your final moments watching everyone you love melt into puddles at your feet. That will be—" He cut off with a grunt of pain and made a choking noise. The staff slipped from his fingers, and he turned his gaze to Rune, who withdrew a bloody blade from his midsection.

The moonlight glinted against a paring knife that Aelyx recognized by its faux-wood handle. She must have stolen it from the cutting board. She plunged in the knife again, this time twisting the blade with the unmistakable fury of a woman scorned.

"Liar!" she hissed. "I won't let you replace me."

She jerked the blade upward while Jaxen's gaze dulled. Blood rose to his lips, and with one final sputter, he doubled over and collapsed to the floor. He dragged the clone down with him, pinning her beneath his torso.

As Cara rushed to pull Rune free and Larish ran to retrieve the staff, Aelyx crawled to Jaxen's fallen body to see for himself the man was dead. Even after checking four lifeless pulse points he still couldn't believe it. "Did that actually happen?"

Cara threw the bloody knife out of reach and knelt down in between Jaxen and the clone. "He wanted a passionate *l'ihan*. Looks like he got one."

Troy limped over, supported on either side by Elle and Syrine. "Note to self," he said, jutting his chin at the clone lying on the floor. "Don't piss off Cara Sweeney."

Aelyx shook his head at Troy's inability to differentiate between his sister and her replicate. If ever there were a perfect demonstration of their individualities, this was it. Cara cradled Rune's head and tried to guide her into a sitting position, but Rune shoved her away.

"Leave me alone. I didn't do this for you."

"I know, but let me help—"

"I don't want your help." Rune drew a loud, rattling

breath that indicated her brief life was coming to an end. Her gaze found the Nova Staff, and she lifted a finger toward it. "The cube accessories are detonators, and the orbs drain and redirect power. The baton stores surplus energy. They all fit..." She trailed off, wheezing.

"Come with us," Cara said. "There might be a way to save you."

Rune curled on her side and nestled her cheek in the crook of her murdered *l'ihan*'s shoulder. "I was born into his arms, and that's how I want to die. Leave me with him and go."

Aelyx used his uninjured hand to cup Cara's elbow. "Give her what she wants, Elire. We don't have much time."

Cara's eyes watered. With clear reluctance, she stood up and helped Aelyx do the same. "I wish things could've been different," she told Rune. "I'll never forget you."

The clone didn't reply. She turned her eyes to Jaxen and slid an arm across his chest. One final breath passed between her lips, and then her face softened in peace.

That was how they left her.

## Chapter Eighteen

Cara blinked rapidly to clear the tears from her vision so she could focus on the pilot controls. After everything the clone had done for her, she had no intention of dying in a random wreck on the way back to the safe house to pick up the extra shuttle.

Directly behind her, Elle prepared to fix Aelyx's dislocated shoulder. She told him to relax. There was a brief cry of pain, followed by a loud pop. When Cara glanced at the backseat, she found Aelyx rotating his shoulder with his head tipped back in relief.

"All right, who's next?" Elle said, and opened the med-kit on her lap.

By the time they landed on the lawn beside the spare shuttle, Elle had treated three cracked ribs, two sprained ankles, a mild concussion, and a year's worth of bruises. Larish, who had sustained no injuries, sat in the front passenger seat inspecting the Nova Staff.

"I see where the accessories fit." He pointed at four prongs attached to the staff head, which currently held an orb identical to the others they'd found. "But I'll have to experiment before I understand how to use them."

Cara peered out the window, scanning the night sky while unfastening her harness straps. At first she noticed nothing out of the ordinary, but then a shadow passed over the moon, and her fingers fumbled on the clasp. Heart racing, she tore off her straps and threw open the door, instantly raising her face to the heavens.

Her whole body turned cold.

In the distance, far beyond the planet's gravitational pull, crept a ship so colossal she couldn't view the whole thing in one glimpse. It was the largest manmade object she'd ever seen. Dark and sleek, the craft resembled a point-ended diamond, like two spearheads connected at the base. Its belly was rounded and slightly darker than the rest of the hull. She wondered if that was the hangar, where the fleet waited to be released.

As she stared up, she remembered what Aelyx had said about destroying the fleet before they launched. He was right. If those ships left the hangar, life on Earth was over.

"We'll have to experiment on the way there," she said, pointing.

Everyone clambered out of the shuttle, and one by one, their expressions transformed into the same masks of disbelief she'd worn moments earlier. Soon all of them stood transfixed.

She snapped her fingers to break them from the trance. "Don't look at it. We can't afford to lose momentum." She wheeled toward her brother. "Troy, will you go inside and get the staff accessories? I can't face Mom and Dad knowing I might never . . ." *see them again.* Just thinking about it loosened the floodgates behind her eyes.

"I'm on it." Troy jogged to the house.

Aelyx dragged a hand through his hair and thumbed at Aisly's shuttle. "We need to decide if we're taking this or leaving it behind."

"I think we should take it," Syrine said. "Two methods of escape are better than one."

"But the more shuttles we use, the harder it will be to infiltrate the Destroyer," Elle pointed out.

Cara hadn't considered that. "How are we getting inside at all?"

"I assume the same way we slipped out of the transport."

"Through a waste chute?"

"It could work," Aelyx said, glancing at the staff headpiece. "If we use one of the cubes to blast open an external port. On a ship that large, the chutes are bigger than houses."

"An explosion will alert them to our presence," Larish warned.

Cara turned up her palms. The six of them were about to invade a ship full of highly evolved aliens, armed with nothing but a staff that nobody knew how to use. This whole mission was a Hail Mary.

Troy came running out the back door, using his T-shirt like a kangaroo pouch for the Nova Staff gadgets. As soon as the door shut behind him, Mom and Dad rushed to the kitchen windowpane, each pressing a hand against the glass.

Cara spun away before the prickling in her eyes intensified. "Let's split up. I'll pilot one shuttle and Aelyx will fly the other. We'll use the onboard com-system to brainstorm a plan while we're in the air."

The group moved quickly, Troy and Elle following Aelyx while Larish and Syrine joined Cara. The pilot's seat was still warm when she sat down to fasten her straps. She cloaked the shuttle and linked her com-system to Aelyx's. After testing the link to ensure they could hear each other, they lifted off and rocketed toward the atmosphere. As they flew, Larish tested the Nova Staff by pointing its sphere at a few random objects he'd rested along the dashboard. None of them moved.

"Keep practicing," Cara told him. "We've got a long way to go."

She'd just reached the five-hundred-foot mark when her com-sphere buzzed. She answered while keeping the link open between both shuttles.

"Talk loud," she told Jake. "You're on speakerphone."

"*Ooo-kay*," he said, drawing out the word in confusion. "I did what you asked and found a link between phosphorus and the Aribol."

"What's the connection?"

"According to my soil samples, phosphorus doesn't exist here. Neither do most elements found in fertilizer, like potassium, calcium, magnesium . . ."

"Nitrogen," Aelyx added through the speakers.

"No, there's plenty of that," Jake said. "The air here is almost identical to the chemical makeup of what we breathe on Earth."

Cara scrunched her forehead. "So why would they want to block our access to phosphorus on Earth?"

"I think I know," came Troy's voice. "In war you go for your enemy's defenses."

Larish shot out a hand from the passenger seat and gripped Cara's wrist. "Our soil is toxic to them. That's why they never returned to either of our planets after the initial abduction that seeded L'eihr."

"But why would they seed planets that are toxic to them?" Jake asked.

"Because worlds that support our kind are in short supply," Cara said. Jaxen had told her so. She blinked as the clues fell into place. This was the reason the Aribol had launched probes instead of making direct contact, *and* why they'd sent the hybrids to do their dirty work. "That's why they need suits for a ground invasion—protection from the elements. Maybe their suits can filter out normal levels of phosphorus, but a pure concentration would be too much." There was only one thing she didn't understand. "So why haven't they destroyed phosphorus mines on L'eihr?"

"Maybe because our population is smaller," Aelyx said. "We all live on a single continent, so there's no need for a large-scale ground invasion. One or two shockwave pulse ships would be enough."

Larish shook Cara's arm. "We have to go back to the ground!"

She checked the altitude gauge. They'd almost reached the stratosphere. "We can't. There's no time."

"For this, we'll make time. We just discovered a weapon against the Aribol—a weapon so deadly they sent Jaxen to destroy it in advance of an invasion. That alone implies their fleet or their suits can be penetrated by the elements."

She bit her inner cheek and slowed the shuttle.

"None of us knows how to use this," he said, gripping the staff. "It might not save us. Go back and let me gather some soil."

"But the phosphorus concentration will be low."

"If it's toxic enough to them, a small amount is all we need."

"I agree with Larish," Aelyx said through the speakers. "You return to Earth. I'll keep going and find the weakest access point on the Destroyer. I'll report back and tell you where to meet me."

Without wasting another second, Cara turned the shuttle around and dropped through the dark, wispy clouds toward the Earth. While they made their descent, Jake finished his report.

"The brainwave-seeking probe picked up signs of life on the opposite side of the planet from where we landed. We're there now. We haven't seen any life forms, but there are definite signs of an advanced civilization here."

Cara glanced at Jake's hologram. He stood in front of a futuristic building, smooth and mirrored in a rounded triangular shape, like a twenty-story shark fin peeking above the ground. Half of its gleaming exterior was blackened, probably scorched by whatever force had decimated the other side of the planet.

"Be careful," she said. "Just because you can't see them doesn't mean they can't see you."

"I'm using the probe to track the . . ." Jake trailed off and turned his head to peer at something out of the frame. He squinted and leaned forward, straining to focus as if he couldn't believe what he'd seen. Then his expression went blank and he ended the transmission without another word.

Cara's stomach sank. "I assume he found those life forms."

"I'll try to contact Ayah," Syrine said.

While Syrine made calls from the backseat, Larish helped Cara navigate to the nearest farm, where the soil would contain a higher concentration of fertilizer. She landed in the middle of a cornfield, blowing stalks in every direction, and cut the thrusters while Larish rushed outside and filled a satchel with dirt. For good measure, he stuffed his pockets, too. Then he was back in his seat, bringing the musky scent of earth with him.

"Nothing," Syrine said as the shuttle lifted off. "I can't reach the Voyagers."

Cara started to suggest reporting the incident to The Way, before she remembered the evacuation. Alona was long gone, and the Voyagers were on their own. But then something else occurred to her, and she snatched her com-sphere to issue a summons she never thought she'd make again.

Alona answered from her seat in the transport dining hall, a bite of *l'ina* suspended an inch from her lips. "Miss Sweeney? I didn't expect—"

"I'm sorry to interrupt," Cara cut in as she sped toward the moon. "But there isn't much time. We're about to attack the Aribol ship."

Alona dropped her utensil. "To what end?"

"To destroy it by any means necessary." *Or die trying.*

"I'm listening."

Cara conveyed all of Jake's information, emphasizing the theory that several elements on Earth and L'eihr were poisonous to the Aribol. "I don't know how far you've traveled, or if you can make it back to L'eihr in time to stop the Destroyer—"

"Or if stopping them is possible," Larish added.

"—but I figured you'd want to know."

The shuttle broke through the clouds, and the Destroyer loomed near enough for her to make out a line of bolts along the hull, each one wider than her craft. "I should go," she said. "I have to coordinate with Aelyx. Good luck, whatever you decide to do."

"And to you, Miss Sweeney."

No sooner had the transmission ended than Aelyx pinged her on the com-system. "I found a way inside. Are you almost here?"

She peered around for his shuttle before remembering they were both cloaked. "Where are you? This mission won't last long if we fly into each other."

"I'm at the ship's northern tip, anchored behind a large, boxy vent. You can't miss it. Land on the side that's been dented by an asteroid."

She approached the ship and veered north, watching the hull pass below her in a blur. If the Destroyer had seemed large from the ground, that was nothing compared to seeing it up close. A cold ball of fear congealed inside her. Anything this massive had to be staffed by hundreds of crew members, maybe thousands—each with the ability to manipulate minds. Even if she infiltrated the ship, how long would she last?

"Breathe," Syrine said, resting a hand on Cara's shoulder, which she hadn't realized was clenched halfway to her ear. "Fear will cloud your logic. Try to let it go."

Cara made an effort to release the tension in her muscles

as she piloted her way to the boxy structure Aelyx had described. She landed near an oblong dent in the hull and contacted him to let him know she'd arrived.

"Stay there. We'll come to you," he said. "That way we can consolidate to one shuttle and leave the other behind as an emergency escape."

"What should I do?"

"On my mark, disable the cloaking mode. I'll dock beside you. Then use the manual override on the ventilation controls and open the door, just like you did when we left the transport."

"Be prepared to help us," Elle called. "The change in pressure is disorienting."

They worked quickly to minimize the time the shuttles were visible. Because they'd done this before, the process went off without a hitch. A few minutes later, Aelyx, Troy, and Elle had joined Syrine in the backseat, the three of them shivering violently but otherwise unharmed.

Troy rubbed his palms together to generate heat. "Smells like dirt in here."

Larish, who'd grown frustrated with the unresponsive staff, set it down and passed his satchel to the back, sprinkling the center console with grit. "Everyone fill your pockets. It might not help, but it can't hurt."

Cara scooped a handful from the bag. "So tell me about this entrance."

"It's part of a ventilation system." Aelyx pointed a dirt-stained finger at the box. "Watch." A burst of steam shot out from the top of the structure, instantly crystallizing into ice. "The grating along the top is thinner than the rest of the hull. We can use the shuttle as a battering ram to break through."

"But where does the vent lead?"

"I have no idea," he admitted.

"So we could be flying into a boiler, or worse?"

"The shuttle is built to withstand heat and radiation . . . to an extent."

"To an extent," she muttered darkly.

"I've been all over the ship, and this is the only access point. All the hatches and exterior doors are sealed."

"So assuming we make it inside and don't fly into something that disintegrates the shuttle, then what?"

"We'll find an airlock that leads to the interior corridors. From there, it's a matter of navigating to the hangar and destroying the fleet."

She bit her tongue. He made it sound so easy.

"I have an alternate suggestion, assuming we learn how to use this." Larish lifted a Nova cube. "I've never met a fuel that wasn't combustible. If we exhaust all other options, one of us can use the staff to detonate the ship's fuel core."

Nobody spoke, but Cara knew they were all asking the same silent question.

*Which one of us?*

Larish found an old protein pack wrapper and began tearing it into thin segments. When he'd finished, he arranged six strips in his hand so only the tips were visible. "If it comes to that, we'll do our best to evacuate to the shuttle before detonation. Whoever draws the shortest strip will stay behind and set off the explosion."

One by one, all six of them pulled a strip. As Cara extended a clammy hand to retrieve hers, she reminded herself that she would rather die by choice than become a puddle of flesh. But despite her bold thoughts, she instantly began comparing the length of her strip to the others.

Hers was the longest.

She released a quiet breath. But her relief turned to panic when Aelyx raised his stubby strip. He set his jaw to put up a brave front, but he couldn't hide the gleam of fear in his eyes.

Cara shook her head.

"Don't," he said in a firm voice. "This is only a last resort, so put it out of your mind."

If he thought she could do that, he didn't know her very well.

The ship's hull rumbled hard enough to vibrate her seat cushion. The noise went on for several moments, reminding her of the motorized drone of a garage door opener. With a gasp, she spun around to peer out the window. From the belly of the ship, a tiny pod burst into the blackness and descended toward Earth. It was shaped like a teardrop, with the same mirrored exterior as the building she'd seen in Jake's hologram.

Aelyx followed the direction of her gaze. "It's not part of the fleet. Anything that small has to be a shuttle."

"That must be Jaxen's ride," Troy said. "We'd better hurry. It won't take long for the pilot to figure out there's no one down there to rescue."

And then the invasion would begin.

"Wait," Elle said. "I assume that noise we heard was the hangar door opening. But after the shuttle left, I didn't hear the noise again."

Cara gripped the wheel and lifted off, bringing the

shuttle around. The hangar could still be open. If she kept the shuttle cloaked, she might be able to fly right inside the ship without the Aribol noticing.

She punched the accelerator and careened toward the underside of the ship. Metal whizzed in her periphery. She was halfway to the hangar when she heard the telltale rumble that signified the hatch beginning to close. The engine couldn't propel her any faster, but that didn't stop her from leaning forward in her seat and choking the life out of the wheel. She rounded the bottom curve of the ship and saw the enormous hatch drawing against the hull, revealing a glint of light from inside. With nothing more than a sliver of space remaining, she barreled straight ahead and clenched her teeth.

The shuttle slipped beneath the hatch with a scrape of metal that sent sparks bursting across the windshield. The craft wobbled. Alarms blared from the control panel. Aelyx leaned up from the backseat to silence the alarms while she squinted through the sparks and steadied her course.

"Please tell me the cloaking mode is still working," she said.

"According to this, it is."

She stabilized the shuttle and slowed the thrusters too quickly, causing her to lurch forward in her harness. From behind, bodies thunked against her seatback. As the hatch sealed shut with a creak of its massive hinges, she silenced her engine and idled in place, taking her first look around the hangar. What she saw made her eyes wrench wide. Endless rows of silvery ships were anchored to the floor, thousands of them stretching in every direction.

"Whoa," Troy breathed. "We're toast."

Cara had to agree. The sight of the entire fleet assembled in one place made her feel like an insect beneath a boot. The overhead lights dimmed, prompting her to scan the room for movement. All was still. "It doesn't look like the ships have been manned yet."

"Maybe we can flush them into space," Larish suggested.

Cara didn't know how they were going to do that, but when she considered the alternative—sending Aelyx to detonate the fuel core—she snapped out of her trance and piloted the shuttle to the far end of the hangar.

She landed adjacent to a sealed doorway and cut the thrusters, then glanced around to ensure they were alone before disabling the cloaking mode. As she stepped out, she took a tentative breath to test the air.

It was breathable, consistent with what she knew of the Aribols' home world. And much like that planet, the temperature inside the ship was sweltering. Sweat slicked the back of her neck and clung to her hair. The room wasn't simply hot. It was downright swampy. A rasping noise filled the air, and when she checked for the source of the sound, she found a floor vent releasing a cloud of steam.

Aelyx had noticed it, too. "They must need heat and humidity to survive. We should split up. You stay here and find a way to destroy the fleet. I'll go inside and look for their thermal system. If I can shut it down, it may solve all our problems." He extended a hand toward Larish, who handed him the Nova Staff. "If not, I'll find the fuel core."

Cara sent him a cutting look. That wasn't an option.

"You'll need this." Larish gave him a cube. "The sphere only captures and redirects energy, not that I was able to make it work."

While Aelyx tucked the cube in his back pocket, Cara approached him and tried to lock eyes with him for Silent Speech. He refused to hold her gaze, instead pulling her into an embrace that felt an awful lot like a farewell.

"No." She wriggled free and held a finger in his face. "No hugs, no kisses, no parting words. This isn't goodbye."

"I'll do what I have to do, Elire," he whispered.

"I know." She gripped her hips and leveled a deadly serious gaze at him. "And if it comes to that, we'll face it together." When he opened his mouth to argue, she cut him off. "What if our roles were reversed? What if I'd drawn the short straw? Would you leave me alone to sacrifice myself?"

"You know I wouldn't."

"Then don't expect me to do it. It's not fair."

He hesitated.

"Promise me we'll face this together," she pressed. "Or I won't be able to focus on what we have to do. Distractions could get me killed." She knew that would sway him.

"All right. I promise."

Troy called, "Hey, check this out." He rubbed a hand over the door, and the material melted to the floor, revealing an airlock chamber. He pulled his hand away, and the door materialized again. "Here's our ticket inside. Let's get a move on."

"I'd better go," Aelyx said.

"I'll hold you to that promise." Cara bowed back as he leaned in for a kiss. "Nope. I meant what I said. This isn't goodbye."

He laughed softly, shaking his head as if he couldn't decide whether he found her stubbornness annoying or impressive. He took a step toward the door. "No goodbyes."

# CHAPTER NINETEEN

As Troy extended a palm to reopen the door, Aelyx caught his wrist and stopped him. Troy delivered a quizzical glance, and Aelyx checked over his shoulder to ensure Cara's back was turned. "Stay with the group. I'm going alone."

"Like hell," Troy cried, then lowered his voice to a hiss when Aelyx shushed him. "I can't do any good in here. I don't know squat about alien tech, but these Marine-issue boots were made for kicking ass." He jabbed a finger toward the interior of the ship. "That's what I can do in there."

Aelyx leaned in and spoke quietly. "I need you to stay with your sister."

"Why?"

"Because I drew the shortest strip." Surely they both knew what that meant. "I need you to make sure Cara evacuates to the shuttle, even if you have to forcibly drag her there and hold her in her seat, which will probably be the case." He gripped Troy's shoulder. "Can you do that for me?"

Troy drew a long breath and rubbed the back of his neck with a heavy hand. He didn't speak, but the tension in his face told Aelyx he'd asked too much. When this was over, Cara would never forgive either of them.

"Look," Troy said. "I know I gave you a lot of grief when you started dating my sister. But I know how she feels about you. She really"—he grimaced—"loves you, so I figure the best thing I can do for her is to go through that door and watch your back."

"But there's no reason for all of us to—"

Troy cut him off by scrubbing a palm over the door and stepping through its disintegrating material into the airlock. "You coming, or what?"

Aelyx strode inside the chamber and resisted the urge to argue. The harder he pushed, the deeper Troy would dig in his heels. If he had to, he would evade Troy and force him to return to the hangar.

The door rematerialized and the chamber filled with the sound of rushing air. Once pressure was optimized, the opposite door dissolved to reveal a dimly lit passageway stretching at least fifty yards into the distance. Aelyx hesitated. Ahead of him, billows of steam rolled across the walkway in thick clouds. The effect reminded him of last year's Halloween festival at Midtown High, when the seniors had filled the halls with artificial fog and strobe lights, and then hidden in wait to frighten unsuspecting freshmen.

"Jesus," Troy whispered, pulling his T-shirt away from his chest for ventilation. "It's like a haunted sauna in here."

Moisture had glued Aelyx's shirt to his own chest. The

choking humidity made him wonder if the Aribol were partially amphibious.

Neither he nor Troy moved until the door began to materialize from the bottom up, forcing them to jump over it into the hall. Aelyx landed as softly as he could and paused, cocking an ear to listen for voices or approaching feet. When he didn't hear anything, he strode forward while Troy followed close behind.

As Aelyx walked, he studied the texture of the wall and noticed it resembled the dark, grainy material of the airlock door. He trailed his fingertips over the surface, expecting to find it slick with condensation, but the wall felt like animal hide, dry to the touch and slightly bumpy. He pressed harder, torn between disgust and amazement. He'd heard of "living ships" made from organic material, but he'd never thought such a thing possible.

The surface gave way beneath his touch, and he yanked back his hand as a patch of the wall opened. There was a pipe on the other side. "Look at this." He craned his neck and followed the pipeline to where it disappeared into a section of ductwork. "If this pipe leads to the onboard humidifier, it's only three floors above us."

Troy tested the pipe, touching it briefly with the pad of one finger. "It's too hot for us to scale. We'll have to find a stairwell."

Aelyx quickened his pace to a silent jog as his insides fluttered with hope. Maybe he wouldn't have to detonate the fuel cell after all. He reached the fork at the end of the corridor and stopped to glance left and right. He noticed bodies in movement and quickly jumped back. His glimpse was so brief he couldn't describe the beings, other than to say they moved upright and stood at least five feet tall.

He pointed to the right and mouthed at Troy, "Someone's down there."

Troy crouched near the opposite wall. "How many?"

"Two, I think. Maybe three."

"Are they coming this way?"

Aelyx didn't know, so he poked his head out from around the corner. About twenty paces away stood two creatures facing each other as if engaged in silent conversation. He could make out their general shapes—two short legs attached to a slim torso; two long, willowy arms; an oversize, oblong head resting atop a thick neck—but their edges and features were blurred. Their flesh seemed to glow, changing color from gray to pale pink to beige and back again. He squinted, unable to bring the details of their faces or hands into focus. It was like viewing a film through a broken projector, and he recalled what Cara had said about Noven brains being unable to perceive the Aribols' true form.

As if sensing his presence, both creatures turned their heads toward him. Aelyx ducked back behind the corner and locked eyes with Troy. "I think they saw me."

Troy hissed a swear and pointed at the staff. "Use it on them."

Before he lost his nerve, Aelyx leaned into the open and pointed the staff at the creatures. Nothing happened. He tried again, mimicking what Jaxen had done, but the orb nesting inside the staff remained dull. Then his brain buzzed with confusion. He could sense what the Aribol were feeling. Their mental activity swelled within him, a force so powerful he shrank back and cringed.

They thought he was Jaxen. His russet skin and long, brown hair matched the person they'd seen months ago on their home world, but his actions were all wrong. They didn't understand his odd behavior, and they were coming to investigate.

"What're you doing?" Troy asked.

Aelyx gripped his head. "You don't feel it?"

"Feel what?"

"They're coming."

"Use the staff!" Troy whisper-yelled.

Fighting to clear his head, Aelyx thought back to the alliance signing last spring, when he'd fired an *iphal* at Jaxen. It hadn't been enough to point and shoot. The weapon's safety mechanism had required intent—he'd had to *want* to fire it. Perhaps the staff worked in the same way. He concentrated on harnessing the power within the sphere, imagined drawing on it like a conduit through his skin. He felt a hum of energy, and the sphere glowed alive.

The first Aribol glided into view. Aelyx thrust the staff forward with all his might, and in the blink of an eye, the creature struck the wall with a sickening crunch and crumpled to the floor. Before Aelyx could lash out at the second one, he felt his limbs stiffen. The creature was inside his mind, shutting down his motor control. He dropped to his knees, the staff disappearing beneath clouds of steam. His lungs seized, and he couldn't breathe.

Troy leaped from his crouching position and tackled the Aribol to the floor. No sooner had they landed than Troy gripped the creature's head and twisted it sharply. There was a crack, and its body went limp. Instantly, the effect lifted and Aelyx was free.

While catching his breath, he crawled forward to study the Aribol more closely. There was a purplish smudge on the wall where the first body had hit. Blood, probably. Even in death, their edges seemed to vibrate at speeds too fast for his eyes, so he used his hands to see, feeling their fingers, which were long and skeletally thin, but with the flexibility of cartilage instead of bone. There were three fingers and an opposable thumb, covered by rough, dry skin that reminded him of fine-grit sandpaper. Despite the moisture in the air, several cracks marred the creature's flesh. No wonder they avoided contact with the ground. Dust could easily make its way inside the bloodstream through these fissures.

Aelyx fanned away the steam and noticed a sprinkling of soil had fallen out of Troy's pockets. "I'd forgotten about that." He patted his own pockets, still full. "We should've thrown some at them."

"I'm sure we'll have another chance. Come on, let's find the stairs."

Aelyx retrieved the staff and followed Troy down the left hallway. As he strode along the corridor, he wondered why Troy hadn't felt the Aribols' emotions or succumbed to the mental attack. Perhaps it was because they hadn't known he was there. Or maybe they could only breach one mind at a time.

Something caught Aelyx's attention, and he paused. There was a whooshing noise coming from inside the wall. He tugged Troy to a stop. The sound came again, and Aelyx followed it a few paces forward to a slim doorway about half the width of the airlock exit. He rubbed a hand over the wall, and it parted to reveal a tube barely wide enough for both of them.

"An elevator?" he guessed.

Troy pressed the toe of one boot into the tube. When the floor held his weight, he stepped inside. "Worth a shot."

Aelyx squeezed in beside him, looking for a set of controls as the door re-formed. The interior walls were bare. He didn't touch anything, but the tube shot up on its own volition and then stopped almost at once.

"This must be the next level. Maybe if we don't touch—" Inertia cut him off as the tube lifted again. Perhaps its default setting was to take them to each floor one at a time until they chose to exit. *Or until someone else wishes to enter*, he thought with a chill.

He held his breath when the tube stopped again. The wait at this floor seemed longer than the last. To his relief, the door remained sealed and the tube shot upward.

"Next floor, right?" asked Troy.

"I think so."

The tube stopped. Aelyx rubbed his palm over the door, and right away he knew they'd reached the boiler level. A burst of heat tightened the skin on his face, and swirls of steam obscured his vision. But it wasn't until he exited the chute and came face-to-face with dozens of Aribol, each basking in the warm mist leaking from massive water tanks, that he realized his shortsightedness. To creatures like these, this location would be the most desirable room on the ship.

Troy froze beside him, and Aelyx felt the same waves of confusion crash over him, ten times stronger than before. There were too many thoughts piercing his skull. *Who are these Noven? Why are they here?*

"Now I know what you were talking about." Troy

clutched his forehead. With labored movements, he pulled both hands down to his pockets.

The creatures' bewilderment turned to a suspicion so intense it was nearly blinding. Dark spots twirled in Aelyx's line of vision, as if he were about to black out. He tightened his grip on the staff and used his other hand to clutch a fistful of soil from his pocket.

"Now," Troy said, and threw two handfuls of dirt into the air.

Aelyx cast another handful at the group and fired the Nova Staff. He couldn't see what happened next, but he heard the smack of flesh against metal. There was a brief reprieve that cleared his vision and loosened the vice around his temples, just long enough for him to scan the area for any Aribol left standing. One of them stood in the background, far beyond his reach. He raised the staff to strike, but with the movement came a pain so sharp Aelyx had to probe his scalp to be sure it hadn't split open. He clenched his eyes and sank to his knees while Troy cried out in agony. Aelyx curled into a ball on the floor, cradling his head. His muscles locked, starting with his arms and legs, followed by his torso, and eventually his lungs.

He willed himself to breathe, but his chest refused to obey. Soon his eyes bulged and his face began to tingle. He thought desperately of Cara. He had no way to warn her; no way to destroy the ship so she could evacuate. More than that, he would never see her again; never watch her blue eyes sparkle when he entered a room. He pictured those blue eyes and held tightly to the image as consciousness slipped away.

And then she was gone.

• • •

Cara touched her com-sphere through the fabric of her uniform, hesitating twice before leaving it in her pocket. Aelyx and Troy would contact her when they were ready. The best thing she could do was let them focus. She'd give them fifteen minutes of uninterrupted silence.

Then all bets were off.

She spotted Larish's legs sticking out from beneath one of the ships. On the opposite side of the hangar, Syrine and Elle were searching for a control panel that might lift the anchors from the landing gear and allow them to flush the ships into space. Cara had checked her end of the room. So far, none of them had found anything.

She scooted on her back to join Larish under the ship. Its belly was open, exposing thick, granular, fleshy-looking tubes that reminded her of the cow's intestine she'd dissected in AP Biology.

"There's no doubt why the Aribol wanted fertilizer and raw phosphorus destroyed," Larish said. "These ships aren't fully airtight. Their filtration systems can block the toxins in errant dust or dirt, but the concentration of elements in fertilizer would be too high for them to screen from the pilots."

"Is that what you've got there, the filter?"

"No, I believe this is the fuel line." He sliced into a tube and frowned when nothing came out. "Or not. Regardless, it must be a necessary component of the engine or it wouldn't exist."

"So if we can open the bellies of a thousand ships and

cut their innards, the engines may or may not operate." She shook her head. "There has to be another way."

"Well, unless we can find a control panel . . ." Larish trailed off as a buzz tore through the air. Loud and steady, it struck Cara as some kind of alarm. She drew a sharp breath and locked eyes with Larish as both of them reached the same conclusion. The external hatch was about to open. Any loose objects—or bodies—inside the hangar would be blown into space with crushing force.

She slid out from beneath the ship and screamed across the hangar, "To the airlock! The shuttle's back!"

After running like hell to the airlock doorway, she flattened her palm over the rubbery panel, and its molecules separated beneath her skin. She and Larish stepped inside while making a *hurry-up* motion to Syrine and Elle, who were sprinting fast enough to leave burn marks on the floor. The buzzing intensified. Twice the airlock door began to re-form, and each time Cara scrubbed her hands over it to leave an opening. When the girls were finally within reach, they dived through the hole and landed hard on their bellies. The barrier had just sealed when the floor rumbled with the force of the enormous hatch opening on the other side.

Everyone released a breath.

The chamber pressurized and the opposite door dissolved, leading to a long hallway carpeted with steam. Instantly, Cara's gaze fixed on the end point of the corridor, where two bodies were slumped against the wall. In the moment before she realized they weren't human, her heart lurched.

She jogged forward as quietly as she could. When she reached the Aribol bodies, she struggled to take in their details. Zane hadn't lied about his kind. She couldn't view

275

them properly. Their forms glowed and shimmered at the edges, almost as if they were made of incandescent gasses.

There wasn't time to study them any longer. Once she darted a glance up and down the intersecting hallway, finding it vacant, she used her com-sphere to contact Aelyx. He didn't reply, not even to deny the summons, which caused her stomach to twist.

"Troy's not answering either," Elle whispered, her lower lip pinched between her teeth.

Syrine pulled out her sphere and began navigating its holographic directory. "You track Troy. I'll lock on to Aelyx." In moments, she displayed his position relative to theirs and gestured left. "This way, up three flights."

"Troy, too," Elle said. "They're together."

Larish adjusted his satchel, shifting the heavy bulk of soil behind him, and then the four of them set off down the hall. As they followed the signal, Cara darted frequent glances over her shoulders. The dim lighting, the dead bodies, the steady hiss of steam, all of it sent a cold finger down her spine. Larish, however, kept his eyes fixed on the walls as they passed.

"Remarkable," he muttered under his breath while touching the surface and watching it part around his finger. "They've constructed the ship using a combination of manmade and organic materials. I wonder what species the walls are derived from."

Cara didn't share his fascination. She would be impressed when the Aribol stopped trying to annihilate her race.

Ahead of them, Syrine stopped in front of a slim doorway and brushed a hand over it. There was a cylindrical chamber inside, too narrow to fit all of them. "This must be the lift. We'll have to go in pairs."

Cara pushed her way to the front of the group and squeezed into the chute beside Elle, who was already inside. The door sealed and they shot upward so fast Cara nearly left her stomach behind. After two more abrupt stops and starts, she touched the door panel and tentatively poked her head out while Elle strode forward.

Cara crept out of the chute. Whatever this place was, the air was so thick with steam she could barely see the back of Elle's head. Heat curled at the nape of Cara's neck, making her dizzy. It was ungodly hot in here. She waved a hand to dispel the steam and noticed several enormous vats, like water towers, each connected by metallic ductwork.

This must be the shipwide humidifier.

Her movement caused the steam to drift, and something at the base of the nearest vat caught her eye. Her heart skipped a beat. A standard Marine issue jacket lay balled up on the floor. Elle saw it, too, and they shared a wide-eyed glance before both of them flew into action. Cara snatched the jacket and used it like a fan to clear the fog while Elle jogged to Troy's beacon, which according to the map was less than a few yards away.

Cara tripped over something and found an Aribol body, and then another. Grit crunched beneath her soles, telling her how these creatures had died. Her pulse rushed as she stepped over more of the dead. She silently prayed her loved ones weren't among them.

The macabre trail ended with Aelyx and Troy lying face up, their hands positioned atop their chests. At once, Cara checked their ribcages, and when she saw them rise and fall, she exhaled in relief. But the moment was fleeting. Just beyond them crouched an Aribol, very much alive and radiating fury.

She barely had time to register fear before she lost control of her body. The next thing she knew, she was on the floor beside Elle, struggling to breathe. The creature was inside her head. She could feel its rage at the lives Aelyx and Troy had taken. It wanted to kill them all, but its leaders had given it instructions to keep them alive until others arrived to probe their minds. Then they would be executed and flushed out the nearest port, while the fleet liquefied the inhabitants of Earth.

Cara heard footsteps, and Larish fell down beside her. She struggled to bring him into focus as her face grew numb and her sight dimmed. Then as suddenly as she'd lost control of her body, it was hers to command again. She sucked in a loud breath. Oxygen rushed through her veins, restoring her senses, and she sat up to find the Aribol writhing on the floor, its holographic skin covered in dirt. Above it stood Syrine.

"It couldn't control me," she said in wonder, brushing the soil from her hands. "I felt it penetrate my consciousness, and I pushed it out."

Elle rose to her knees. "I tried blocking my thoughts, and it didn't work."

"So did I," Larish added.

"Maybe it's because of the 'emotional healer' thing." Cara crawled to Aelyx's side and tried to rouse him. He wouldn't wake. Neither would Troy. "It did something permanent to them. Can you remove its influence like you removed Aisly's?"

"I can try."

"Others are coming," Elle cautioned. "I sensed it."

While Syrine bent over Troy and gently pried open his eyelids, Cara looked for a place large enough to hide all six of them. *Behind the vats*, she thought. But that was a temporary fix. She noticed the Nova Staff on the floor and picked it up, glancing at Larish. "Parts of the ship are alive, right? If the walls are made of flesh, maybe burning the elevator doorway—"

"Will cauterize it and lock out the Aribol," he finished. "It's worth a try."

"We have to hurry," Elle said as she helped pat down Aelyx for the cube. "Now that the shuttle has returned, there's no reason to delay the invasion. I'll use my sphere to scan the ship for its fuel core."

Larish tipped his head at the boiler equipment. "I'll look for an off switch. A drastic loss of humidity may very well kill them."

Cara tried to ignore the number of *may*s and *might*s in their plan, focusing instead on removing the Nova sphere from its cradle and replacing it with the cube she'd pried from Aelyx's back pocket. As soon as the cube clicked into place, she cradled the staff in the crook of one arm and ran back to the elevator.

Steam and soil had formed a thin layer of mud on the floor, causing her ballet flats to skid past the chute doorway. After righting herself, she took two backward steps, then two more, unsure of how large a blast to expect from the cube. Finally she raised the staff and brought it down, focusing on the door's fleshy membrane as she aimed.

She wasn't prepared for the surge of energy that passed through her. Before she could brace herself, she landed hard on the floor. She stood and rubbed her tailbone, then limped toward the elevator to find she hadn't simply scorched the doorway. She'd obliterated the entire chute and three walls behind it she hadn't even known were there.

"Bad news," she shouted to Elle and Larish as she ran, slipping, toward them. "Instead of sealing the doorway, I blew it wide open."

Syrine didn't look up. She was still bent over Troy. Aelyx was out cold, and Larish had disappeared to somewhere behind the boiler vats. Only Elle answered, talking to Cara while studying the holographic map she'd displayed in midair.

"I scanned the ship for traces of radiation and found this." Elle pointed to a dot on the map that pulsed like a beating heart. "It has to be the fuel core."

Cara traced a finger along the path from their current position to the core and noticed they were on the same level. She turned and studied the walls she'd opened behind the elevator shaft. The fleshy membrane had begun to repair itself. "We can travel between walls. If we're quiet, no one will catch us."

Elle charged forward and pocketed her sphere. "Let's go."

"Wait," Syrine called, still peering into Troy's eyes. "I've almost reached him."

"There's no time," Cara told her, following to the wall Elle had just opened. "We'll check in once we make it to the core. If no one's found a solution by then . . ." She didn't finish the sentence, but the slowness of Syrine's nod said she understood.

The time for evacuation was over.

• • •

Aelyx awoke abruptly from the deepest sleep of his existence. One moment he was all but dead, and then his eyes snapped open and he was fully alert, as if someone had switched him from *off* to *on*.

He sat bolt upright and registered his surroundings. He was still inside the boiler room, but someone had moved him in between the wall and a floor-level air duct. He heard male voices, Troy's and Larish's, though he couldn't see them. Then Syrine touched his shoulder and asked if he was all right, and all his memories returned in a jolt.

"What happened?" he asked, pushing himself onto all fours. "Where is everyone?"

Syrine helped him stand. "Larish is looking for a way to shut down the boiler." A grunt echoed in the distance, and pain sliced through Aelyx's skull. Syrine winced, indicating she'd felt it, too. "Troy is holding off the Aribol reinforcements with what's left of his soil. Every time one of them dies, we all feel it."

Aelyx shook off the pain and glanced around for the Nova Staff. He needed to find the fuel core so the others could escape. "Where's the staff?"

Syrine avoided his gaze.

"Where is it?" he repeated.

"Cara and Elle have it."

His brows hitched, and on instinct his thighs tensed to run after them. "No! I drew the short slip."

"None of that matters. It's too late. Either we neutralize the Aribol so they can't pilot the fleet, or Cara and Elle will detonate the fuel cell—whichever comes first."

Aelyx forced himself to clear his mind. "Point me to Larish."

He found the scholar on his hands and knees, peering beneath a cylindrical tank. Larish sat back on his heels with a pained expression that told Aelyx he hadn't liked what he'd found. "Nothing," Larish said when he noticed Aelyx approaching. "I can't find a single way to compromise the system."

Aelyx crouched down. "Explain to me how it works. Maybe I'll see something you missed."

"Well." Larish pointed at the ductwork near the elevator. "Their humidity system operates similar to our body's circulatory system. The intake ducts are like blue veins, pumping deoxygenated blood to the heart. They channel recycled air here"—pointing at the series of connected vats—"where the vapor is infused with fresh oxygen and steam, and then sent through these ducts, which are like red veins, feeding all the vents inside the ship."

"Okay," Aelyx said. That made sense. "How do we figuratively slit its wrists?"

"We can't. There are too many failsafe seals. If we destroy the connection between one tank, the system is designed to reroute to the next, and so on."

"So we'd have to destroy everything on this level." And because the pressurized steam would kill them all in the process, that plan was no better than detonating the fuel cell. "Or poison the bloodstream."

A mass summons issued on their com-spheres. Cara's image appeared alongside Elle's, both of them huddled in the dark. "We're here," Cara said. "The fuel cell's on the other side of this wall." She paused for a pregnant beat before asking, "Any luck on your end?"

Troy and Syrine hadn't answered the summons, likely

because they were engaged in battle on the opposite end of the room. Larish cocked his head and began muttering gibberish to himself, which left Aelyx to deliver the bad news. "So far, no."

Darkness concealed the fear in Cara's gaze, but she couldn't hide the tremble in her reply. "We can't let them launch the fleet . . ."

"How far away are you?" he asked, and used his eyes to say the rest. He'd promised to face death by her side, and that was what he wanted. When the universe reclaimed their bodies, they would go together as one.

The subtle shake of Elle's head said *too far*.

He fought against the fresh ache in his chest, determined not to let his voice waiver. "I love you," he said, strong and sure. "Both of you. And I regret nothing."

"I love you, too," Cara said. "I'm glad we went down swinging. You were right. What we have is worth fighting for."

Aelyx didn't know what more to say. They were out of time. "No goodbyes?"

"No goodbyes," Cara agreed, and the transmission ended.

Aelyx's shoulders rounded. This was happening too fast.

Larish continued muttering under his breath until he abruptly shouted, "Poison the bloodstream!" and grabbed Aelyx's wrist hard enough to wrench it from his hand. Larish took off like a comet, towing Aelyx toward the elevator shaft. "I have an idea," he yelled. "Tell her to wait!"

Cara stepped through the wall's opening into a small compartment that reminded her of her late grandmother's storm cellar. The ceiling here was so low she had to stoop over to avoid hitting her head, and the only source of light was the faint glow leaking through the seams of a boxy fuel tank in the center of the room. Unlike the rest of the ship, this area was bone dry, but still blisteringly hot.

It was about to get a lot hotter.

Elle approached from behind and laced her long, slim fingers between Cara's. It might've been the first time Elle had ever initiated touch, and it made Cara smile. They shared a watery glance that overflowed with all the things they didn't have time to say. With one last squeeze, Cara released Elle's hand and strode toward the fuel cell.

Her pulse was pounding and her breaths turned raspy, but she eased her fear by thinking of her parents, safe on the ground. They would survive, and that was enough. She issued a quick prayer and raised the staff as high as she could in the squat room.

She was ready.

Her com-sphere buzzed, but she ignored the summons. There wasn't a moment to waste, and she might lose her nerve if she didn't do this now. So she rotated her arm to send the ship into oblivion.

Suddenly, a blinding pain sliced through her skull, and she lost all scope. She couldn't be sure whether she'd detonated the cell or not. Her body seemed to vanish, and all that was left was the panic and agony of a thousand deaths. She felt herself sinking into a cloud of collective suffering, and only then did she know she had succeeded.

With a lifted heart, she followed those souls into the light.

# CHAPTER TWENTY

*Elire.*

The word was soft and distant, like a melody floating on a breeze.

*Elire.*

Closer now, it came as a whisper of breath that stirred inside her ear. The tickle puckered her skin into goose bumps and made her shiver, but in a good way. She wanted to feel the warm breath again, so she turned her ear toward it for another caress. Only silence followed.

Frowning, she cracked open one eyelid, then the other, and found Aelyx peering down at her, his silver gaze shining as brightly as the moon.

"Elire."

He said it aloud this time, curving his full lips into a smile. As he bent over her, his hair began to escape his ponytail one lock at a time until it spilled out and framed the strong angles of his jaw. She grinned in return. She loved seeing him this way, rugged and disheveled, his hair forming a curtain of privacy around them.

Her tummy quivered. Maybe this was heaven.

But any illusions she had of an otherworldly paradise vanished when Elle appeared out of nowhere and jabbed a hypodermic needle in her arm. Cara flinched, sucking in a breath as fluid bloomed beneath her skin.

Unpleasant as it was, the burn helped restore her senses, and by the time the needle pulled free, she realized several key facts. Chief among them, she was not dead. And judging by the hard press of metal beneath her back and the high ceiling above, someone had dragged her into one of the ship's corridors.

Elle lifted the empty syringe. "Not the gentlest way to wake up, but we absorbed a lot of radiation when we were passed out in the fuel chamber. This will isolate the radioactive particles and flush them from your system."

Cara rubbed her arm and tried to sit up. Her stiff muscles didn't want to cooperate, so Aelyx helped her. She opened her mouth to ask how long she'd been asleep, but then she remembered she'd been two seconds from blowing the ship to kingdom come, and she snapped her gaze to Aelyx's while her heart lurched.

"It's all right," he assured her, brushing back her hair. "You blacked out before detonating the core. The ships never launched."

"The Aribol . . ."

"Are dead. We killed them before they could man the fleet."

Cara wrinkled her forehead and glanced at her

surroundings. The air smelled different, slightly musky, but otherwise nothing had changed. "How?"

With a click, Elle closed her medical kit and stood up, her movements as brisk and efficient as ever. If Cara didn't know better, she might think the entire night had been a dream. "I'll let you take it from here," Elle told Aelyx. "I want to give Troy an injection, too, since he's the one who pulled us from the chamber."

She strode away, and Cara raised a questioning brow at Aelyx.

One corner of his mouth hitched up. "It's probably best if I show you."

After situating himself more closely beside her, he cupped her chin and leveled their gazes for Silent Speech. His eyes softened, and as she opened to him, she felt his presence glide inside her mind, sweet and familiar, like a finger of warm honey. At first she sensed his emotions—the euphoria of having cheated death and the anticipation of new beginnings—but he soon gained control and replayed the events leading up to her awakening.

*She was in the boiler room, looking through his eyes. Larish was yelling, "Poison the bloodstream!" and running like a madman to the ductwork near the elevator, where Troy and Syrine had just pitched another handful of soil down the chute. The two of them looked weary, their sweat-slicked faces streaked with dirt.*

*"Stop her," Larish shouted while opening his satchel. "Tell Cara to wait!"*

*Aelyx issued the summons while watching Larish throw one handful of soil after another into a slit in the ductwork. He thought Larish had come unhinged. Then he looked closely at the dry soil, which disappeared inside the duct as if sucked into a vacuum, and he understood. The slit was some sort of intake vent none of them had noticed before. They'd had it all wrong. Instead of eliminating the steam—a conduit to every living creature on board—they needed to taint it.*

*Aelyx grabbed the heavy satchel and raised it above his head. His biceps burned as he shook its contents into the vent. Once the bag was empty, he shouted to Troy and Elle, "Give me everything in your pockets." He didn't know if it would be enough.*

*Just then he realized Cara hadn't answered the summons, and his stomach dropped. What if she detonated the fuel cell before he could reach her?*

Aelyx averted his eyes to close the connection. "You nearly gave me an aneurysm when you didn't answer," he said. "I thought it was too late."

She huffed a dry laugh, marveling at what he'd shown her. Now she understood the musty scent in the air. "It's a good thing I blacked out." She recalled the torrent of pain that had crippled her senses. "That must've been when they started dying. I could feel them—it was horrible. I thought I was dying, too."

"We all did, I think." He stroked her cheek with his thumb, his gaze drifting as if replaying the memory. "Except for Syrine. She stayed conscious and kept a clear head the whole time. When I came to, she was conferring with Alona, explaining how to defeat the Aribol."

Cara's breath caught. "Are the L'eihrs going back to fight?"

"They were already on their way when Syrine called."

A thread of hope wound itself around Cara's heart and gave a mighty tug. Everything might be okay. And in large part, they had Syrine to thank for it. Cara checked over her shoulder. "Where is she?"

Something dark settled over Aelyx's features. He dropped his gaze to his hands. "She said she was going to sweep the ship for survivors. It made sense, so I didn't question her at the time." He glanced up. "But right before she left the boiler room, she started fidgeting with her pear-seed pendant, and I knew what she was really going to look for."

"Oh." Cara brought a hand to her chest. "The elixir Aisly promised her."

He gave a slow nod. "I don't think it exists."

Honestly, neither did Cara. But that wouldn't stop her from tearing apart every inch of this ship looking for it. Maybe she would find a second chance for Syrine and David. Maybe not. Either way Cara would be there to lift Syrine up, because they were friends, and that's what friends were for.

She extended a hand to Aelyx. "Come on. Let's prove ourselves wrong."

"Elire, it's time. If you don't hurry, they'll start without you."

"Okay, coming," she called.

On her hands and knees, Cara backed out of the dark, narrow service shaft and clicked off her flashlight. The shaft was another bust. She hadn't expected to find any medical marvels in there among the layers of mold growing on the passageway walls, but after three days of fruitless searching, desperation had set in, and she'd broadened her scope to include the ship's dank nooks and grimy crannies. She knew she was grasping at straws, but she didn't care. She would leave no stone unturned.

She stood up and brushed the mildew from her pants, then handed the flashlight to Aelyx. "We can mark that one off the list."

He pulled up a holographic map and tapped their location to darken it, indicating the area had been searched. Of the ship's massive interior, only a few scattered blocks remained unchecked.

Though not for lack of trying.

Two days ago they'd donated their shuttles to the Earth Council because the planet was still under a blackout. The Council had made good use of the crafts, ferrying aboard hundreds of dignitaries, soldiers, and scientists. Since then, the corridors had been teeming with people scavenging for useful bits of technology to take home before the ship's impending demolition, which was scheduled to take place tomorrow at zero six hundred hours. That didn't leave much time to look for the elixir, but Cara agreed with world leaders that the ship and its fleet had to be destroyed before it fell into the wrong hands.

"Take this with you." Aelyx extended a protein packet. When she wrinkled her nose at it, he added, "I know you skipped breakfast again."

"No, I'm pretty sure I . . ." But her stomach growled and made her a liar.

He pressed the packet into her palm. "Eat it on the way there. You're already late." He pointed the flashlight to the next section on the map. "I'll clear this area, and we'll finish the rest tonight."

She stood on tiptoe for a brief kiss and then set off down the corridor toward the nearest elevator tube, cramming a handful of protein cubes into her mouth as she walked.

She nearly spat out the first bite when the chute plummeted toward the lower level, where the Council had staged an impromptu command center in a room near the hangar.

As Cara jogged to her meeting, she passed a pair of men in biohazard suits carrying a stiff Aribol body between them, either en route to the airlock for its disposal or to an isolated lab for its dissection. She caught a whiff of death and quickly lost her appetite. Shoving the rest of her lunch into her pocket, she turned aside and gave the men in the hallway a wide berth before continuing to the command center.

The meeting was already in session when she entered the room, which was sparsely furnished with four rows of folding chairs facing a sheet music stand that served as a lectern. Colonel Rutter stood behind the makeshift podium, debriefing the council on the status of blackout repairs. He told them Larish had shuttled to the ground to join the collective think tank in Washington DC, and he was confident they'd have the power grid up and running within the week. He glanced up from his notes and spotted Cara, then waved her over to an empty seat in the second row.

"Now I'll turn it over to the L'eihrs for their report," he said, and shifted the angle of his com-sphere so Alona's hologram moved to the area beside him.

Cara took her seat and peered between heads at Alona, scanning her face for hints of good or bad news. The L'eihrs had defeated the Aribol, but not easily. They'd struggled to infiltrate the Destroyer, and during the battle for control of the ship, it had drifted into the planet's gravitational pull and gone down in the ocean. Several shuttle pods had ejected before impact, and it was unclear how many Aribol had escaped or where they'd gone. Then there was the issue of the Voyager crew, none of whom had made contact since the day Jake Winters went offline.

The head Elder lifted her chin, surveying the group with her cool gaze for several moments before she spoke. In true Alona fashion, she started with a bang. "The escaped Aribol are alive and in my custody. I have issued a summons to their leaders to discuss the terms of their surrender."

Cara sniffed a quiet laugh and sat an inch taller. She was proud of her title as Chief Human Consultant to the most badass woman in the universe.

"I expect a reply momentarily," Alona went on. "In the meantime, we can discuss our demands."

"What demands?" barked a representative from the third row, a husky bearded man whose name Cara didn't remember. "I want them all dead."

The woman seated next to him nodded in agreement. "The blackout killed two thousand people in my country, and those are just the casualties we know of."

"We lost five hundred in our hospitals alone," another woman said. "Without life support systems, we're losing more by the day."

The bearded man stood up, raising a fist. "Their attack on us was unprovoked. Instead of accepting surrender, I say we launch a counterattack and finish them off."

"With what ships?" Cara asked. The Aribol were in possession of the last Voyager craft, and the only intergalactic transport that remained was on L'eihr. Technically they could send it to war, but that would be a foolish risk. "We're landlocked at the moment."

"Then we'll use this," the man said, splaying his hands at

the fleshy walls around them. "We'll learn how to pilot the fleet and attack the Aribol with their own ships."

Cara didn't like where this discussion was headed. She wanted the battle to be over, not to escalate the war. The Aribol, however many of them remained, would fight back if attacked, and who knew how many Destroyers they'd stationed throughout the galaxy? Besides, the Council had already agreed to demolish the ship and its fleet. Nothing this deadly should be allowed to exist.

Alona didn't offer her opinion. She folded her hands in her lap and followed the conversation until a high-pitched whine from her quarters announced an incoming transmission from Zane. She lifted a hand, and the Council fell silent.

"Greetings," Zane said when his façade appeared in midair beside Alona. It didn't escape Cara's notice that for once he didn't call them children. "My leaders have reviewed your summons and authorized me to discuss the conditions of a truce."

"A truce?" Alona repeated. "Do you mean surrender?"

"I do not."

She arched a brow at him. "What conditions do you propose?"

"We have established the following boundaries for your review." His mask vanished, and in its place flashed a series of star charts Cara couldn't read, one unfamiliar constellation after the next, until finally his face reappeared. "Peace will be maintained for as long as you observe your distance from our system. I must also mention this offer is conditional on the return of any of our kind being held prisoner on your worlds."

Angry chatter broke out, murmurings of *offer?* and *conditional?* filling the room. The representative from China stood up and bellowed, "You're in no position to dictate terms. We have the power to drive you into extinction."

Despite the threat, Zane's computerized voice remained as impassive as ever. "Your Voyagers are alive and in stasis on board their ship. As a courtesy for the release of our prisoners, we will return yours as well."

Cara leaned forward, waiting for Alona to accept the offer on behalf of the Council. Maybe the terms were a bit restrictive and Zane's delivery less than humble, but as long as the Voyagers returned home and everyone lived in peace, who cared?

Apparently, several people.

"What about restitutions?" demanded one representative.

"Forget restitutions. They should pay with blood!" shouted another.

"Total extinction!"

"It's what they deserve!"

"Stop." Cara stood from her seat and faced the group, beseeching them with wide eyes. "I have no love for the Aribol. What they did to us was unforgivable. They almost wiped out two civilizations just because they were afraid we'd team up against them. But there's an entire crew of humans and L'eihrs on that Voyager ship who risked everything to give us the information we needed to survive. Now they're counting on us to bring them home."

"What about the dead?" argued the bearded man. "And their families? They're counting on us to vindicate them. We must never forget their sacrifice."

"We don't have to forgive—or forget. We only have to

look forward." Cara spread her arms and told the Council a simple truth. "The last few weeks have taught me that life is worth fighting for. And life is made up of a series of moments like these—*choices* like these. It's those choices that define us. Our decision today will affect the future of three worlds. So what will we choose? To avenge the dead, or save the living?"

She peered from one pair of eyes to the next as silence thickened the room. A few faces turned down in contemplation. Others shook their heads or set their jaws. She didn't know what more she could say. She'd delivered her best argument, straight from the heart. If that didn't sway them, nothing would. So she squared her shoulders and faked a confidence she didn't feel, then made a formal motion before the Council.

"I move to accept the Aribols' terms and bring our people home. I move to fight for the living. Who will second it?"

Night had fallen, but with no windows inside the ship, Cara didn't realize it until Colonel Rutter appeared in the doorway and announced, "Pack it up, kids. This is your last call. Everyone to the shuttle."

Cara pulled her head out of a storage cubby and clicked off her flashlight. She sat back on her heels and looked at Aelyx, who was elbow-deep in a waste chute at the other end of the lab. From there, she shared a glance with Troy, Elle, and Syrine, all of whom had paused with various alien artifacts clutched in their hands, their eyes round with the same realization.

The elixir wasn't here, assuming it existed at all.

"Can't we have a few more minutes?" Cara asked. "There's one area we haven't searched."

"No can do, Sweeney." The colonel thumbed behind him. "The nuke's here. I have to prep for the remote detonation, and my team can't bring the warhead on board until everyone's gone. It emits radiation—low-level stuff, but you know, safety regulations and all."

Nobody spoke or moved. All eyes shifted to Syrine as if waiting to see how she would react. Cara held her breath, and she knew the others did, too. None of them had expected to find the elixir, but they'd wanted more than anything to be wrong.

Syrine set down a metal object and brushed off her hands. Her expression was neutral, as though she'd already made peace with David's fate. When she joined the colonel at the door, the rest of them did the same.

Elle cupped Syrine's cheek and shared something through Silent Speech. Whatever she said made Syrine smile, and the two linked arms and led the way into the hall. But before the rest of them could follow, Rutter blocked their path.

"I need a word." Rutter snagged Troy by the sleeve. "You, too, Sergeant."

Troy stiffened his backbone and saluted the colonel.

"At ease."

With his feet spread hip-width apart, Troy relaxed his posture and folded both hands behind his back.

"First of all," Rutter said, beaming at Cara, "that was some smooth talking you did back there at the Council meeting. I didn't get a chance to tell you, but I'm mighty proud." He clapped her on the shoulder. "You've come a long way from that shell-shocked girl I met last year in the principal's office."

Cara's face heated. She didn't know why, but praise always made her more uncomfortable than insults. She lifted a shoulder and gave a small grin. "Thanks. I'm just glad enough people agreed with me." The vote had been close.

"As for you," the colonel said to Troy, "I pulled some strings with the president, and she awarded you a full pardon for assaulting her secret service officers."

Troy released a lungful of air. "No court-martial?"

"That's right, son," Rutter told him, then inclined his head. "As for my decision to relieve you of duty, I'm more than willing to rescind that order . . ." He trailed off, using his sharp, gray eyes to deliver a message. "*If* that's what you want."

A slow smile spread over Troy's face. When he darted a glance at Cara, her heart lifted because she knew what his decision would be. "Thank you, sir." Troy stood at attention, flattening both arms by his sides. "It's been my honor and privilege to serve as a United States Marine, but I respectfully request to join my sister on the L'eihr colony."

Rutter brought a hand to his forehead in a salute. "Request granted, Sergeant Sweeney. Consider yourself honorably discharged." He grinned and vigorously shook Troy's hand. "Now get your asses on that shuttle so I can start the fireworks."


When the first blush of dawn kissed the horizon, Cara and Aelyx sat cross-legged on one of many patchwork quilts spread over the safe house lawn. The countdown had begun, and with ninety seconds left to detonation, soldiers whooped and hollered as they jogged away from their posts and settled in to join the party. The excitement was infectious, like the Fourth of July and Christmas wrapped into one, and at the heart of it all were Mom and Dad, smiling as they carried trays of white paper coffee cups from one blanket to the next.

"Everybody take one," Dad said. "I added a nip of something special."

Troy took two cups. While handing one of them to Elle, he sniffed the coffee and flinched, then let out a low whistle. "*Yeah,* you did."

"What's in it?" Elle asked him, side-eyeing the brew.

"Jet fuel," Troy joked.

Cara hesitated when Mom brought the tray to her blanket. "Go ahead," Mom said with a wink. "It's a celebration."

As she and Aelyx helped themselves, someone shouted, "Thirty seconds!"

Dad tossed aside his empty tray, his face positively giddy. He waved Mom over to a quilt in the front, and while she tiptoed in between blankets, Mom raised her cup. "Quick, a toast. What should we drink to?"

One of the soldiers hollered, "To victory!" and his comrades cheered.

Everyone lifted their coffees in unison and chanted, "To victory."

When Cara tapped the rim of her cup against Aelyx's, she glanced into his eyes and caught him watching her with so much adoration that she forgot to take a drink. Something fluttered behind her navel, and for a long moment, there was only the two of them, drunk on love and the promise of the lifetime that lay ahead of them. If it were possible to feel any happier than this, she didn't know how.

Brightness flashed from high above. It started as a pinpoint of light in the center of the Destroyer and quickly multiplied into a blinding fireball that forced Cara to shield her eyes and clench them tight. Even through closed lids, she could see the explosion, like a second sun. The boom came next, stronger than a hundred thunderclaps. On and on it went. The roar tore through the heavens for so long Cara peeked between her fingers to make sure mankind hadn't broken the sky.

The Destroyer was gone. All that remained of its hull were the north and south spear tips, growing smaller by the second as they spiraled into space. Smaller chunks of metal had fallen into the atmosphere. They caught flame and streaked toward the ground, hurtling, Cara hoped, into the oceans or deserts instead of more populated areas.

Before long, the sky cleared and the early rays of sunlight painted the clouds light pink. Cheers and applause broke out, and then turned to shouts of delight when the front porch bulb flickered on and off a few times and glowed steadily. Cara set her coffee aside and clapped her hands, thinking of Larish hard at work somewhere in a government think tank.

He'd done it.

She was still smiling when her senses prickled, as if she were being watched, and she glanced over her shoulder to find Syrine sitting on the front porch steps, hunched over with her arms wrapped around her knees. She wasn't looking at anyone in particular, just staring blankly over the lawn.

Aelyx had noticed her, too. While the celebration raged

on, he and Cara strode to the front porch steps and sat on either side of Syrine. Aelyx handed her his coffee.

"Drink it," he said, and flashed a teasing smile. "It contains a substance rumored to manufacture cheer *and* put hair on your chest. Humans call it whiskey."

Syrine played along, taking a sip and then peeking down the front of her shirt. "The rumors don't appear to be true." She returned the coffee to him with a weak smile. "You don't have to do this. I'll be all right."

"We want to help," Cara said. "What can we do?"

Syrine rested her chin in her hand and turned her gaze to the trees. "Not much, really. I'll need help retrieving David's body from where I hid it. Then when the transport arrives, I want to lay him to rest on the colony. That's what you can do for me. Take us home."

Cara rubbed Syrine's back. "I can do that." Then the three of them sat in silence and watched a new day unfold. There was no more that needed to be said.

# CHAPTER TWENTY-ONE

## United
### MAY THE SOURCE BE WITH YOU

THURSDAY, SEPTEMBER 28
L'eihr: The Final, *Final* Frontier

Guess what! After three weeks of waiting for the L'eihr transport to arrive, another two weeks hurtling through intergalactic wormholes, and five more days in quarantine, I'm finally writing to you from the colony in my new apartment on the third floor!

Why a new apartment, you ask? Because the old one—as seen on pages 52-54 of *Squee Teen* magazine—was damaged by a tidal surge when the Aribol Destroyer crashed into the ocean. Brief as it was, the surge really packed a punch. Our first season's crops are ruined, half the solar-powered cars washed out to sea, and I found something in my underwear drawer resembling a jellyfish with spider legs instead of tentacles. (Aelyx says it's harmless, but I still plan to burn those undies.)

Fortunately, we colonists aren't afraid to roll up our sleeves and get our hands dirty. Which I'm about to do in the literal sense. Those seedlings that arrived from the continent aren't going to plant themselves.

If you've applied to join the colony, please be patient with us as we rebuild. Construction is underway for a new fleet of transports and Voyager ships. Once they're ready, we can open the cosmos for new immigration and visits from family members. (I'm talking to you, Mom and Dad.)

Until then, please be good to each other and savor every moment on that beautiful planet of yours. It's not every day mankind dodges an apocalyptic bullet and lives to party on.

*Posted by Cara Sweeney*

Cara had just closed her laptop when the distant rumble of thrusters drew her attention to the window. She set her computer on the futon cushion and rushed to the glassy pane, a smile lifting the corners of her mouth as she watched a fifty-passenger shuttlecraft touch down on the beach.

"They're here," she called to Aelyx in the bedroom. "The Voyagers are home."

Actually, the Voyager ship had arrived four days ago, just one day behind the transport from Earth, but strict quarantine protocols had delayed the colonists' reunion until now. Cara bounced on her toes as the shuttle hatch opened and a set of stairs was unfolded below it. She couldn't wait to throw her arms around Jake Winters's neck.

Funny how much had changed.

Aelyx sauntered, half-dressed, through the bedroom doorway and snagged a clean tunic from the storage bureau on his way out. The sight of his bare chest stunned her into a momentary daze, and clearly he noticed, because he proceeded to pull on his shirt and lower it with exaggerated slowness. Finally when the last sliver of his bronze, buttonless belly was concealed, he cleared his throat and blinked innocently.

"You were saying?"

Cara slid him a challenging glance. She was tempted to give him a taste of his own medicine, but the competition would have to wait. "The volunteers just landed, and I think their colony reps"—she pointed back and forth between them—"should be there to welcome them. Don't you?"

By way of answer he extended an elbow, which she accepted, and the two of them strode into the hall and hooked a left toward the stairwell. They were halfway to the stairs when the door to her brother's quarters slid open and Elle sneaked out, obviously wearing the same uniform as last night—her clothes were never that wrinkled at eight o'clock in the morning—and carrying her shoes in one hand. She started when she noticed them, then blushed and offered a quick wave before darting down the hall in her little socked feet.

Aelyx snickered to himself and shared a knowing glance with Cara. Troy had convinced Elle to join the colony weeks ago, when they were still on board the transport, but instead of declaring themselves as *l'ihans*, they'd announced they were "taking it slow," which apparently meant pretending to sleep in separate bedrooms while they dated each other. Cara thought they were being silly, but she held her tongue, and for the most part, so did Aelyx. Their siblings could be as neurotic as they wanted to be, as long as they were here.

Nothing else mattered.

Outside, the morning dew gathered on their boot tips as they crossed the grassy pathway leading to the beach. Beyond the dunes, mist clung to the ocean waters, hovering in a way that promised another humid day with no breeze. The sand shifted beneath Cara's soles, and she squinted against the rising sun toward the shuttle's landing place to find a group of humans and L'eihrs stretching their legs and stomping their feet playfully on the ground, having not felt it in weeks.

She called hello and waved. A few people shielded their eyes, bending forward to bring her into focus, and waved in return. She picked out Jake easily, a lone blond head among dozens of brown ponytails. His teeth flashed in a smile when he spotted her, but as the distance between them closed, Cara noticed a slight tenseness in his posture, a certain respectful formality, and she decided at the last minute to offer him a handshake instead of a hug.

"Welcome home," she said as Jake shook her hand, and then Aelyx's. When Ayah joined them, Cara greeted her with the standard two-finger press to the throat. It warmed Cara's heart to see Ayah rest her head on Jake's shoulder. As Cara glanced around, she noticed theirs wasn't the only interspecies coupling that had bloomed among the Voyagers. "Guess there was love in the air," she mused.

Jake chuckled, his ears going pink. "Yeah, well, I wasn't kidding when I said the whole end-of-the-world thing was a good pickup line."

Cara perked up when she realized new matches would mean more colonists, assuming the Voyager commander released the crew members who'd paired off with humans. "We're glad you're back. I'm sure the last thing you want to think about is work, but we need the extra hands."

"Oh, um, about that . . ." Jake cringed sheepishly and pulled Ayah into a sideways hug. "We decided not to stay."

Cara's mouth dropped open.

"It's not you," he assured her with a lifted palm. "I just . . . I don't know, I feel like I found my niche on that ship. I like discovering new worlds. And I'm good at it. So when the commander offered me a permanent position, I couldn't say no. Especially when he said Ayah could come, too."

Aelyx clapped Jake's upper arm. "Congratulations. I confess I'm jealous. I wanted to join the Voyagers when I was a youngling, but they denied my application."

"And it's a good thing they did," Cara reminded him with a pat on the chest. She turned to Jake. "I'm sorry to lose you, but I understand."

"Hey, listen." Jake checked over both shoulders and moved in close, lowering his voice to a murmur. "The reason I shuttled down was because I have to give you something." He dug in his pocket and pulled out a metal box the approximate size of an egg. "It's a message." He leaned in closer. "From Zane."

Cara jerked her head up so quickly she almost clocked Jake in the nose. In a blur of motion, Aelyx thrust a protective arm in front of her and positioned himself before the device as if throwing himself on a grenade.

"No, it's safe," Jake whispered. "I scanned it a dozen times, I swear."

Cara tried to peek around Aelyx, but he wouldn't let her near the object. He flashed a palm at Jake, a warning to stay back. "How did you get it?"

"I woke up from stasis and it was in my pocket," Jake said. "I knew it was there and what I was supposed to do with it. Zane must've put the information in my head. He said he had Cara's DNA from when he cloned her, so he programmed the box to respond to her touch. She's the only one who can open it."

As Aelyx relaxed a bit, Cara leaned around his arm

and studied the device. The box looked harmless, and she couldn't think of a reason for Zane to want to hurt her. She was the one who'd argued for a truce when half the Council had wanted to annihilate his kind.

"I want to hear what he has to say," she told Aelyx. When the corners of his mouth pulled down, she added, "The one good thing I can say about Zane is he never lied to us."

"Except when he said the alliance was a threat."

"Well, it *was* a threat . . . to the Aribol," she pointed out, which earned her a dirty look. "My point is he made demands and he backed them up with actions—actions he told us about. He wasn't sneaky."

The firm set of Aelyx's jaw said he wasn't convinced, but he stood aside and swept a hand toward Jake, who extended the box only to draw it back again. Jake shifted his weight from one foot to the other and peered at Cara through his lashes. He seemed hesitant to release the object.

"Oh," Cara said in understanding. "You want to listen, too?"

He relaxed into a smile. "Do you mind? The curiosity's killing me."

Figuring it was the least she could do, she waved him toward an expanse of leafy underbrush near the dunes, where they could listen to the message in privacy. Aelyx came too, while Ayah stayed back to keep anyone from wandering too close.

Once they were a safe distance from the beach, Cara formed a huddle with Jake and Aelyx. Jake licked his lips, more eager than a kid on his birthday, and rested the box in her palm.

The cube was lighter than Cara had expected, no heavier

than a silver dollar. She lifted it higher and rotated an ear toward it. For a moment, all she heard was the gentle rush of surf over sand, and then the object hummed. A pin-size hole opened at the top, projecting a miniature hologram of Zane's porcelain mask.

"Greetings, young representative," he said in his computerized voice. "I hope this recording finds you well. Per the terms of our truce, it will be my last initiation of contact." His mask morphed briefly into an image of Jake's face. "While probing this human's mind, I discovered memories of his conversations with you. One particular discussion drew my interest, regarding a promise made by the hybrid Aisly to a Noven female called Syrine."

Cara drew a breath and glanced at Aelyx.

"You were correct in assuming that promise was false," Zane went on. "Such an elixir does exist, but the hybrid had no authority to access it. However, I was moved by your speech to the Council in favor of a truce. Your efforts helped preserve the lives of many, so in return I offer you this gift of life. Please accept it with my compliments."

The cube's outer shell began to fall away until it flaked into a circle of dust surrounding a thick disc the size of a pillbox. The bottom half of the disc was made of metal, and atop it rested a clear bubble filled with yellow liquid.

"To use the elixir, place the device on the flesh above your patient's heart. Bear down with your palm cupping the dome, and much like this message, your touch will activate it. When the enzymes have fully dispersed and the process is complete, the device will detach on its own. Your patient will be restored from all ailments, even those that preceded his death." Zane paused for a beat, then abruptly droned, "Goodbye."

The hologram vanished in a wisp of white, leaving Cara staring blankly at the bubble in her palm. *This* was the elixir? It looked like something she'd find in a gumball machine. She didn't know what to think. Despite her former argument that Zane had never told a lie, doubt tied her tongue.

For a long while, nobody spoke. Jake was the first to step back from the huddle, followed by Aelyx, who couldn't stop rubbing his lower face. Cara blew the dust off her palm and stepped into a beam of sunlight, holding up the fluid-filled bubble for inspection.

"We can't tell Syrine," Aelyx said. "Not until we know it works."

Cara agreed with him. More than a month had passed since Syrine had let David go. She'd finally begun to heal. To give her false hope now would be the most vicious act Cara could imagine. She almost wondered if trying to bring David back was the right thing to do, especially since scientists could use this sample to study its properties, but she quickly shut down that train of thought when she imagined how she would feel if Aelyx were the one lying in a cryogenic box.

"Did you bury him yet?" asked Jake.

Cara shook her head. "There wasn't time."

"How long does it take to thaw a frozen body?"

Aelyx lifted his chin, his silver gaze hardening in determination. "Let's find out."

• • •

The answer was six days, much longer than Aelyx had expected.

They'd learned that in order to prevent the outer layer of David's body from decaying before his internal organs had a chance to thaw, they would have to refrigerate him at a constant temperature for nearly a week.

That week had passed so slowly it seemed to go in reverse.

Aelyx had barely slept, and what brief hours of slumber he'd achieved were filled with nightmares of failure. His most frequently recurring dream had been walking into the medical lab to discover David's body had been moved to the crematorium. No matter how fast Aelyx ran, he could never reach his friend in time.

His waking hours were no better. He couldn't count the number of times he'd entered a room and immediately forgotten why he was there. But most difficult of all was Syrine. After the fourth day of refusing to engage in Silent Speech with her, she'd begun watching him with narrowed eyes. She knew him too well for him to hide anything from her for long.

So the morning the laboratory called to report David's body had reached optimal conditions for a burial dressing— the excuse they'd given the technicians—Aelyx stood from the dining hall table, grabbed Cara by the hand, and set off for the medical center without bothering to finish his breakfast.

David was resting on a table in an unused room in the medical lab when they arrived. The technicians had prepared the body according to Aelyx's instructions: clothing removed, skin bathed, a thin sheet draped over him from waist to toes. Though the temperature in the lab was frigid, Aelyx found his hands sweaty as he slid the door shut and locked it.

He stood across the table from Cara and swallowed hard as he regarded his friend, or what remained of him. In this state, David was barely recognizable. His blond hair, cropped close to his scalp, seemed abnormally dark contrasted against skin the color of wax. Aelyx tried not to look too closely at David's chest cavity, where a hollow-point bullet had torn a path clear through him. A memory flashed from that day, of the blood that had pooled across the floor. There had been so much of it.

A sickening thought occurred to him. "What about blood? His veins must be empty."

Cara frowned at the bubble-topped disc, tipping it to and fro. "Zane didn't say anything about a blood transfusion. I think he would've mentioned it if it was important. Maybe the elixir helps the body create new plasma."

Aelyx released a long breath. He wanted so badly for this to work.

"Let's try it and see," Cara said, and without further delay, she set the device above David's heart and firmly held it in place. A second passed, then two, before she jerked her hand away as if she'd touched an open flame. "It shocked me. I guess that means it's working."

Aelyx bent down to study the disc's metal underside, which appeared to have fused itself to David's skin. There was a slight odor of burnt flesh, and then the liquid-filled dome began to pulse, beating like a heart. Its contents drained gradually with each compression until the serum was gone. Even after the bubble emptied, it continued pumping, strong and steady, as the minutes turned to hours.

Cara pulled two chrome stools over and sat down on one. Aelyx tried to do the same, but each time he lowered to the seat, his restless legs forced him up again until he finally abandoned any pretense of serenity and paced the floor. With every other pass, he noticed something new taking place inside David's body. First his muscle fibers began to knit together, after which layers of tissue closed the hole in his chest. David never breathed, and his heart remained still, but before long, a hint of color blossomed beneath his skin—not much, just enough to indicate the presence of fresh blood.

It was then that Aelyx allowed himself to hope.

He and Cara bent down to study the progress. One of David's fingers twitched, and suddenly the bubble delivered a massive blow, like a shock to the chest, that startled Cara off her stool. David's ribcage lurched upward, and he drew a loud gasp, disengaging the metal device, which plinked to the floor. His eyes snapped open, and in that instant, Private David Sharpe awoke from the dead, flailing his arms and legs as if he'd fallen from the sky and landed on the examination table.

Aelyx rushed to help his friend, who was now shivering violently and clenching his eyes in pain. Cara darted to the storage cabinet and brought back a heated blanket, which they activated and wrapped around David's trembling shoulders. The warmth seemed to help. David groaned through chattering teeth for another minute or two, then turned onto his side and drew the blanket up to his ears.

Aelyx pressed two fingers against David's wrist, noting a strong, steady pulse. The first question he asked his friend was, "How do you feel?"

David expelled a dry laugh and cracked open one eye.

"To quote my old drill sergeant," he rasped in a delightfully familiar voice, "like a bag of smashed assholes."

Cara smiled as she crouched down to meet his gaze. "Sounds about right, considering the circumstances."

"Considering what circum—" David cut off, his gaze flying wide as realization set in. He rolled onto his back and began frantically patting his chest.

"It's all right," Aelyx said, and held him still. "You were shot, but a lot has happened since then." He didn't mention that David had died. It was probably best to dole out the information in bite-size pieces. "If you calm down, I'll tell you everything."

Cara smoothed a comforting hand over David's head. "You've been in cryogenic storage for about four months. You're on the L'eihr colony now, fully healed." As if to confirm her statement, David glanced beneath the blanket. "Your genetic disease, too," she added. "At least that's what Zane said."

"Zane?" David asked.

While Cara fetched David a cup of water, Aelyx explained what happened after the shootout last winter, including the fact that David had died. David seemed to take the news well, or at least to conceal his anxiety as he listened to the story of the Aribol threat and their subsequent defeat. Aelyx had just begun to describe the elixir when a knock sounded at the door, and a voice called, "Aelyx? Let me in."

David's face lifted in a hopeful grin. "Is that Syrine?"

Aelyx made a shushing motion. He hadn't reached the part of the story where they'd decided to use the elixir without Syrine's knowledge. He wanted to give David a full medical checkup before telling her the news, and then break it to her gently, not slide open the door and jar her with the sudden resurrection of her *l'ihan*.

Maybe if they were quiet, she would go away.

She pounded her fist harder. "I know you're in there, Aelyx. I tracked your sphere."

*Fasha.* "I'm busy," he called to her. "Go back to the center. I'll meet you there later."

"The technician told me you're preparing David for burial." A new heaviness in her voice tugged at Aelyx's heartstrings. "I deserve to be with him. If you don't open the door, I'll have the technician do it."

David blinked in surprise and looked back and forth between Aelyx and Cara. "She doesn't know?"

Cara caught Aelyx's eye and whispered, "Go talk to her."

Aelyx nodded; there was no avoiding it any longer. He positioned himself to block the view of the examination table when he answered the door. On the other side, Syrine gripped her hips, looking equal parts furious and hurt.

He moved forward half a step to force her to back up, but she refused. She tried to dart around him on either side, and he blocked her with his body. "Wait," he said. "There's something I have to tell you."

Before he could say anything more, David called Syrine's name, and her hands slipped from her hips. The color in her face drained away, and she went stone-still. Not even her eyes moved from their position fixed on a point behind Aelyx's shoulder.

"Let me explain."

She moved to push him aside. This time he let her. As she drifted forward, he shadowed her every step, prepared to support her when shock set in. And it did. The moment

313

she found David, very much alive, sitting on the exam table with a blanket twisted around his torso, she lost her breath and swayed on her feet.

Aelyx caught her by the elbow and held her steady. "I didn't want you to find out this way," he told her, but she didn't seem to be listening. Her glassy gaze never left David's face.

Beside the table, Cara wrung her hands. "We didn't know if it would work. That's why we didn't tell you. But I swear we were going to as soon as . . ." She trailed off when it became clear Syrine wasn't listening to her either.

When Syrine began to tremble, even David showed signs of concern, opening and closing his mouth as if afraid to speak and push her over the edge into actual, medical shock. Her eyes flooded with tears, but not necessarily the happy kind. Aelyx traded a nervous glance with Cara. Maybe they'd done more harm than good in hiding the elixir from Syrine. He often forgot how fragile her gift made her.

But then, still staring ahead, she drew a shaky breath and exhaled in a barely audible whisper, "I love you."

David lifted a blond brow.

"I love you," she said, the words louder this time but broken in half by the thickness in her throat. She wriggled away from Aelyx and strode toward the table, chanting through her tears, "I love you."

Overcome by emotion, David didn't speak. His eyes glittered with moisture that welled over and spilled down his cheeks. He lifted one corner of the blanket when Syrine reached him. She crawled beneath it, and they embraced each other with so much passion Aelyx was forced to avert his gaze.

There was no more talking after that, only the sounds of sniffles and quiet sobs. He glanced at Cara to find her smiling at him with tears streaming down her face. He offered her his hand, and when she took it, they walked out of the room and closed the door behind them.

The checkup could wait.

They strode outside, where the sun hung low over the ocean, signaling the end of the longest day Aelyx could remember. Activity bustled on the front lawn of the living center where a group of humans appeared to be teaching several L'eihrs how to play soccer using a ball made from rubber bands wrapped around old uniforms. The "ball" wobbled in a wayward path when kicked, but the group played on, laughing and cheering.

"It's funny." Cara watched the game as she led him along the sidelines. "Not *ha-ha* funny, but strange, how it took an intergalactic war to make everyone put aside their differences. Two months ago, none of these people would talk to each other."

Aelyx made a noise of agreement. The threat of extinction had forced both their worlds to unite against a common enemy. In doing so, they'd also discovered a new planet populated with their kind, although the Earth Council and The Way had decided not to initiate contact. Aelyx was glad for it. A few years of stability might be nice for a change.

He was so deep in thought he didn't notice where Cara had led him until sand shifted beneath his boots and ocean mist dusted his face. His stomach grumbled. He'd thought they were walking to the dining hall. "Where are we going?"

The breeze tossed Cara's braid over her shoulder as she

towed him past the dunes. "You made me a promise, and now it's time to deliver."

Aelyx pursed his lips. He didn't recall making any promises, but he hoped it involved skinny-dipping. "Give me a hint?"

"Nope. I want you to remember it on your own."

As it turned out, their destination was the secluded northern tip of the beach, where sand gave way to stone. Cara indicated a spot and motioned for him to sit down. He did, and after he settled on a comfortable drift of sand, she sat between his legs, facing away, and reclined with her back against his chest. He wrapped his arms around her and looked out at the white-capped waves. The view was pleasant, but he still didn't know what they were doing here.

At least not until the sun slipped over the horizon and a trio of moons arose to take its place. The darkness allowed the stars to shine, and there, high in the heavens beyond the third moon, stretched the angel nebula he had described to her last year. He tipped back his head to admire the swirling clouds of pink and violet. Then he recited the words he'd said to her so many months ago.

"Every time you see it, I want you to think of me. Soon we'll stand together and watch the L'eihr sky from our colony." He gave her a teasing squeeze. "Though sitting is nice, too."

She gazed dreamily upward. "You know, the whole time we were apart I kept looking for this in the sky, but I couldn't see it from the Aegis. It's like the nebula wanted us to see it together."

"We have," he reminded her. The nebula had once been visible from their apartment window.

"But not like this. Not like I imagined we would." She pondered for a moment. "Why didn't we take the time to really appreciate it?"

Aelyx didn't say so, but he imagined that was because they'd spent all their free time in their bedroom during those first few weeks on the colony. Not that he was complaining. "We were distracted by other things, I guess."

She snuggled closer and rested the back of her head on his shoulder. "Well, let's make time from now on. I don't want to forget how hard we fought for this or how close we came to losing it."

He hugged her tightly and pressed a kiss to her temple. The truth was he had never taken Cara for granted, and he didn't need a nebula to make him appreciate how fortunate he was to have her with him. But he kept that thought to himself. "I promise."

"So beautiful," she said to the sky.

Aelyx was watching the freckled outline of her nose. He agreed. *So beautiful.* Eventually he joined her in turning his gaze skyward. He didn't look to the constellations as humans often did, seeking glimpses of his destiny or predictions of the future. Instead, he propped his chin atop Cara's head and let the pace of their breathing fall into sync. *She* was his future.

He didn't need the stars to tell him that.

# Acknowledgments

Many thanks to my editor, Susan Barnes, for guiding me through the revision process with thoughtful, in-depth suggestions that took my story to the next level. Additional thanks to Gene Mollica for a beautiful cover and Maria McGrath for stellar copyedits. It was a pleasure working with all of you. Endless gratitude to my agent, Nicole Resciniti, for finding a loving home for this book. Speaking of which, big hugs to Mary Cummings and the entire team at EverAfter Romance for helping me deliver a seamless conclusion to this trilogy. (Anyone reading this book in hardcover has EverAfter to thank for it.)

Much love to authors Lorie Langdon and Lea Nolan for manuscript critiques, support, and friendship. I'm so glad to have you in my life. As always, I'm grateful for my family and friends, whose support has never wavered.

Completing this trilogy is bittersweet. Part of me is delighted for my characters and all they've overcome, but

I would be lying if I said I was happy to see the journey end. Aelyx and Cara have lived inside my head for so long they've become a part of me. I hope they've become a part of you, too. For that reason, I'm grateful to *you*: the readers, librarians, bloggers, booktubers, and reviewers who've made this series a success by talking about it. You're the ones who'll give life to my characters for years to come. Thank you!